Mark Palasek

Letters From My Uncles

Copyright © 2016 by Mark Palasek

All rights reserved. No part of this publication may be reproduced or transmitted in any form or by any means, electronic or mechanical, including photocopy, recording, or any information storage and retrieval system, without permission in writing from the author and copyright holder except by a newspaper or periodical reviewer who wishes to quote a brief passage in connection with the review.

All transcribed letters and photographs are from the author's family collection except the photo, "Stephen Palasek and bride, Stephanie Wrobel" used by permission from the collection of Nina Wall.

Front cover photograph © 2016 Mark Palasek

www.lettersfrommyuncles.com

Preface

The story that follows is a true one: true, in as much as the characters are based upon real people; and true in the fact that the letters transcribed to bring the story alive are actual letters, as written by these same people. The thoughts these brave men wrote on paper with whatever pen or pencil was available were not always written with perfect grammar, or correct spelling, or in terms that would pass for politically correct today. Had they been altered significantly, they would not reflect the individuals who took the time to write them. The balance of this story, told between the letters, comes from diaries, tales shared, personal recollections, and memories of a time long gone, as well as historical notes.

Though some of the people in this story may have a larger part in its telling, or faced a more difficult time during the war than others, all should be considered heroes. They were all willing, if able, to fight and to die for our country, should that be their fate. It is a great honor, and with no small amount of pride, that I am able to share with you the stories of these brave men and their loving families during a most difficult time in history.

Chapter 1

Every story has a beginning. This story has more than one.

The first beginning comes from the contents of a box. Not a special or magical box by any means, but a very simple, old, dusty, brown corrugated cardboard box measuring 12" X 8" X 5", with a label addressed to my father from the Flagstaff Foods company in Perth Amboy, New Jersey — once a purveyor of coffee in tins. The box was discovered in my mother's basement, beneath the last step of the grey wooden staircase, resting on the concrete floor seven months after my mother had passed away. My family was in the last hours of a two-day tag sale to sell those household items and pieces of furniture that none of us wished to retain. While in the basement, I realized there was an easily removable sheet of plywood covering the area beneath that rough wooden staircase; when I removed it, I found an old table lamp with a bright floral design and some equally old beige suitcases we could sell. Fortunately, I also noticed the cardboard box as something my mother had shown me years before. Though I had completely forgotten about it since that day, I immediately recognized it as something my father, Stanley, had wanted to keep.

As anyone who has ever been away from home knows, staying in touch is important for the traveler and for those waiting for his return. Whether it is merely to let a loved one know that you arrived safely at your destination for one night away or that you were thinking of your family after months away from them, communication is important for the spirit as much as anything. It is also a way to keep one's mind busy when away from home. So, in the 1940s, without the simple methods we all have at our fingertips today for instant communication, people would regularly sit down and write letters. To be away from home and in the military with the strong probability that you may one day be in a situation where you do not know when, or if, you will see those you love again, hand-written letters were more important than ever. Somehow, that simple cardboard box was able to preserve the events, thoughts and emotions that a family shared during such a time.

This story also begins about 100 years earlier in Poland. In 1906, Stanislaus, the son of Josef and Marta Palasek, left the small farming village of Porzadzie in the east central part of that country. Booking passage from Hamburg, Germany on the S.S. Stattendam, a rather weathered turn-of-the-century steam vessel, he travelled to the "New World" as so many others he knew were doing at that time in search of a new and better life. It was quite the daring undertaking for a man who had never been more than 50 miles from his home. He settled among other family, mostly cousins, in the town of Port Washington on the north shore of Long Island. He found a job as a laborer and worked hard lifting and digging to build the homes and country clubs for those of considerable means who enjoyed the Gatsby-era good life that the "Gold Coast" had to offer.

Other immigrants from the same region of Poland moved to that area of Long Island, hoping that settling among people from the same homeland and with similar customs would lend a greater ease to the process of starting over — perhaps even, as with Stanislaus, among acquaintances and friends from back home. Seven years after Stanislaus made his one-way trip to America, a young woman named Marjanna Najmolla (the "J" is pronounced like a "Y") left the hamlet of Wyszkow, Poland, a mere twelve kilometers away from Stanislaus' hometown. She traveled with family to Hamburg, Germany, where she boarded the S.S. Patricia, yet another steam vessel of considerably less refinement than others at sea. The final destination was also New York. Marjanna and Stanislaus crossed paths often at the weekly gatherings fellow Poles would have in their community, fell in love, were married soon after and the next year, 1914, Marjanna gave birth to the first of eight children, Stephen. Only one of the eight children she would eventually have was a girl who sadly died shortly after her birth.

The Najmollas' departure from Europe came at a time when the continent was about to suffer through the "War to End All Wars," which also failed its nickname to be the last of all great wars and is better known today as World War One. This war did change the European map considerably, shifting borders based upon agreements set forth by the Treaty of Versailles. Much of these territorial changes directly affected areas that Germany had possessed and now would lose, such as the Western Prussian territory that was returned by Germany to a unified Poland. This had little effect on Stanislaus and Marjanna Palasek in 1919. The Palasek family in America was growing, having already added sons Carl and John and most recently in 1919, Joseph. The family would continue to grow, struggle and search for a better life as the years passed with Stanley, William and Alexander coming into the world over the next seven years while the world was more or less at peace. With the stock market crash of 1929, Stanislaus found it hard to find work to support his home and family as few who had wealth retained it, and those that did retain some of it were averse to funding new projects through which Stanislaus could find even menial employment.

As with most families, then and now, hand-me-downs were passed between the Palasek boys. Even the sturdiest garments were threadbare by the time the younger ones would get to wear them, as illustrated by the cold winter day in 1928 when second grader Stanley was surprised to be stopped in the hall by John J. Daly, principal of the Sands Point School that served half of Port Washington. Mr. Daly saw that the shoes Stanley wore were opening at the seams and worn through at the sole, with paper serving as the only protection between Stanley's foot and the frozen ground. Mr. Daly kindly took young Stanley to a shoe store in town and bought him a simple, but new, pair of shoes. Perhaps it was just the right thing to do in Mr. Daly's mind, but the memory of this gift lasted for decades with Stanley. (Many years later, the school was renamed in John J. Daly's honor.)

The family tried to find a new lifestyle that would allow them to be more self-sufficient. Leaving behind friends and relatives, they moved to a farm in the small upstate New York town of Ballston Spa. The town was known for its sock mill and a chocolate factory near the Mourning Kill creek, where the Palasek boys would swim with the scent of chocolate in the air. It was a good life for young boys, but not one that was earning enough for a family of nine. Before long, they returned to Port Washington with the hope that opportunities would improve as the nation moved past the shadow of Black Friday, 1929. Two of the Palasek sons, Steve and Carl, joined the Civilian Conservation Corps (CCC) in 1933 to help the family. They worked hard and were away from home and family for the first time, as laborers on government projects. It was similar to the work their father had done for years. They were supplied with food, clothing and shelter at the location or camp where they labored, and sent most of their $30 a month home to their families as a part of their agreement with the CCC. The experience gave Steve and Carl their first taste of independence as they approached the age of 20. This would have a considerable effect on how they conducted their lives in the future.

Chapter 2

As Stephen and Carl Palasek were on their way to work with the CCC in 1933, significant events were occurring overseas. The economy in Europe was struggling. The German Mark had been virtually worthless for over a year. With several political parties struggling for power based on the promise that they would turn the German economy around, the Nazi party representative, Adolf Hitler, was chosen as Chancellor of the new coalition government. Within one year, the sole party in control of Germany was the Nazi party. After the death of German President Paul Von Hindenburg in August of 1934, the German military recognized Adolf Hitler as the leader of Germany and declared him as "Fuhrer." The word simply meant "leader" before World War II. Henceforth, it would stir emotions in people as if the meaning was considerably darker. Moving swiftly with a desire for power, Hitler disregarded troop and military limitations set upon Germany by the Treaty of Versailles and, without consideration of the protests from other European nations, built the largest army in Germany's history. Looking back, it is difficult to fathom that this military buildup did not stir more of a global concern to bring it to a halt. One must also consider that each nation was struggling to rectify its own problems brought on by the Depression; focusing on other countries that did not directly affect each other at the time was not important to their own recovery.

Germany was not alone as it began a less-than-subtle move for power during hard economic times. In Italy, Fascist dictator Benito Mussolini moved troops into Africa to take control of Ethiopia. About this same time, Hitler moved troops and the machines of war into what was known as the Rhineland, an area close to the Netherlands that had been demilitarized by the aforementioned Treaty of Versailles. These moves were occurring in the early and mid-1930s; though protested by many nations, they were not declared acts of war, nor did any nation outside of those directly affected raise a finger in battle to stop these aggressions. On the other side of the globe, Japan — one of the designers of the League of Nations agreements — disregarded this pact outright and, in 1932, moved its army into a Manchurian state of China and occupied it.

In 1936, Civil War broke out in Spain when General Francisco Franco moved army officers from Spanish Morocco across the short strait between Spain and Africa to overthrow the recently-elected republican government in Spain. Both Mussolini and Hitler supported Franco's overthrow of the government with troops from Italy and Germany, but the powerful French and British nations did not wish to interfere. France and England's position of staying at arm's length from the war was apparently seen by both Hitler and Mussolini, who called their partnership the Rome-Berlin Axis, as a weakness in Europe. That nations would not stand in support of each other in war could work to their mutual advantage. The United States, having developed a frame of mind that its involvement in the First World War may have been a mistake, enacted the Neutrality Act, which was signed by President Franklin Delano Roosevelt. This act prohibited the use of troops, ships and weapons of the United States in wars on foreign soil — yet another factor that Hitler and Mussolini considered as being a weakness that they could use to their advantage.

As for Americans like the Palasek family, the top concern of the day was not of foreign affairs, but rather the everyday struggle to earn enough money to feed and clothe the family. There was a growing concern among newer immigrants to America, dependent upon where they had immigrated from and how involved their native land was in the changes that were taking place overseas. Yet the majority of immigrants came here to escape the troubles back home and seek a better life in America, even in these hardest of times.

In 1938, Adolf Hitler took advantage of a growing movement of support for the Nazi government in Germany to force Austrian Chancellor Kurt Von Schuschnigg to give up control of Austria to

Germany based upon their Germanic connection as a form of unification, known as the Anschluss. Again, France and England stood back silently. It seemed that Hitler's aim was to place all lands with historical ties to Germany under his control. In what may be one of the biggest errors of capitulation, in an attempt to retain peace, British Prime Minister Neville Chamberlain agreed in a meeting with Adolf Hitler, Benito Mussolini and French Prime Minister Edouard Daladier that the Sudeten region of Czechoslovakia (which was rich in German heritage) should allow itself to be occupied by German troops. Mr. Chamberlain proudly returned to England waving the piece of paper signed by Hitler in his raised hand, declaring to the people of England that he had achieved "peace in our time." This proclamation could not have been further from reality.

The forceful actions of Nazi-controlled Germany pressed on more boldly in late 1938 and England began to consider whether it might have been a mistake to allow Germany to control the Sudeten region of Czechoslovakia. Concerns became increasingly grave when the Germans took revenge against Jews in Austria and Germany in retaliation for the murder of a German diplomat in Paris by a Polish Jew, who was of German birth. Known as Kristallnacht, or the Night of Breaking Glass, windows of homes and shops belonging to Jews were shattered as over 90 Jews were killed and thousands were arrested. Hundreds of synagogues were destroyed. Soon after, the German army moved into Prague and Lithuania under the guise that these areas were also predominantly of German background. The Danzig region of Western Poland, close to the borders of Germany, shifted after the First World War to the control of Poland, unifying Prussia and Poland. Hitler stressed that the Germans there were oppressed and should be a part of Germany, but Poland was resistant and received a promise from England that it would help to stop any such takeover — a first sign that nations may step in to assist other nations against German aggression.

Months of negotiations between leaders of Germany, the Soviet Union, England and France (with some meetings more secretive than others) took place through the summer of 1939. Tradeoffs were discussed, concerning who would take what regions of which countries in exchange for respecting Germany's aggressive wishes. Or would it be better to stop Hitler's moves completely? On the first day of September 1939, Germany invaded Poland with a considerable amount of the military might it had built up with no fear of retaliation, due to the slow response from France and England's rebuilding military to actually show that they could protect Poland as promised. On September 3, 1939, with great reluctance, England declared war on Germany, thus beginning another war between nations only 25 years after the War to End All Wars had concluded. Though some nations were drowned in this flood of aggression, other nations that were yet not directly affected did not see it as their concern.

    Rather than turning into a political takeover, the military attack on Poland resulted in nations across Europe taking diverse positions. These were at first largely dependent on how important a trading partner Germany was to each particular nation. Denmark, Sweden and Norway, major trading partners with Germany, at first took neutral positions regarding the attacks on Poland. Lithuania and Switzerland, smaller nations with borders where German goods moved, refused to allow any military supplies to pass through if intended for any country with leanings toward the Axis powers of Germany and Italy. Italy itself, a partner in the Pact of Steel, was also keeping its political distance from the attacks on Poland. The Soviet Union, claiming that its nationals living in Poland were being mistreated as a lower class of residents, began its own attack campaign from Poland's eastern front, the opposite direction of Germany's attacks.

    Stanislaus and Marjanna Palasek were becoming distressed that the homeland they had left behind was now under siege. What was to become of family and friends that they had left behind? More of their growing boys sought out work appropriate to their ages, in order to support the family. Newspaper delivery routes, laboring at small factories, learning to put slate roofs on houses were sometimes big jobs for young men, but they did whatever they could to contribute to the family as the difficult financial times continued.

    With the United States suffering from the effects of financial depression when he took office, President Franklin Delano Roosevelt chose, as one of his methods to calm concerns of the nation, to present on a regular basis his "Fireside Chats." Broadcast on the radio, these chats were a way for the President to explain what the government was doing to bring recovery in simple, everyday language. To let America know that, as he stated at the start of his Presidency, "the only thing we have to fear, is fear itself," and that recovery was possible. As the affairs of the world were now becoming as great of a concern as the economy and recovery, President Roosevelt stated in one of his chats, "I have seen war and I hate war." Yet, as time passed he realized that there was a need to repeal the Neutrality Act that he had previously signed so that aid in the form of arms could be supplied to troops who were trying to save Poland while still keeping American lives out of harm's way. By the end of 1939, the American weapons embargo was lifted, a sign of American sympathies toward France and England. In the Eastern hemisphere, Japan was beginning to lose its grip on Chinese provinces it had previously taken following unsuccessful battles with Chinese nationals and Soviet troops bordering the Japanese-held areas of China.

The German Secret State Police, the Geheime Staatspolizei (better known as the Gestapo), began herding Poles — particularly, but not solely, Jews — into areas of cities where they were cut off from the outside world. Cruelly treated in these "ghettoes," many were killed with little reason by the Gestapo. Other Poles were being sent to "work camps" for forced labor. News came that half of the 9,000 residents of Marjanna's hometown of Wyszkow were taken prisoner just for being Jews. All Stanislaus and Marjanna could do was to go to St. Peter's Church in Port Washington or to Saint Hyacinth across the harbor in Glen Head (if transportation was available), where mass was said in Polish, and pray with others they knew for peace and salvation for their homeland. They were fully aware of the problems friends and family back in Poland faced, but what was there to be done by poor immigrants in a land that was an ocean and many days removed?

Hermann Goring, a German pilot of considerable merit in the First World War, had risen through the Nazi party and was appointed leader of the German military under Hitler. He immediately made plans to expand German control into Norway. In Poland, Germany's Schutzstaffel (which loosely translates to "Protection Corps" but was better known as the "SS") began setting up concentration camps for the interment and eventual genocide of

Jews and other resistors who were to be sent there from occupied Poland as well as well as cities such as Berlin in Germany. The Russians were making their own aggressive moves on Finland from the east as Germany expanded its attack on Norway and moved troops into Denmark that spring.

A major transformation in power occurred in England that spring of 1940. Having given Prime Minister Neville Chamberlain a vote of no confidence, Parliament forced him to resign. Chamberlain did not believe, at the outset of German aggressions, that there would be an expansion of hostile movements beyond certain regions of Poland. In 1938 when Chamberlain had signed an accord with Germany, Winston Churchill stated, "You were given the choice between war and dishonor. You chose dishonor, and you will have war." Two years later, Churchill would be chosen as the new Prime Minister of England, replacing Chamberlain.

German tanks moved into Belgium, the Netherlands and France that same week in May. Within days, the Netherlands surrendered to Germany and its queen, Wilhelmina, took refuge in England. Belgium fell soon afterwards. British troops, holding the port city of Dunkirk on the northern coast of France, destroyed as much of the seaport as possible in order to make it useless to the Germans, then left the city (as well as the northern coast and the people of France) without defense against the Germans. The British troops were no longer capable of defending Norway, and left as that nation fell in June of 1941 to the Germans. It was only a matter of weeks before Paris itself fell to the Germans and Nazi troops marched through the streets. Italy, possibly seeing the course the war was taking and having its own plans for domination of other countries, declared war on England and France and invaded France from the southeast, showing its alignment with Nazi Germany. France's government felt that it was left with no other option than to sign an armistice agreement with Germany and Italy. Even though the government and many of the people of France had succumbed to the invaders, France became a divided nation, if not on the map, then at least in the hearts of the French people. The north of France was controlled by Germany, the German military having moved south and west from the English Channel and Germany. A new French "government," completely under German control, aligned itself with the Axis powers of Germany, Italy and now, with some surprise, Japan. This new French body, which was primarily formed to police the southern portion of the nation on behalf of the Axis, was known as the Vichy government, using the name of the city where its installed Premier of France, Phillipe Petain, sat. Another France also came into existence: Free France. Unrecognized by the Axis and considered a terrorist, underground group by Vichy, this group — led by French General Charles de Gaulle —primarily comprised French soldiers who had escaped Paris before Germany's invasion of that city and those who sympathized with the belief that France must remain free of Axis control.

This war and the insatiable yearning for control and dominance did not stay within the boundaries of Europe or, in the case of Japan's aggressions, Southeast Asia. Anyone who has been to northern Africa today would surely notice that many of those nations still reflect an influence of France, as many of them were once under French control. Many natives speak French as one of their languages and, for example, just as in the motion picture "Casablanca," the police in Morocco still dress in the uniform of the French Gendarmerie. But with France seemingly under the control of the Axis powers by mid-1940, the Axis now felt it necessary to be sure that France's influence in Africa was actually that of the Axis through the Vichy government. In July of 1940, Italian forces had moved into the Sudan and Kenya in Africa. Two months later, Italian troops moved into Libya and soon after, Egypt. The war had now expanded to a third continent and was becoming more global.

In 1940, President Roosevelt was re-elected to an unprecedented third term, which the Constitution still allowed at that time. The nation sought strength and stability as the possibility of once again being involved in a global war loomed darkly over its collective shoulder. Not long after his inauguration in 1941, Roosevelt signed the "Lend-Lease Bill," which would allow the U.S. to supply billions of dollars in U.S. war materials to Britain, "Free" France, the Soviet Union and China for their defense. In July, the United States made its first movement of troops relating to the war, even though these troops would not see action. In support of England, U.S. troops were moved into Iceland in order to replace British troops who were stationed there. This move would allow the British troops to fight in Europe and Africa against the Axis.

Early in 1941, German troops moved into northern Africa in response to England loosening Italy's grip on the region. Germany's Panzer tank divisions, led by General Erwin Rommel, "The Desert Fox," swept across the Mediterranean coast of the "Dark Continent" toward Libya and eventually into Egypt. Before the middle of the year, Yugoslavia had fallen to the Axis powers and Germany was also moving its troops into the Soviet Union. A new word entered the military lexicon: Blitzkrieg, a concentrated mechanized attack behind enemy lines. The blitz of German bombings upon England escalated with heavy destruction in London, and the temporary closing of the port in Liverpool.

Japan's aggression in the eastern Pacific increased as well. It was the stated belief of the Japanese foreign minister that the Oceania region — which extended from Japan through Southeast Asia, the island nations of the Philippines and Indonesia, all the way to Australia — was the land of the Asian people and whites had no right or purpose to be there. Over one million Japanese men were drafted in order to prepare to fight the British and most likely the positioning American troops in the Asian rim, in order that Japan might occupy French Indo-China. Assets of Japan in England and the United States were frozen based upon these and other aggressive stances. The spread of the German war machine and Nazi cruelties were becoming intolerable, leading the United States congress to allow American ships, not just foreign freighters to unload supplies and weapons of American origin in England, thus bringing an end to the Neutrality Act.

December 1941 was the month when America's role in the war changed from military assistance to deep involvement. At dawn on December 7, the American Naval base that had been set up in the Hawaiian islands was attacked by over 300 Japanese fighters, bombers and the infamous kamikaze planes which were essentially manned torpedoes flown by pilots who knew they would die "with honor" upon delivery of the plane and its explosives directly into their target. Over 2,000 Americans died and another 1,200 were wounded that morning. The following day, President Roosevelt called it a "day that will live in infamy" as he declared war on Japan and officially brought the United States into the global conflict. A mere three days later, with Japan now in a declared war against the United States, its Axis partners of Italy and Germany declared war on the United States. The threat on American interests and Allies around the world had been increasing week by week for the past few years. Now, the threat was not only against others close to the United States, but on the United States and its territories. The hopes of staying out of the war were dashed and Americans resoundingly stepped up to answer the call to battle in whatever way they could. The Palasek boys were to be no exception.

Chapter 3

Stan Palasek was the fifth son of Stanislaus and Marjanna. Born in 1920, he was above all a young man with his sights on career goals he dreamt to achieve. He loved modern technology and though he had jobs as a slate roofer's assistant, a cabin boy on a local yacht and a golf caddy, he studied the field of electronics and electronic communication, mostly from borrowed books. He could also be considerably headstrong. Always willing to learn, but also forceful in his opinions based upon what he learned in his studies, he felt that he was almost always correct in his personal feelings about religion, politics, science and life when speaking with others.

On a warmer-than-usual October day in the fall of 1939, Port Washington High School was playing a football game against nearby rivals from Roslyn High School at noon. Stan, a graduate of the Port Washington school, decided to take a girl from Roslyn he had been seeing on occasion to the game. Helen Krayewski was tall with platinum blonde hair. To Stan, she was a glamorous beauty. Helen liked the idea of going to the game but asked if they could make this a double date. She wanted to make a connection between her friend from nearby Roslyn Heights, Mary, and another friend, Richard. Her friend, Mary Rykowski, was also quite beautiful in her own simpler way. Much more reserved than Helen with a subtle, Mona Lisa type of smile and brown hair, she was more the type to politely giggle than to laugh out loud as Helen might. Mary's date, Richard Henderson, was outgoing and loved to laugh, having no qualms concerning his suitable nickname, "Chubby."

After the game ended with Port Washington's victory, the four headed back to Roslyn, climbing into Stan's 1932 Plymouth. "Climbing in" is a particularly appropriate term, especially for young Mary and the portly Chubby, as they had to ride in what was known as "the rumble seat." The two-door convertible coupe had only a small storage area behind the front seats; behind that, where the trunk of modern cars would be found, was a hatch that flipped open to reveal a cushioned seat that faced forward but was exposed to any and all elements or hazards that were in the air that particular day. On the poorly paved roads of the times, there were many hazards to watch for. Additionally, the seat — located directly above the rear wheels of the car — had a tendency to give the passengers more of a "rumble" than those in front. As the four friends headed back to Roslyn along West Shore Road at considerable speed, the car hit a pothole and Mary went face first into the unpadded steel of the car's body directly in front of the rumble seat. Stan and Helen both failed to notice her injury, and Mary made no issue of it until they pulled into the dirt drive of the Rykowski property on Powerhouse Road. Mary's right eye was swelling shut and the area was severely reddened. Her three companions helped her from the car and into the house. Mary's mother, Theodora, was not at all pleased to see her daughter come home in such a state, much less in the company of her friend Helen and two men Theodora did not know. Mary went to bed with as much ice on her eye as could be had in a house with only an icebox for refrigeration.

The next day, after Sunday mass at St. Peter's in Port Washington, Stanley headed back to Roslyn to check up on his injured passenger. Mary's mother was not home, as she was visiting cousins with her husband Adolph — her weekly tradition after church. Mary's younger sister Sophie, who looked much like Mary, answered the door and Stanley breathed a small sigh of relief, as he believed her to be Mary — and she wasn't even bruised! Then, Sophie introduced herself and Stanley asked if Mary was home. He was let in and found Mary in the kitchen with a less swollen but seriously blackened eye. Stan offered his apologies and the two sat and talked for much of the afternoon.

Stanley returned several times that week. Soon his dates with Helen ended and they went their separate ways. Although Mary found Stanley to be a bit quirky and certainly outspoken, there was something about him that she liked. He would go on about all of the things he had done and hoped to do some day, particularly in the areas of new engineering concepts. At the age of 15, Mary was becoming very interested in spending her time getting to know Stan.

One week after Mary's 17th birthday, she and Stan were married at St. Peter's in Port Washington in a simple ceremony that was followed by a party at the Palasek house on School Street. Stan and Mary lived at that Palasek house at first, but worked to get their own place. They soon managed to get an apartment at the Nielsen Building at 62 Main Street next to the Port Washington train station, and close to the firehouse with its sirens that would wake their infant son, who was named after his father. The relationship between Stanley and Mary was never a simple one. Before they were married, Mary wrote love letters to Stanley with affectionate words such as "sweetheart" and "darling," which were "sealed with a great big kiss" assuring him of her love in response to more somber cards and notes from Stan. But marriage and motherhood for this 17-year-old woman were a change that she was not prepared for at first. She struggled. Serious arguments ensued between the couple, causing doubts in both of them of how they could stay together during their early years of marriage. With the added pressures of life during wartime, such as rationing and a difficult economy, things were not often happy in their apartment. But as much as they struggled in obvious ways and within their souls, they made it work.

Chapter 4

In July of 1940 — 15 months prior to the Japanese attack on the American fleet in Pearl Harbor and the United States' declaration of war on Japan, which was followed days later by a declaration of war on the United States by Germany and its cohort, Italy — America was already preparing for the inevitable. The Two-Ocean Navy Act was signed and set the industrial wheels in motion to produce hundreds of military ships and aircraft. Two months later, preparations were further raised with the initiation of a peacetime draft to commence in September 1940. The possibility that troops might be added to the ranks of those already in the service as career military could not wait until the last moment.

In the 1940s, communication was all but non-existent when compared to what we enjoy today. There was no internet, email, text messaging, Facebook or Twitter. Electronic communication was in its infancy, with television in its earliest stages of development and certainly not something that an average person would have in their home. Instead, visual media was limited to those who could afford the 15 or 25 cents to go to see a motion picture. There, in the darkened theater, one could see a 10-minute newsreel before the feature film. Radio was becoming a much more prevalent in-home medium, with news of the war coming between serial adventures such as "The Shadow," romance stories, and variety shows featuring stars of vaudeville and motion pictures such as George Burns, Gracie Allen and W.C Fields. Telephones were also becoming more common in some homes, but in many cases during such hard times they were still an unaffordable luxury. If one was able to have a phone, it was most likely a "party line" shared with two or three others in homes nearby; people would have to check if the line was clear before making a call, and you had to listen for your particular ring pattern to know that someone was calling you.

To Stanislaus and Marjanna Palasek, a phone was a luxury item that was certainly not necessary for their humble lives. They spoke very little English even years after moving to the United States from Poland, mostly by choice, so there was little they could understand on the radio, though they would listen. Their sons, who were all born and educated in Port Washington, were well educated and spoke English as well as Polish when necessary at home with their parents and Polish neighbors. When the time came for the boys to get involved in the war effort and leave Port Washington, there were not many ways to stay in touch with home.

As one by one, they went away, they wrote letters home — each in their own way and with the regularity that suited his personality. The letters had to be in English as they were in most cases reviewed and sometimes censored or redacted by people working for the government, whose sole job was to assure that information on military locations or strategic matters could not be seen by the enemy should the letters be intercepted. As the letters were in English, the Palasek boys did not address letters home to their Polish speaking parents, but to wives, brothers and others who spoke English back home, knowing that what they wrote would be told to their parents. For reasons to be discussed later, my father, Stanley was one of the sons who did not serve in the military. He became a relay point in their hometown for much of the communication from his brothers who did serve. That is what I discovered under that basement staircase in my mother's home on that December day in 2001: a box that held the stories of war and daily life, at home and abroad. Letters and documents in their original form as mailed and delivered to my father. It is here that this story begins yet again.

Chapter 5

In 1942, the war was mounting with strengthened ties between nations of both the Axis and Allies. The Axis powers gained territory and forced more countries into allegiance with Germany, Italy and Japan. The Allied powers, in an attempt to save both themselves from attacks upon their own countries and their independence (as well as to help other nations from domination under the Axis) strategized together and grew in strength. As a part of this, the United Nations pact was signed and was to eventually have its first headquarters on a piece of land adjacent to the Sperry Company in Lake Success, New York. With important U.S. naval victories against Japan at the Battle of Midway, hopes were rising for Americans that this war would be over sooner rather than later. More men were being brought into the armed forces in the United States day after day, both by conscription and by volunteering. It was only a matter of time before the Palasek boys would have to be involved in some way.

By the close of 1942, a gallon of gasoline cost 15 cents and bread was nine cents a loaf. But average annual wages were less than $2,000 and gas was rationed to assure sufficient supplies for the military and government. The average civilian was only allowed to purchase three gallons per week. Movies such as "Bambi" and "Casablanca," the latter telling a tale of the Moroccan city under the control of the Germans and Vichy-France, were released in theaters.

The U.S. Government began issuing war bonds. Known as the Third War Loan, war bonds were a popular method to raise money for the war effort where citizens could purchase bonds confident that the funds would be used for the war effort with the promise of redeeming the bonds with interest after the war was over.

Stanley Palasek was 22 years old and developing his career in electronics to support his small family in late 1942. Having worked in wireless communications with Press Wireless, a division of the Marconi group that helped with communication between the military overseas and the U.S., he later went to work for Sperry Gyroscope on Long Island, a company that was developing systems to improve methods of navigation for the American military. During the summer of this year, he applied for a job that merely mentioned that electronic engineers were amongst those needed for a position that would be supporting the war effort. He excitedly went for an interview at the Empire State Building in New York City, in an office only marked by the room number. There, beside the interviewers in suits, was a man in a dress military uniform showing considerable rank. As the interview concluded successfully, with no mention of the job's duties or even a company name, Stan was asked if he would be willing to move to Tennessee. Stan considered how things were difficult for he and his wife, Mary, who was at times questioning if getting married and starting a family so young were the right choices for her. He put family first and stated that the move would not be possible at this time and explained his reasoning. Stan was thanked for coming in and asked the interviewers what the job was to have been. They simply said that it was classified and they could not discuss it further. So Stanley and his family remained in Port Washington, rather than move to Oak Ridge, Tennessee, the headquarters for the Manhattan Project — which developed the atomic bomb.

William "Willie" Palasek, the next to youngest of the brothers, was 20 years old in 1942. The sixth of the seven brothers, he looked much like his next older brother, Stan. But Willie was slight of build and unsteady in his gate and coordination. He was also easily distracted with a poor memory. One might have thought he was too much of a daydreamer. Several years later, Willie became seriously ill and the lingering illness took him while he was still a young man.

John Palasek, 25 years of age in 1942 and the third eldest of the Palasek boys, was enjoying being a free-spirited young man with no indication of settling down any time soon. He worked at construction jobs learning to be a mechanical engineer. He spent his off hours enjoying what nightlife a small town like Port Washington offered at that time. This would usually include hanging out with friends at a local tavern, drinking a shot of whiskey with a beer chaser, appropriately known then as a "boilermaker" because the heat of the whiskey being quenched by the cold of the lager would stir the idea in one's mind of steam in a boiler (that, and getting drunk fast was the other more immediate and actual result). John got into more than his fair share of fights, but more often, merely stuck by his friends and drank until closing time, flirting with the women who happened to be there and eventually leaving with a slightly crooked smile on his face. He had a furrowed brow, even as a young man and always displayed a slight smirk. Some would rightly say that he looked like a "poor man's Humphrey Bogart". Never boasting, and caring about his parents above all, he moved to 1126 Spruce Street in Chester, Pennsylvania, and worked at the Sun Shipbuilding and Drydock Company South of Philadelphia, one of the largest manufacturers of ships to the military during World War II, while waiting anxiously to be called up into service. Sun primarily built T-2 tanker ships but was also known for producing hospital ships and freighters. They also built "Liberty Ships," British-designed freighters that were quick and simple for Sun and other shipbuilding companies to make, and for the speed at which they could be built, surprisingly durable. These were perfect when the country was trying to assemble a Navy for itself and at the same time supply the same ships to its allies.

    In late fall 1942, Stanley began writing to his brother John in Pennsylvania. The letters from Stanley to John, and later to the rest of his brothers who were in the different branches of the service during the war, are lost to wherever his brothers left or kept them. Most of the letters that Stanley received from all of his brothers were saved in that simple cardboard box and in various places over decades. The letters were all handwritten and, more often than not, in the style that the particular author would speak if he was face-to-face with the reader (their brother, Stanley). At times they were terse, personal, angry or heartwarming. In reprinting these letters, it seemed appropriate to maintain many of the punctuation, spelling and grammatical errors, as well as the occasional comment that in the 21st century would be considered improper. Though they may not always sound politically correct by today's norms, this is done with no disrespect to these brave men who served our country. It does uphold the fact that these men were not college educated, but honest, hardworking and very real people.

We begin our story with two letters from John to his brother Stan from his work site at the ship building dock in Pennsylvania after he had been there for several weeks. The United States had an urgent need for ships for battle, particularly after recent warfare in the South Pacific area of Guadalcanal had taken a toll on the Navy. The ships were not only needed for combat; the freighters being built were urgently needed to supply countries that had been cut off from imports and basic needs by the war. For example, the tiny island nation of Malta, strategically located in the center of the Mediterranean, found its people were starving after massive bombings by the German air force, the Luftwaffe. The Allied mission "Stone Age" brought four freighters full of supplies, guided by armed ships. Malta, then a British territory, suffered greatly at the start of the war. It was the only incidence of an entire nation being awarded the George Cross, England's highest award for valor, for what they faced. That cross is borne on their flag to this day.

Our first letter is from Stan's brother, John, wherein John credits Shakespeare with a quote from Rudyard Kippling's "The Vampire."

From John P., Chester, PA, November, 1942 – *Dear Stanley, Boy it sure is pretty cold and breezy nowanights. Last Tuesday we had a wicked rainstorm. More like a squall at sea than anything else but it came down in buckets for a while. I didn't work that night and neither did anyone else. The next night it turned cold and the staging at the top of the ship I was on had ice on it. Last night we had our first snow here. It started like a blizzard but it only lasted about forty-five minutes. Right now we have a cold northwest wind blowing.*

I was transferred to instructing a gang of niggers Monday night and I've been working with them on the open deck. I kept warm walking around from one guy to the next but its pretty hard to keep warm doing nothing. Most of the niggers are from down south so they can't take the cold very well.

The boss told me he's working on my raise the other night so I guess I'll get it pretty soon, I hope.

Here's something I almost for got about. I received a notice from the draft board Thursday. I am now classified in 2B until May 6, 1943. So the card says anyway. [Authors note: A rating of 2B was issued to those employed in the defense industry.]

You know Stanley, I was just thinkin'. They ought to have women working on the ways then the instruction would be a lot of fun. You're a married man anyway so you won't have as much fun teaching them as I would. I think I'll try and get me a job like you got, teaching women I mean. That's just kidding though, but just between me, you and the lamp post, I'd rather teach men. I think women in general are a royal pain in the neck and the farther I stay away from them the better off I'll be. Shakespeare's definition of them is perfect. You know – "A rag, a bone, and a hank of hair."

So much for that, I'm trying to stretch this letter that's why I'm writing anything that pops into my head. I hope it reads allright. I wouldn't know since I never go back and read what I write. I guess that you know that Steve and William were here overnight. William said he liked the place but I think he was just talking. I hope he doesn't pass his examination for his own good. I really feel sorry for him if he goes. After seeing how he behaves away from home, I know he won't fit with a bunch of rough guys. Although he's 20 he seems like a little boy to me. However, its only my opinion, and I wish you wouldn't mention it to him. Well I guess that covers the situation and I don't know any good jokes, or any bad jokes either so I guess I'll sign off and until I receive a communique from somebody, I'll put me pen away. Johnny P.S. The mosquitoes are bothering me something awful (B-r-r-r-r) P.P.S. – (Some joke) – kinda korny-

One year prior, on December 7, 1941, the Japanese made a dawn air attack on the U.S. Naval base at Pearl Harbor in Hawaii, which at that time was not a state, but a territory. The attack, as mentioned earlier, brought the U.S. to declare war on Japan and began military involvement in the Second World War. On the first anniversary of this attack, the U.S. Navy launched 15 ships, an act as steeped in symbolism as it was in necessity. In a speech that day, President Roosevelt spoke encouragingly to America, pointing out victories in the Solomon Islands, Midway and North Africa. Signs, he stated, that the Allies were on their way toward victory. However, the fact that over 58,000 lives had been lost in that first year at war tempered any idea of celebration with the reality that war was indeed hell and a long, difficult road lay ahead.

From John P., Chester, PA., December 7, 1942 – *Here I go again. Better late than never though. Since this is Pearl Harbor Day, we launched two ships at 1.30 this A.M. Nice night for a launching although its cold and we have snow on the ground. It snowed most of the night Saturday so by daybreak we got quite a bit of it. I guess you've got some too.*

Things are going along as usual for me. I got the raise I was telling you about so that's that for the present. I just took a count and I find I got sixteen pieces of fan mail last month and I think I've answered them all. I've got a tough time remembering whom I wrote to and what I said so if I repeat anything just overlook it.

I don't know what you want with a gun but if you want me to investigate any arsenals in Phila. just tell me which ones and I'll take a trip. It only takes about fifteen or twenty minutes for me to get there and I can find my way around pretty well even on the subways. You just let me know what you want done and I'll do it.

Boy, this guy that rooms with me is sure snoring. He works day shift and he's always sawing wood when I come in. How do you stop a guy from snoring anyway? This guy is an artist he can snore with his mouth either open or closed. Most annoying!

I get letters from Steve and Stephanie too. I manage to write different letters to both of them. Steve wrote me about the guy who committed sewer pipe [Note: a colloquialism for suicide]. *His name was Siconolfi. I knew him and his brothers too. I also read about it in the Port Washington News which Stephanie sent me last week. I wonder what ever made her think of sending it to me.*

I sent a couple of bonds home Saturday and now I'm on my eighth one. The seventh is paid for as I should get it before Christmas. I also decided to go home for Christmas if everything goes right and I can get a train. Its only a little over two weeks away and since it will be about 3 months since I've been home I guess I should make the pilgrimage. The months seem to fly by for me for some reason or other.

I went shopping for a suit Saturday and boy, this place is more crowded than New York is. You have to elbow your way any place you go. I'm getting a suit tailor made. Just the coat and pants plus victory cuffs. I'll get it in about a week.

Well I guess that covers the situation to date and since its 5.30 I guess I'll hit the hay. I usually go to bed around six o'clock and seldom sleep to eleven.

Don't forget to let me know about that gun and if I can help you, as I said before, I will. Meantime, "Keep 'em flying." John

John makes reference here to "Victory Cuffs." Being at war with Vichy France at the time, French cuffs were commonly called by this name — not completely unlike the 2003 changing of the name of French fries to "Freedom Fries" in the U.S. Congress cafeterias due to France's opposition to U.S. actions in Iraq.

Chapter 6

In early 1943, the war was escalating in Eastern Europe between the Soviets and invading German armies with the Soviet Union showing considerable dominance in defense of Stalingrad and other cities. The Allied leaders were meeting in a liberated Casablanca, Morocco, months after Humphrey Bogart's film told the tale of the city under Axis influence. The Allies were making progress with increased air strikes on Germany and a few significant victories in Northern Africa but also suffering with struggles against the German tank commander, Rommel. The Jews within the Warsaw ghetto, under German control, staged a revolt, as places like Auschwitz in controlled Poland were becoming little more than crematoriums for those interred there by the Germans.

The year 1943 in the U.S. and in Port Washington led to the further rationing of shoes, canned food, fresh meat, dairy products and cooking oils for the war effort. Port Washington's Beacon Movie Theater on Main Street became a collection spot for "scrap drives." Here, people could bring old metal objects and empty cans which would be recycled to be used in building tanks, ships and ammunition. Collected paper was reused for packing of goods to be shipped to factories and overseas for the military. Used oil from cars and fat from kitchen cooking was to be recycled, the fat to make explosives. A familiar sign in a town shop window that was accepting certain items read, "Bring Your Fat Can Here."

Rationing was a necessary hardship. One day, Stanley Palasek's young wife Mary joined her mother-in-law Marjanna on a trip by train to Queens, New York. The word had gotten around that a market there was going to have fresh chicken available, something that was becoming a rare treat. The women returned home from their trip, having spent most of the day traveling and standing in line to find when they unwrapped the chickens from the butcher paper that the chickens were spoiled and inedible. A long day and money had been spent for nothing. It was the year that the penny was made of steel rather than copper, as copper was needed for ammunition shells and other tools of war. "In The Mood" by Glenn Miller was a hit on the radio and "Lassie Come Home" was in the movies. Even with all of the restrictions on what Americans had access to in terms of food and products, the economy was improving now that industry was in high gear producing goods for the military. And women were moving further into the workforce to replace the men who went to war, even in heavy industry, becoming known as "Rosie the Riveter."

***From John P., Chester, PA, January 19, 1943** – Dear Stanley, I haven't anything to write about and when I don't answer everybody's mail, somebody always winds up getting sore so maybe its just as well I don't write at all. Even though I don't feel guilty about anything, I wrote Stephanie [n.a.: Steve's wife] a letter apologizing for any damage I might have done. She never answered my letter so I guess she must be mad. Women seem to have an awful lot of foolish pride in my opinion but there isn't one alive that will make me crawl. Her old man made a dirty crack to William about* me so maybe somebody owes me an apology. I'll admit that I should have been home on Christmas Eve and also should have gone to church but its just one of those things I guess. I was having a lot of fun and even though nobody approves of it I still had a good time. And though I say a lot of things when I'm pickled, I don't mean them when I sober up. I know everybody has ideas about what I do down at the shore but its nothing to be taken as seriously as they take it. I have fun my way and I don't get much chance out here so if anyone else was in my boots they'd do the same, if not worse. Too bad people have such gossipy tongues around Port [Washington]. I'll always enjoy giving them something to talk about. But you can take it from me that whatever you may have heard about me at home, you know, about me hanging around with a certain girl is nothing serious just a lot of fun for me, it was anyway. You'll admit its nice to have one hanging around your neck for awhile but as far as I'm concerned not for life. I always had my own ideas on the subject and we'll discuss it to greater lengths sometime. I will say that I don't believe in love anyway. It's only physical attraction and that wears off with age. But so much for that, I never intended to wander off in so many different directions in this letter so, as I said, we'll cover that subject another time.

    I just answered a letter I got from William. He seems to think that his going to work will cause me to be drafted. I told him that it wouldn't make any difference either way since I'm not a married man and whether or not I get in the army is a matter of time only. He'd be crazy in the head if he didn't go to work because if I could get another deferment it would only prolong the agony. You've got to go sometime and no matter how essential a man's job is, he's going as soon as he can be replaced. Besides, if he was working I could save some money maybe to get my teeth fixed which is something I have to do and it would be a big help to me. So tell him that will you?

    We have an epidemic of small-pox around here as you might have read in the papers. According to the latest report there were 36 blocks quarantined here in Chester. The company is supposed to vaccinate all employees but we're still waiting. If it ever breaks out in the yard there will be hell to pay what with 35,000 employees there.

I've got a new roommate now. Another guy moved out and I'm damned glad too since he worked day shift and used to snore like hell. This guy likes to drink and works third shift so he comes in around 10 A.M. most of the time which is okay by me. He doesn't snore either.

We had a little excitement one night last week. One of our men burned a nice hole about 6" x 8" in the shaft alley which is where the propeller shaft is. I had a hell of a time fitting the piece in again and I ground it down after a welder welded it up. Its not noticeable now but if the Maritime Commision Inspector ever sees it they'll have to rip out the whole plate which is about 20' x 6' and its all welded solid. That's it for now. John

Also signing up to go to war in 1943 was Joseph, the fourth son. A young and handsome 32-year-old, Joseph was a warm and friendly young man. Joseph had met Margaret as 1940 approached, during some of America's hardest years. Margaret appeared to be and presented herself to be much like the "girl next door" but to the Palasek parents, immigrants living in a small town, she was from a different life in some ways to what they were familiar with as Polish immigrants. Margaret was born and raised in the borough of Manhattan in New York, a train ride of almost an hour away, and she would visit cousins who lived in Port Washington. Her father commuted daily to Port Washington where he worked at a metal pipe factory. While they both happened to be attending a semi-professional baseball game in Port Washington, Joe and Margaret met and began talking and they discovered that her cousins lived within a short walk of the Palasek home. Always smiling, she was the perfect companion to Joe and his cheerful, "things may be tough but they could be worse" attitude. One considerable stumbling block did exist in their relationship. Margaret was not of Polish decent and therefore she had a lot to prove to be considered worthy of mother Marjanna Palasek's approval. But Marjanna was apparently willing to give Margaret a chance. Marjanna, who loved to be in the kitchen or shopping, shared time in both pursuits with Margaret, as she had with the women in the lives of her other sons. Even though Margaret spoke no Polish and Marjanna usually did, whether by habit or purpose, Margaret — who Joe affectionately called Maggie — was quickly welcomed on her visits with Joe and became very close to Marjanna. The rest of the family warmed quickly to her and before long, she and Joseph were wed in New York City — which was quite an experience for this family from a small suburban town. Joe, who was well aware of what his brothers were planning in regards to the war, believed wholeheartedly that it was right, and joined the Army. At this early stage of U.S. involvement, men who had small children were not permitted to enter the service without a written letter granting permission to do so from their wives. There was no stopping Joseph from his intention to sign up, so Margaret regrettably signed what was necessary and sadly sent her brave husband to serve his country, leaving her and her young son Joe at home.

German troops occupied many territories they claimed were rightfully theirs across the Soviet border, and the battles between the soldiers of these countries were intense that spring. More and more people were being placed into the German-run concentration camps with little chance of ever seeing their loved ones again. And the German U-boats were attacking Allied vessels as they crossed the Atlantic from below the surface with great success, with at least 50 ships sunk between February and March of 1943.

Fort McClellan in Alabama, named for the less-than-successful Civil War general, had been established in 1917 as a military camp in the Chocolocco foothills. Renamed as a fort in World War II and continuously maintained and upgraded prior to the war as a basic training center, it was the source of the first trained troops that were sent to war after the attack on Pearl Harbor in 1941. Almost half a million soldiers trained there during World War II. As contemporary of a facility as it was, it was deep in the hot south, a different type of place for many of the men that trained there from the northeast, including Joe Palasek.

From Joe, Fort McClellan, AL, Spring, 1943 – *Hello Stanley, Hows everything. As for me I've got about 8 weeks of basic trainning here in Alabama then the shipped you to another camp for about 3 to 4 months then they ship you over. Stanley please get me a good fountain pen and pencle and Maggie will pay you for it. And tell her to send those rationning books in and if you haven't got any thing to do write me even if you don't here from me for a short* time that will be because I haven't time and if you whant me to send you a pillow case| That's about all they got here so send me some stamps and I'll get you one there pretty there gold and have Fort McClellan on them I want to send one home to and tell Maggie to send me some stamps and paper but I forget to write|

Please tell Maggie to send me a little pocket knife just a small one. Hows Mary and Little Stanley is he walking yet. I haven't got nothing else to write so I am signing off Your Brother Joe

From Joe, Fort McClellan, AL, April 11, 1943 – Hello Stanley Hows every thing back home. As for me i think that my legs are wearing out every day. And the weather here is hot as hell the temperture goes up as high as 110-120 and boy that hot. And these godam mountains are full of rattle snakes and copper head.

Listen Stanley you asked me what the IRTC standed for well it means Infantry Replacement Training Center. And you know yourself that the infantry covers a lot of things so I know I'm in the infantry. But what branch of service well I'll find out in my next camp.

Listen Stanley if you want my advice about the army. Well wait till they draft you. It doesn't matter how much you know about radio you still got to go through your basic training and as much as I wrote and told you how tuff it is I'm only telling you in a letter but that 13 weeks you suffer and I'm not lying there ain't a bone in your body that doesn't ache. So you see even these officers I mean Luetenats where Buck privates and they had to go throw the mill and it's a tuff one to. So just wait till your time comes and I don't think youll go wrong.

Another thing you asked me whats the nearest town well were 6 miles from the town and it's a little jerke town called annerston [n.a. Anniston] its right on the border line of Georgia. Another thing Stanley we never have time off. I write all these letters in 10 fifteen minutes between things, when were all through drilling weve got to take our guns apart wipe all the dust of and oil it and that takes about 2 hours in order to pass inspection. Then we got to wash our legging shine our shoes scrub the hut and when were all through is about time to go to sleep and start and start the old army grind. And that's the same old story every day we don't even know what day it is.

This Alabama is hot as hell in the day and full of rattlesnakes and copper head. But the nights are cool as hell. And I wont take a shower so I'll be rareing to go tomorrow so it so long for a while. So its Good night and God Bless you and Mary and the Little Battle, Joe

The Axis' hold over North Africa was being solidly crushed as the spring of 1943 progressed. Nation by nation, the Allies were gaining more control in the Mediterranean and preparing for an assault on Italy. By July, Italy had all but given up, having arrested dictatorial leader Benito Mussolini upon his return from Berlin, after a vote of no confidence by the other government leaders of Italy and upon the direct orders of Italy's reinstated King.

Not all of the mail received from the Armed Forces at 62 Main Street was from one of the Palasek brothers. Mary, Stan's young wife, had a brother named John Rykowski. John was three years her senior, and she loved him dearly — not only because they were the closest in age to each other, but that they were true friends as much as they were siblings. After the birth of Mary and Stan's son, Stan Jr. in March of 1942, John was thrilled to be the young boy's godfather. John was a poster boy for new men in uniform with his good looks and cheerful smile. He was of mild demeanor and loved his family and his new godchild. During the spring of 1943, he went off to the Army. As with many soldiers from the area, he went first to Camp Upton on Long Island to be inducted. Within days, he travelled "deep in the heart of Texas" to Camp Bowie, which became the largest basic training facility in that state during World War II.

From John R., Camp Bowie, TX, May 27, 1943 – *Dear Mary and family, I'm in the Army know, for about two weeks, and I didn't have much time to write.*

I'm down here in Texas. It toke us sixty-one hours to get here from Camp Upton. I'm in the tank division it is called the suicide squad. The food was pretty good for a week, then after that we got stew for dinner and supper for three days straight. I'm down here with quite a few friends from Roslyn.

*You ought to see the emblems we got to put on our shoulders, it's a tiger with a tank in its mouth, its outstand, orange and black. Well I can't think of anything much to write, until I here from you. Another thing we were told that we might be shipped to Wisconsin within a couple of weeks. Give my regard to the rest of the folks.
Your Brother, Johnny*

    As spring evolved into summer in 1943, the Allies were making considerable gains over the Axis hold on northern Africa with battle victories in Tunisia followed by the Axis surrendering there in May. The British RAF (Royal Air Force) was now staging its own air raids over German cities like Stuttgart in retaliation for the blitzes across England by Germany and more importantly to damage the German war machine. The Germans, on the other hand, were continuing to toughen efforts to destroy the rebellions in the Warsaw ghettoes and send the residents to concentration camps. By July, Allied troops invaded Sicily by sea after airstrikes there were not successful. It was to become the first time the Allies took control of an area within the homelands of any Axis power. Stateside, John Palasek had been cleared for service in the U.S. Navy and was excited to be leaving his job at the Sun Shipyard.

    Stephen Palasek was the eldest son at age 28 years old when he volunteered for the Army, seeing it as his patriotic duty. He was an easygoing young man, quick witted and kind with dark, wavy hair. He loved his family and preferred holding back his own feelings and thoughts if it would keep the peace, but when an idea was set in his mind, he was insistent on carrying it through — hopefully with his family's support.

    A few years earlier, Steve, became friends with the sons of the neighboring Wrobel family. Steve would go to visit the boys and would always end up chatting with their mother, Mrs. Wrobel, in Polish. Stephanie, the eldest daughter in the Wrobel house, was tall with blonde hair and eyes that seemed to twinkle when she smiled. She was quite taken by Steve's good looks and kindness to her mother. When Steph was busy with chores or reading a book, she would also spend as much time glancing over to her mother and Steve talking. She felt sure that a popular fellow like Steve would not be interested in her. But he would visit with her father and brothers at the nearby Grumman aircraft factory on Manhasset Isle near their homes, and he always took time to visit Stephanie, who was also working there. Before long, Stephen, who was four years older than Stephanie, asked her to a dance. She accepted and more dances followed where either local musicians formed combos or 78 RPM records of the latest hits were played on Victrolas. It was a way for them to enjoy time together without having to spend too much of the money he earned in order to help with the Palasek family bills. Several months passed and as they left one of the dances in town, an unexpected summer rain was coming down faster and heavier with every step they took from the hall. As they crossed at a bend in the Long Island Rail Road tracks on the way back to the Wrobel home, a train was bearing down on them — seemingly from nowhere. Perhaps the heavy rain drowned out the sound of the train, or it was merely eclipsed by the joy of two people distracted by love, but the lights of the train were approaching quickly. Steve squeezed Stephanie's hand and hurried her clear of the tracks. They took shelter from the rain beneath the porch roof of a small store that was closed for the night to catch their breath. It was then that Stephen asked Stephanie to marry him, an idea that 17-year-old Stephanie's parents were adamantly against. Stephanie was as strong-willed of a person as could be imagined for all of her life, and insisted that she was going to marry Steve one way or another. Months later, the two were wed in a ceremony as grand as the times and the families' means would allow.

  In 1942, Steve broke Stephanie's heart with great regret when he decided he had to serve in the Army. They had a five-year-old little girl named Regina and Steve would not be allowed to serve without the same written permission from Stephanie that Joe had acquired from Margaret. Stephanie loved Steve dearly; she hated to see him leave for the war and did not want to feel that she was signing a paper that may get the man she loved killed. She also sensed in her heart that if she did not sign, Steve would possibly resent her and it may be an issue between the two of them for years to come. With the deepest of sadness, she signed and sent him to the Army, a matter that she refused to discuss for decades after.

From Steve, Camp Upton, Long Island, NY, August 17, 1943 – Hello Folks, Remember me I a soldier at Camp Upton. I guess Upton is still winning because we are still here. Before I ask you about my doings here I want to ask you how are you all? Hope you are all well and keeping the wheels of Progress turning.

Now I just want to tell you a little about myself here. We got to Camp Upton quarter after one Fri. and this is my fifth day here. All the boys from Port are still here but in different Barracks. We see each other at night. I am loose always. I am orderly in my barrack, in charge of 42 men. All day I sit alone in the barrack because that's me job. I have plenty of responsibility.

Well I don't know when we shall get shipped I hope it is soon. The army is not so bad if one could take it. But lord you should see the weepers we have. I only pity the boys when they go to the next camp and start basic training.

By the way Stanley I want to tell you about my test here. I took an I.Q. also a mechanical apptitude test, also have been interviewed by the different officers in Technical Dept. I don't get no details or K.P. at no time. My job is to get the boys up 5.30 A.M. see that they wash make there beds the army way clean the barracks up and out for breakfast. I give there mail out and keep all names on a roster as after breakfast they all go out on different details such as cutting grass, making side walks, picking up trash machine shops, clerical work and a thousand other jobs. I get my barracks orders through a speaker from headquarters and I answer through a mike. I wake the different boys up at 3.30 A.M. for K.P. So you see all I do is write a list every day for guys who disobey orders. To my figures and from the Sargeant I hear that I will be in the Engineers or tanks. But I sure had an oral test of 50 questions and 100 written test. I don't mind they took me back from the day I left school, to the day I entered the army. All the record goes into my service book. I got two shots so far, all of my equipment.

Well folks I must sign off now and please excuse my scratching for I have no pen or ink. In conclusion I am wishing you all lots of good luck my best regards, God bless you and keep you. So I say so long for a while. Steve

By midsummer of 1943, Camp Hanahan outside of steamy New Orleans was changed from being solely a staging area for soldiers to prepare to board ships for the war to a full-blown basic training center, even though it still maintained that "staging area" title. Here Steve mentions the importance of receiving letters from home.

From Steve, Basic Training, Late August, 1943 – hello Folks, Well, here we are in Louisiana. Each weekend we have tests written and oral on all one weeks progress. We work from schedule and have 5 minutes out of each hour to take a smoke. This Army life is tough but a good one. If you can take it and try to comply with the rules and regulations. It's a tough fight still we are gaining slow but sure. We have faith in the good lord to guide us and watch over us. A soldiers life is in the open under the stars in the heavens, good old solid mother earth to tread on, the open spaces. Good news a letter from home is his consolement, his morale builder his courage and determination to make the best of it with what you have. So far these are some of the things we under went in training.

One The Care of our Weapons and Gas mask, Recognition of enemy planes tanks and vehicles. Obedience and Discipline. Natural use of Cover and Concealment Appreciation of Terrain Security, Fire and movement Prompt Reports To Combat intelligence, Plus Common Sense, which each soldier is supposed to use the appliance of the above mentioned will carry any soldier through hell.

Well Stanley I covered an awful lot of territory I guess I'll have to be shortening up a bit. Yes is it's all in the game. I don't know what the next move will be, but I hope it's a good one. Well Stan, I did write Joe mail, but I haven't had an answer as yet, I guess he isn't settled as yet so let's give him time. I wish him the best of luck for he and all of us will need it. If you should hear from him let me know for I to would like to know his where abouts.

Well folks I am getting my field pack ready plus good many other things ready for action, so I say so long for a while my best wishes and regards to your little family and the rest, May God Bless you all I sign off a good soldier one of yours always. Steve

From Joe, Fort McClellan, Alabama, Summer 1943

– Hello Stan, How you all as for me I never felt better in my life I'm in 1A condition and hope you all are the same. Well Stanley, how do you like your new apartment I'll bet its nice. Well I got myself one but these 15 borders in here with me and they don't want to move out. But I really think that they can't they tell me they got a lease here and are going to stay here just as long as I am so you see there's nothing I can do about it so I guess they just have to stay. Is Uncle Sam still giving out these free apartment in Port W. Well maybe someday we can move out and come back to civilian life but right now we got a little job to do and the quicker we do it the quicker we can wear a white shirt and a sport suit but I guess there's no use in getting to anxious because will get a chance at those guys across the pond that think that they can lick the hole world well I guess they bit off more than they can chew when they bumped into the United Forces.

Well Stanley you say in your letter that Mary's brother went AWOL. I Don't know what he got for it but in this camp they really suffer. One guy was AWOL just for missing a formation and he got 3 months of hard labor and had to pay 13 dollars a month out of his own pocket. Another guy went 14 days AWOL and he got 6 months of hard labor and 24 dollars a month out of his own pocket so you see it's not worth it because after this mess is over you got to make that time up and you don't get paid.

Boy this basic training is tuff but it's worth to go through this routine and get toughened up then now nothing and get over there and get your head blown off. I know I wasn't tough when I was in civilian life but now I'm as hard as a rock and am ably to take this grind we go through and it's only for our own good. So I never thought I'd now anything about the M1 rifle were issued made by Garand. Hell I can take it apart in the dark and put it together because every night we got to clean our rifles and pass inspection or we get gigged. [Author's note: "Gigged"was a term used in the military if one should receive a demerit.] But I think I like the Carbine rifle better than this M1. The only thing wrong is that the sights are not so hot so you can't get a good sight picture. But the M1 is the rifle. You can sure squeeze of the shots and get the correct windage and its accurate as hell.

The B.A.R. [Browning Automatic Rifle] is some weapon but it's to heavy to move around but it shure is a buiety. We fire the rocket out of the Imfield and that thing can put a tank out of commission the damn thing can go through 5 inches of steel so you see what it can do to a tank if you hit it in the belly.

Boy I sure am anxious to find out what branch of the infantry I'm in but I guess I just have to wait and find out when I get to my next camp. What I really like is to be is a machine gunner. But I think they'll probly put me in one of them heavy tanks. But I don't care where the hell they put me. You no one thing that if it wasn't for the Infantry we wouldn't have taken Tunisia. You now the infantry does the mopping on up. The plain [Author's note.: planes]go first then the heavy tanks then the infantry with fixed bayonets has to go and drive them the hell out and this M1 is the weapon that can do it.

Well Stanley I think I have to quit now because I have taken my gun apart and get ready for inspection so be good..and take care of yourself. Your Brother Joe Blow

Chapter 7

Basic training for men who went into the U.S. Navy was not much different for John Palasek in comparison to the training his brothers had been going through in the Army. Familiarization with and use of weapons, physical training and time in the classroom learning procedures and strategies were basic for all recruits. Instead of a pack that could be worn on ones back with all of your gear in it, sailors were issued a sea bag, sort of a duffel bag they could carry on and off ships, that would include a hammock and small mattress to be hung in a rocking boat rather than a sleep roll that a soldier would use on solid ground. In John's case, he had been sent to basic training at Coaster's Harbor Island, just northwest of Newport, Rhode Island when he wrote to his brother.

From John P., Naval Training Station, Newport, RI, July 3, 1943– Dear Stanley, It seems you're kind of mixed up about where I am. You wrote to me about New London which is a submarine base in Connecticut while Newport is a training station in Rhode Island and as far as I know New London is quite a ways *from here. We're not allowed to go anyplace while we're in quarantine for three weeks and after that they only give you about six hours liberty each week and the only place you can go is to Newport, 25 miles away and we're not allowed to buy beer. If anybody is caught selling beer to a boot he gets a five thousand dollar fine. So I guess beer is out.*

Thursday we got our double shot of typhoid at 12.15 and by six o'clock the guys were dropping like flies and the ambulance was busy most of the night. The shots didn't bother me much outside of giving me a sore arm.

Today we had captain's inspection for which everyone has to appear spick and span. About four battalions were on the parade grounds. We had to go through the semaphore, physical drill with and without rifles with the band keeping time and its really an impressive site to see. The "Constitution" which used to be named "Old Ironsides" if I'm not mistaken, is laying at the pier near the parade grounds. I've been over the obstacle course three times already and I think its pretty good. The first time over it you really get pooped but now I can run for a half hour without breathing hard.

There's a lot of submarines, PT boats and planes dropping dummy torpedoes around the bay. The place we're on is a little island off Rhode Island and there's only a bridge connecting both. I've got to cut this off right here because the lights will go out in five minutes. John

Stanley's brother in-law, John Rykowski, was not as prolific a writer. He was progressing in training rapidly and was relocated to Camp McCoy, which in 1943 was the largest infantry training area in the Midwest of the U.S. and remains active into the 21st century. It was located near the small town of Sparta, which was the hometown of its namesake, Major Robert McCoy.

From John R., Camp McCoy, Wisconsin, July 8, 1943 – *Dear Stanley, Mary + Buddy. I hope you are all well. I'm feeling pretty good myself. I received your letter today and its nice and long.*

So your brother goes through with his basic huh well how does he like the Army. That must be something to have all your Brothers to go into the Army. Did you ever talk to him. I mean my friend Eddie that was on the bus. Ho yes I got Helen Schultzes birthday card, and by the by tell her to write me and thank her for the card.

We've been going on the range all week long from 4:45 AM. And don't get in until ten o'clock or eight. I've fired every weapon we have for a rifle up to a 3" gun and we shoot the three inch with 22 shells, for practice only. We're having some hot weather hear and plenty of rain too.

Give my regards to your mother and family. Give little buddie a kiss for me and my love. I hope to take a few pictures of myself soon. Well so long now. Your loving Brother + Godfather Johnny

P.S. Excuse the pencil, I've loan my pen to the cook.

After a brief home leave that coincided with his brother Steve's time off, Joe Palasek found himself deep in southern Mississippi at Camp Shelby. The training received at Camp Shelby was not as broad as at Fort McClellan. It was here men would wait to be shipped overseas to combat with training designed for their specific assignment on arrival in hostile territory.

From Joe, Camp Shelby, MS, Summer, 1943 – *Hello Stanley, Well Stanley I received your letter and was glad to hear from you. Because hell I've nothing to do with myself these days. Specially when a guys broke. One thing I can say is its lots easier than McClellan and to tell you the truth they don't now what to do with us guys. Listen Stanley you say that Johnny's going to the pascific well Stanley as I told you when I was home that we were going over well Stanley we are waiting to be shipped and the only person that can stop us from going over this time is the Good God Omighty and that's on the leval. So next month if you don't here from me for a long time you now where I am.*

Listen Stanley you say that Steve was little nervous well I don't now if he nows what hes stepped into but I talked to him when he was home and he wouldn't listen to me. So the only way he'll learn is the hard way. I do wish him all the luck in the world but theres one thing about the army and that's there's no favors. And he'll find out that its not like back home were he can go were he please's and come in when he please's and I'm sure he'll find life different all together. Listen Stanley when you find out where he stationed at right and tell me. Well Stanley I haven't got much to write and I sure am glad to hear from somebody because I didn't hear from home any more I don't know whats wrong with every body but in one way I'll be damn glad when I do get shipped because I'm sick and tired of something that I would tell you in person but in a letter it would take me all night to write. So Stanley I'll sign off now because I've got to borrow a dollar of a guy to get some butts and if I don't hurry up he'll be in town and I'll be in a fix for another week. So take care of yourself and the family till we meet again and that will be a..........? Joe

In August of 1943, a tropical depression dropped almost 20 inches of rain on the lower part of Louisiana. Not unusual for the area but not a welcome change in the weather for those in boot camp there, as Steve was. The war bond selling effort was also in high gear at that time and The Hollywood Bond Cavalcade visited 16 cities across the US in 21 days with such stars as Lucille Ball, Dick Powell, Judy Garland and the music of bandleader Kay Kyser. It not only helped to sell scores of bonds, but it boosted the morale of all who were present.

From Steve, "Staging Area", New Orleans, LA, August, 1943 – *Hello Folks: Here I am once again trying to scribble a few lines. Well folks how are you and hows everything else in that part of civilization. I am well and doing all right in this outfit so far. I don't know whether or not you read in the papers about the storm raging through here that is Louisianna. We have been fighting a hell of a flood here. Good many other camps shipped out. We did our best in the bivouac area until this storm washed us out. We worked in shifts trying to stave off the flood waters. For one whole week its been storming emergency crews are out day and night. Most of my equipment is shot to hell, plus a cold I developed staying in wet clothes. Today is Sunday and its raining worse than* ever. We are now back in barracks at the staging area where I first came to in New Orleans. In the bivouac area we slept in tents, done things by candle light ate sitting on the ground, washed out side, and what not. Here we have all the comfort in the world. Although something tells me we are going to leave this area if the storm keeps on. Here where the gulf stream comes through storms are terrific I never saw anything like it in my life. Boy we are only a few miles from the Mississippi levies, if they let go we go to where I don't know.

Well Stanley although we are stopped in our basic training on account of these floods, we have been under a terrific strain we have had a taste of what soldiers go through in Guadal Canal or any part of those islands. I know my manual of arms plus the Springfield bolt action 30 calibre riffle and the M.I semi automatic 30 calibre riffle. I know each part in it, the description of the M.I. is, it's a U.S Army riffle, model M.I. 30 calibre, It is gas operated, air cooled, clip Fed and is a shoulder weapon, takes 8 shells in a clip, fires 16 shells in 60 seconds rapid fire Is very effective at 3,400 yards its made by Gerand.

All the parts I had to take out learn the names of and put the riffle to-gether with a Leuitenant watching and instructing. The Springfield riffle is similar hasn't that many parts, it comes apart in three parts, Stock the bolt and barrel assemblies.

Well I guess its about enough of this I'll continue with something else. Yes we most likely have to start our basic all over again, after which we go to Technical schools in our trades, where our colors will show. If we make good we may get Technicians stripes in the many branches we are attached to. I tell you I lost all my equipment everything I had but the fatigue clothes I had on me. To top the situation the 6th battalion got busted up after illness in the mess and that is why I am here in the fifth battalion forming a new Company. I have to start basic training all over again bad luck on top of bad luck. I feel slightly depressed over all this mess, still I guess its all in the game. I also got a beautiful cold wading in the waters up to my can. No dry clothes no sleep just carry on James orders is orders. It's all over now thank god I am well and able to tell this yarn and that is the truth. I have seen and been in a forest fire out West but a flood is the worst thing that can ever occur. Yes

Stanley it is a tough life but I know things will turn for the best in the end. The situation here is well in hand everything is getting around to normal. As you know this place is noted for storms heat, snakes and lizards. We have plenty to account for. We had a real taste of front lines right here. We only get ten minutes out of each hour here we train study see pictures on different training from which we take notes also go to lectures all these things we have to know like a book. Let me tell you if I get out of this alive I will be able to write a book. A story that will be and is now history in the making. I guess folks this story is most likely boring you so I'll switch to something else for a change. After clearing up the mess after the hurricane the City of New Orleans holds a bond rally at which a contingent of Hollywood stars were to take part in. So the army sends the guard consisting of 1,000 men to hold the crowds back. I am picked as one armed to the teeth. I get the post at the stage door. Therefore I had the honor of shaking hands with Mickey Rooney, Fred Astaire, Harpo Marx and James Cagney. Plus Kay Kaiser. Then came Greer Garson plus lots of lady stars I don't know the names of.

    They sold 39 million dollars worth of bonds some pile of bonds and some response to the great call and aid to the attack that's real support on the public showing patriotism, helping most likely there sons and relatives in the armed forces many who already have passed on to the new world. Well folks I guess I covered all the news on my part here.

    Now I am getting on to Joe I wrote him a few letters to Camp Shelby, but now that you have forwarded me his new address I will write him at once. I am glad he is still here and god keep him here for the duration. Also glad to know John is around I did write him as yet have no answer. But for my sake to the two of them tell them I asked for them send them my best wishes and regards thumbs up boys. We are all in it for the same cause. I haven't much more time to write so I must conclude here with the best of luck to you and all the families, my best regards may god bless you and guide you to success may all your hopes come true. Carry on until the boys come home. I remain on of yours a good soldier. Steve

In the middle of August 1943, Stanley received this letter from his brother Joe. Although Joe's next step was not certain, even for him as he wrote, he knew that the time to go overseas was near. Nearer than he expected as he wrote.

From Joe, Camp Shelby, MS, August 1943 – Hello Stanley, Just a few lines to tell you a few things that I wanted to tell you. Well Stanley were going over and I don't want you to tell Maggie for a while till I am well on my way. So Stanley I think the fooling around in the States is all over and were going to get the 'real thing' now. Well I always wanted to march throw Berlin and now I guess I'll get my chance.

I think we" be out of here by Sept 1, and I hope I get a chance to drop you a few lines because they won't let us right when we get in P.O.E. [Port of Entry]. So if you don't hear from me in a couple of months you no were I am. I do hope that when I get over there I bump in to Tommy or some of the boys from back home but one thing is it might be years before I ever come back. And don't think that I am not because this was the day that I was waiting for and I'm tired of fooling around in the states.

So Stanley the next time you hear from my will be from so place in Europe so be good God Bless you all and take care of your self and your little family. Joe

Joe's expectations were met head on within days. General Dwight Eisenhower intended to take Italy, which had shifted its allegiance away from the Axis powers politically. The Germans and an Italian militia of those who remained faithful to the Axis were still a force with significant control in Italy, even after those who ousted Benito Mussolini, the former leader turned political prisoner, signed an armistice. Eisenhower planned to completely liberate Italy. The British would strike the island of Sicily, resulting in Axis forces shifting from the west coast of the Italian mainland toward Sicily's defense. This Allied operation was known as "Operation Baytown." U.S. troops would then move into the western Italian areas of Salerno and Naples once those defenses were down in what was called "Operation Avalanche." Joe Palasek was a part of a pre-operation force, which was to lay the groundwork for Avalanche. Shortly after he landed, he suffered minor wounds from enemy bullets, which only curtailed his fighting for a short time. He was awarded the Purple Heart for these efforts.

Carl Palasek was the second son of Stanislaus and Marjanna and two years younger than Stephen. He was also much different than Steve, keeping to himself and rarely sharing in his feelings with his siblings or parents as he grew older. At about the same time as Stephen, in the late 1930s, Carl met a beautiful, raven-haired girl who was working near the factory outside of Port Washington where he also worked. In contrast to Carl, Violet was more outgoing and loved to talk to anyone who would listen about her daily life and what was happening in her world. They had a simple, small wedding, which best suited Carl's desire. Carl now felt free from the burden of his family and was ready to start a new life in a new home away from the Palasek homestead. No longer would he have to see his father struggle or feel oppressed by his mother's domination, issues that brought him feelings of anger. Unlike Stephen and Stephanie, Carl and Violet chose to live in another town, closer to Violet's family. For Carl, the further away they lived from Port Washington, the better.

John Palasek's wait to go to sea was comparably brief. For reasons of security, soldiers were not allowed to state their location in mail sent home from overseas. However, letters sent to soldiers, by way of Army Post Offices (APOs) in the States, or in the case of the Navy, Fleet Post Offices, were forwarded in batches to the those serving and family members at home would play a bit of a guessing game or write riddles to attempt to gain some idea where loved ones and friends were located once they left the states. Here, still in training mode, John Palasek writes from what would later be discovered as being the Pacific fleet near San Diego, California.

From John P., August 23, 1943 – *Dear Stanley, You must have received the letter with my present address pretty quickly. Again I have to admit that you're a pretty good guesser because you guessed my location on the nose. About a week ago I had some pictures taken but I doubt whether I'll be able to get any of them because the guy who took them has the film and can't get it developed. After reading in your letter that my friend Armand had been in town I sat down and wrote him a short letter. I was under* the impression that he was in the service. I hope he'll drop his beer long enough to answer me. You know he's not much for writing letters, something like Carl only that he always starts out with good intentions and keeps putting it off. He never had use for much writing. I also wrote Steve today using the address you'd sent me and I hope he gets the letter without its having to detour by way of New York because that is only a port of embarkation address. I heard from Joe three weeks ago and he said he had been in a hospital in Naples but that was a long time ago. He never hints as to where he might be at present except for saying he's away from the front and taking it easy. Speaking of swimming though, the other day I was about to go in when I saw two good sized sting rays in the water, so I changed my mind about going in. They looked too tough for me to wrestle with and I wasn't sure whether they'd be very congenial. Well, I don't know how much longer this waiting around is going to continue but I'm pretty well used to waiting by this time so it doesn't bother me very much except that there are a lot of other places I'd rather wait around in than here. There's no use bitching about the heat and this place though because the next place usually turns out to be worse. I haven't received any of the packages you mention and since packages usually take longer than ordinary mail I guess they won't be along for a while yet. So Carl has got himself another job. If you hadn't let me know about him every now and then I guess I'd be pretty much in the dark as to how things are with him. Maybe it won't be very long before the boys start coming back home and then guys like him will have to live pretty crowded instead of like hermits. Maybe he won't care for our proximity and have to haul ass to where the grass seems greener. One of these days I'll have to put together a nice letter to him just so he'll know I'm still around.

  I notice in almost every letter you keep saying that that wasn't the reason why you're not in the navy. You've kind of got me up a tree trying to figure the thing out. Unless you throw some light on the subject I'm afraid I'll have to stay in the dark as far as that point goes. I hope that everything is squared away as far as you're concerned and since I'm at the bottom of the page and can't think of anything further to write I'll drop the mud hook here and will write again soon. John

Chapter 8

September 1943 found the war in Italy intensifying since the initial Allied invasions began, which is where Joe Palasek was wounded. The U.S. and England were moving in from the south and west, but German soldiers heavily guarded Rome. Benito Mussolini — who had been arrested by the new Italian government — was freed by a group of Italian paratroopers still faithful to his Fascist rule from the mountain confinement where he had been held, and he was taken to Berlin.

The struggle back in the U.S. was getting more difficult with increased rationing and some feelings of resentment from a vocal minority of civilians. Stanley was also dealing with inner conflicts of his own and the realities of married life. His bride, Mary, found it difficult to be a very young mother living in a tiny, one-bedroom apartment. Arguments often ensued and Stanley was thinking more and more that he would be better off signing up to be in the Navy. He felt he could lend his skills in electronics to them, perhaps at a base on some Caribbean island (an unlikely scenario for a new recruit). For now, his dreams would remain as such.

After about five months of training, Steve — who was not given much of a choice as to what he would be doing in the Army — was finally discovering that the Army had plans for him. Just what they were, he was not fully certain, but he was willing to perform whatever duty he was asked.

From Steve, September 3, 1943, New Orleans, LA –
Dear Stanley, Writing you a few lines to let you know that I am well and hoping to hear the same from you. The ban is lifted and you can write to me when you have the opportunity. To start with I must tell you about my self and where I fit in this mans army. In the first place we are a none combat unit, known as Army Service Force. As I have mentioned we are Transportation and supply service, meaning men and material. By air, sea and rail we have to repair machinery and take charge so the different supplies get to the destination. If one or two of the men have to go with it even if its over seas, we make a return trip. We are now in a bivouac area for

about 4 weeks of basic training and let me tell you it's a cinch. Well so far I consider my self lucky, the insignia worn in this outfit is a blue star enfringed with white and red rimmed circle. After finishing here we get shipped again to some other training center.

One thing I will tell you the heat is terrific here and snakes and mosquitos are plentiful. We sleep under mosquito nettings and in tents. Anyway you can tell that four weeks of basic is not making a fighting out of this unit. All I can say they can ship me out of here any time its to damn hot. Otherwise the sunny South is a wonderful country through and through.

All men with mechanical knowledge are put in this unit. This as you may know is a port of Embarkation and lot here is a military secret. You know how it is in one of these places. I am getting along fine in this mans army. I do hope I get shipped to a good place in my next move where I will be more permanent.

Now I want to ask you whats new in the civilian life and what goes on. Tell you the truth I don't know what day it is I am pretty busy shuffling around here. Well folks I am signing off for a while with my best wishes and regards to you once in a while, Good luck and god bless you. Steve

The use of APO and FPO addresses for servicemen made it possible for Americans to write to their loved ones at war without using international mail. However, the location of a serviceman's post was not always directly associated with his APO. One might mail a letter to a loved one via New York even though they were stationed nearer the Pacific. Here, Steve mentions his brother, John, being near New York, when he was actually located on the West Coast.

From Steve, "Staging Area," New Orleans, LA, October 13, 1943 – Hello Folks, Here I am right on the ball as we say in this man's army, Feeling fine in pretty good condition. Heres hoping this letter finds you all in the best of everything. According to your letter Stanley I am very glad to hear the good tidings and the wheels of progress are turning. Thank you a million for the long and interesting letter I have received from you to-day. I'm also glad to hear John is still around. I hope he does stick to the wonderful island for the duration. As far as Carl is concerned I have nothing *against him, only I do know, what good would it be for me to write him, his wife would only sneer at my words I guess you understand Stanley. Carl is allright but his wife she just hates me so I must quit on this subject if you see him again tell him I asked for him, I wish them the best of health and prosperity plus all the good luck in the world. So I will get back to your letter Stanley you say it won't be long before you go in the service, well Stan, it is true that you will rate high in your type of work in any part of the service. One main object there the adventure is one way to take it still the job you expect to attach yourself to especially running to the islands, I think it's a great risk, it may be all right for a man who is single. You may think different, but my estimation, think of Mary and little Stas he is to tiny and your wife would suffer something terrible. Don't be hasty Stanley watch your moves and lose, of course its only my idea, you will do whatever you think best. You have a beautiful child there, I advise you keep your little family to-gether stick by them as long as you can. I wouldn't say this Stanley if your little boy was older you know what I mean. Anyway please don't get me wrong, or get mad at me for these words, after all you may say why did I join, well mine was a different case and my chances were better. Well Stan I am again going to change the subject, before I do I want to wish you good luck in no matter what you do which ever way you decide. After all we are all in it up to our necks, The only way to win is one for all and all for one.*

    Now I shall step off the beam and just tell you of some of my actibities to date. I have received all of my shots plus vaccination, we have been driven like mules in order to complete or basic training. No matter where we go we are the Army service Forces. Some will be in Railroad Battalions and operators. Others in Port Battalions, Transportation and supply, Ordinance, Quartermasters and Motor Pool. These main branches of our armed forces are bombed more times than anything else. Therefore we have had lectures on bombs especially incindiaries, how to control them. We have gas masks and went through gas chambers with the different type gases. We have to know more than the infantry although we wont be in the front lines. Still supply lines are bombed warehouses railroads and transportation the most important factors in this war. We are an outfit being trained for overseas duty where we are needed most. Unless the war comes to an end before we are ready to take off. By the way how is the war coming along. Well folks this story of mine is most likely going to bore you to death, Still this is the army and the truth, the hell we have gone through to date is the same any soldier goes through over there the conditions are the same on the same principal. I sure will have some experience to tell, to talk about in due time, more than I can write you here. I am being a damn good soldier taking my training very seriously. I know my eleven general orders, like the M.I. riffle. Well folks I'll have to be going on guard duty soon in this weather so I will have to be cutting off here somewhere. Another little thing before I conclude I wish to add, how in civilian life people sqawk about gasoline, tires, chisel on food with ration stamps, cry about this and that, if they came here to watch what there sons there loved ones are going through without a peep they certainly would crack down, change there moods say a prayer and do there utmost to cooperate with this soldier and give him there best all the support and back bone is there is there in the civilian army. They sure would be doing something real for themselves and there country. In my basic I lost eight pounds but I sure got tough. Now folks I am no preacher I write you the sincere truth as time goes by in this mans army. So I conclude with my best regards to you Stanley, Mary and Stanley Junior my best wishes, may god bless you and keep you, until the boys come home to a grand reunion. Solong for a while, heres hoping I hear good tidings from that little island. I remain one of yours truly. A good soldier, Steve

By the end of October 1943, the Germans were struggling to keep their foothold in Italy as their war with the Soviet Union intensified. Perhaps in response to this, and to reduce the numbers who were counter to them, the death sentences meted out in concentration camps like Auschwitz were increased.

As the numbers of men and women who were no longer in the U.S., but instead stationed overseas grew, the number of letters home also increased dramatically. The need to stay in touch was never more vital. But handling the mere size and weight of so many letters home needed to be addressed. "V mail," or Victory mail, was a method of communication where hand written letters from soldiers were reviewed and censored after they wrote them on special stationery. After review, the letters were photographed and the small roll of film could hold numerous letters in a much smaller space and weight for shipping to the states. On arrival, they were printed at sixty percent of the original size, and mailed free to the addressee domestically.

In 1943, popular crooner, Bing Crosby, released a hit song for the holidays. The tune, popular to this date, was "I'll Be Home For Christmas." For a few of the Palasek brothers and Mary's brothers as well, that musical Christmas message would only tug at their heart strings as the lyrics were not going to come true that winter.

From Steve, "Staging Area", New Orleans, LA, November, 1943 – Dear Stanley, Hello Folks, just received a letter which I could never write, even though I tried. Stanley you sure can gather enough material with news and views for a weeks reading. Anyway I thank you ever so much for this you really don't know how much I appreciate it. At a time like this when we the Company of Eng. is actually on the alert. There is great tension, twitching and waiting this calm before the storm. I tell you Stanley we have been this way for a few weeks, the idea is no one knows where we are going or whats in store for us. Everything is a real military secret. The rumor is that our destination is near by, another hell hole if I must say so. The company is so on edge that some have gone over the hill one went crazy. Shows to go you it really takes cool nerves to wait like this. After 17 weeks darn near of creeping, crawling, hiking, firing the boys just crave action. We have special duties which I am restricted to give any detail on. That's army life this is really the time one appreciates the mail he receives and gladly answers them to the best of his ability. I can see Joes point before he left for over seas. Some guys here get tougher and rougher others weaken so that they can't go on finally the main crack up. You see lots of strange this happen in this mans army as time goes by. You see when they put you in the alert like this they some times hold you for a month or more. Company has an examination in everything they had during basic training. One group of men pitches tents, another rolls full field packs. Another gives a description of four war gases and what effect they have. Others may have to use *camouflage natural and artificial, Break a machine gun down also the M.I. Riffle and carbine name the parts. Still others will give details on explosives and demolition which is used plenty in the Eng. Corp. There are one hundred other things to go over during this review. If the company fails it means basic training all over again. So far our Company has been on the ball at all times and to date is the pride of our Battallion which consists of three other Companies. We are quite an outfit. That is why it is so hard to tell when we will get a furlough, we are about ready to shove off so maybe we will some how get one in the next camp. I had all my shots and vaccination, all stamped on my dog tags. Now all I get is a booster every six months. That damn Tetenus is a mean shot and the worst of the lot, let me tell the cockeyed world. Anyway that is the whole set up as far as training is concerned.*

Now Stanley you write that you are about to join us boys in some branch of the service. You also state that you feel like a slacker. There is no reason for this for I sincerely know that you have a real essential job in which not many men can work at. You are doing your bit for your country and your little family. You claim that this does not put bread and butter on the table. I don't actually think your that far off the beam. You seem to have the urge to get right in the mixup. Stanley I think you should stand fast right on the job , doing your utmost to stay out. Someone has to be holding the fort until the boys come home. I say buck up fellow, don't let it get you, for I will admit its one hard life.

One sure bit of news I gather from your letter is about Joe. So he is receiving our mail, that is great and tickles me pink to know my letters are also getting to him. Now Stanley you mention V. mail, to tell you the truth I really haven't seen any or quite know what you mean. I am puzzled is this a different kind of paper or is this a certain stamp you put on the letters. Or I think I am dumb as hell not to know. Can you beat that a soldier in the army doesn't know what V mail is, well live and learn as they say.

Now let me tell you a little about the weather here, it is just as hot as ever but the nights are real cold. Strange here it is November getting on to winter still there is no sign of it anywhere. The trees are just as green as ever, every thing is in full bloom so you see folks, this is the sunny south land but to my estimation they can sell it to the Indians.

I guess I covered some territory folks and I am coming to a photo finish, hears hoping I see you all soon, maybe around Christmas time, I hope for I am counting on this so much. So long for a while and the moment we shift some where I'll be able to write moreof whats been going on here. So far we are restricted from spilling the means. So here I go again adios and I remain one of the flock always your brother. Steve

Alexander, the youngest of the Palasek sons at 17 in 1943, yearned to join his brothers in the service. He was ambitious and the idea of being at home when there was something he could be doing was a part of his ambitious spirit. He looked up to his brothers, at times envied them and to a degree wanted to show them that even though he was the youngest, he wasn't the least of them. And in stature, Alex was anything but a lesser brother. Alex was what some might call "built like a bull," never one to shy away from hard or heavy work, nor to shy away from letting his temper get the better of his strength and putting someone in their place by physical force in a heartbeat. He was another of the brothers who was anxious to serve.

From Joe, Italy, November 22, 1943 *– Dear Stanley, Thanks for the letter you wrote to the Motor Vehicle Bureau about my liscense. Ill hold on to that letter an bring it to those guys some day. Im glad you and Johnny are having a good time drinking beer. Johnny stays in the states I also hope Alex gets home for Christmas. For Steve and I have a roundevou here for a little while before we get back there so you hold up the fort.*

There isn't much to write about Stanley. I wish you all a nice Thanksgiving and a great big turkey for you, Mary and your little guy. Till we meet again it's solong for a while and don't forget to keep the home fires burning. Your pal, Joe

Meetings were being held in places such as Cairo and Tehran between U.S. President Franklin Roosevelt, British Prime Minister Winston Churchill and, alternatively, China's Chiang Kai-shek and the Soviet Union's Joseph Stalin. Tactics needed to be agreed to for a common strategy both in the Pacific and in Europe. Still, in New Orleans, plans continued to take shape for Steve.

From Steve, New Orleans, December 3, 1943 – Hello Folks: Here I am once again writing you a few lines just to keep you and all informed of developments as they are and have been today. In the first place I just wish to state that I am well heres hoping this letter finds you in same. Well Stanley, things have snapped here, there have been changes made. To begin with my story, well as I have mentioned to you in my previous letter that we were on the alert also having a class A inspection. Yes Stanley my company the 712th Bn. has left for Camp Clayborne La. 56 of us men who have been the top notch bunch in the Engineers have an assignment a detail to complete. We were picked by the high ranking officcers as a group who can really take it. This of course I am proud of because time I get through I may have some kind of rating, due to my experience. In the begginning as you know Stan I was in the 6th Bn. Post also a Casual Company until I completed my basic training. Then transferred to the 5th Bn. Then the 712th and now Co. C. of the 8th Bn. We have a tough assignment let me tell the cockeyed world. I am proud of my-self not bragging, but I sure have blazed a trail to date as far as I have gone and the fifth month I am starting in this mans army. Due to this assignment the real heart breaker is this I won't be home for Christmas, although some thing may break. You know Stanley the army is a strange place and a guy never knows to much, because the army has to many surprises for yu especially when you count on something. After going through all the hell which we have we won't be able to get home around Christmas time. Lord only knows what they intend to do with this bunch of 56 which the high toppers picked. Over 1700 men in this battalion left this camp the band marched them off to the train and away they went. I have it figured this way, if I don't get a furlough now, I will get one in my sixth month, I have now started my fifth month in the service. Time sure does fly here, most of us are kind of upset about not going home around Christmas time. We did look forward toward this so much I guess you understand. I hate to think of this day which comes but once a year, but there is no use crying about it. Just got to be a good soldier as I have been in the past. We the 56 men who have been picked here have trades and can do our jobs well, we also have the best scores, as far as basic training was concerned. Yesterday I was called in to headquarters once again interveued, they asked me if I could drive, truck tractor speak foreign language fluently, have I supervised any job at some time or another. They also took my C.C.C. record. The Leuitenant told me that in due time they have to make 3 Tech. sargeants and my name is on the list. Well I do hope it turns out to be so.

    Well the way I got it figured out most of these 56 men are due for ratings, there fore it is why we have been cut off from our main body of men. I sure would like to be with you all this Christmas, but now I can only dream about it, just like being over seas cut off from the rest of the world. I have talked to our Leutenant here, he would let us all go still theres the Captain and Major they want this mission completed. We have undertaken a great job here and I figured this would hold us back from our loved ones back home. Yes basic training is all over, but not forgotten and never shall be.

    I wrote you Stanley that I did not know what V. mail was well I do now, because I received two letters from Joe over seas god bless him and I thank him for this. I wish him a Merry Christmas and Happy New Year, heres hoping we are all back together again some time next year. Tell him this Stan in your next letter, my best wishes and regards to him from a soldier to a soldier. I keep writing him now more often knowing that he is receiving my mail. Did you by any chance here from John as yet. I'll bet he is in some strange country. Yes we are scattered through out the world. Heres hoping this mess is all over with soon.

    The weather here is the same and no sign of change. The trees are just as green as ever There is no leaves falling here. I guess this is the South land all right. Must be true what they say about Dixie. But the way I think, it stinks give it back to the Indians.

    This here Co. C. which we have tied in with, well we are only boarders here in there barrack. They have plenty of room so we shoved in with them temporarily. Now getting to the word furlough, I can say this much, I will be home around January sometime which will entitle me to 15 days. So I don't know just what to say folks I just have to take it on the chin for a while, unless a miracle turns up before that time. *You probably don't know how I feel when I think of not being with you as I have hoped to. I was counting on seeing every one, especially Alex knowing that he is preparing to step into the ranks. I am now coming to the end of the line with my best wishes and regards to all our family, god bless you and keep you in good spirit and good health until I come rolling in on that Pullman. You can bet your life I am in one tough outfit when I do get home I'll have some thing to talk about. If we go overseas well I know just where this outfit is scheduled to go. I'll save this for later. So long for a while and keep the home fires burning. I remain one of the seven, your Brother, a soldier. Steve*

As mentioned, Willie Palasek lived at home with his parents at 12 School Street in Port Washington. He was becoming nervous and anxious about his brother Joe being so far from home, especially since he had been wounded his first week there. Willie and Stanley often shared the letters they received with each other. Joseph would be spending his first Christmas away from home. Joe understood Willie's anxiety and tried to ease his mind.

From Joe to Willie, Italy, December 23, 1943 – *Hello Willie, How's everything on the home front. I guess you're the boss now since Alex is going in the Navy. And you have a big job ahead of you taken care of the house and Mother and Father.*

Hows Mother an Father are they in good health. I hope so for when everyone is happy back home, I'm happy myself over here in Italy. And don't worry about anything but you people back home. So tell Mother an Father not to worry about me for I'll be there when this mess is over with and we all can be happy once more. But right now you know there still lot to do here and once its over with then the hell with Europe take me back to New York. I guess I'll cut it short know Willie. Solong for awhile and don't forget keep them home fires burning. Your pal Brother, Joe

From Joe. Italy, December 24, 1943 – *Hello Stanley, Hows everything on the home front. I hope this letter finds you in the best of health and happy ness. I myself am in good health and now miss the good old states helluva lot. But whats the use of* *worrying it can't last forever and I guess there is better days to come. So I might as well take the good with the bad while I'm over here on my nice little vacation and every day that goes by is a day closer for us to our land, good old America.*

Well Stanley how did you spend your Christmas I hope you enjoyed yourself. For I now it wasn't like the one's we used to have when we all were together and I guess its tough on you people back home, for it must be awful dead around town. But Better days are coming and when they do come that going to be the time to roll out the barrel. Your pal Brother Joe

And so, the lyrics and melody to Bing Crosby's wonderful Christmas song sadly remained little more than that.

Chapter 9

The 18th-century writer, Alexander Pope, wrote that "hope springs eternal." There are few who do not feel this way as they anticipate the start of a new year. For millions in America, Asia and Europe, that hope was rarely as universally fervent as it was at the dawn of 1944. With advances in Europe against Germany along the Russian Front, Allied moves into Italy, Royal Air Force bombings of Berlin and pressure increasing upon Japan in the Pacific, perhaps this would be the year that the fighting would end and loved ones would hopefully return home, safe and sound from wherever the battle took them.

These same notions were expressed at the start of the year, in what was almost a prayer that Stanley wrote in his diary on the last day of 1943. "My hope for 1944 is that this bloody conflict comes to an end and all our boys come home safely and we can all live again like human beings. Having all faith in the lord I know that god will help us," he wrote. He hoped to work hard to establish himself "intelligently in a skill for the benefit of family and community." He also wrote, "It's an awful nightmare this war. We are all living under a terrific nervous strain and so we become tired and haggard as the war drags on. Each day I am anxious for my brothers, and I try to keep so close to them as possible through letters." The war was not only hard on Stanley, as he wrote, "William has acted very nervous since my brothers left for the service. I am going to do all I can to help him straighten himself out. Mother is carrying on and hiding her feelings and grief." His entries further show the importance of these letters that were exchanged by the Palaseks. Stanley wrote plaintively, "I wrote to John and Joe today and had a letter from Joe. If only John would write, I would enjoy myself. But he hasn't written so I hope he is safe and we hear from him soon."

A small party was held that New Year's Eve in the Main Street apartment, with Stephanie and Margaret, the wives of Steve and Joe respectively, attending along with a few other family friends. Also, Stan's brothers — Alex, who was anxious to serve, and Willie, who always seemed to be in a state of worry — were there as they "ushered in the New Year in a reserved fashion," in Stanley's words. Stanley's loner brother Carl even came by around 1 a.m. for a "few night caps." Though the celebration was small, it was at least a celebration. Little did any of them know that hours before the clock struck midnight in New York, the new year had already begun in Italy, where Margaret's husband was quietly spending the evening in the mud of a foxhole.

In 1944, a loaf of bread cost about 10 cents and a gallon of gas about 15 cents, when one could actually get them due to continued rationing. Even oil used for heating most homes in the Northeast was in short supply, making many homes, including Stan and Mary's apartment, cold. Hollywood bombshells Rita Hayworth and Betty Grable were not only hitting the top of their careers stateside, but their likenesses were showing up overseas in American soldiers' backpacks and as painted images on the fuselages of their planes. Big bands and their singers, such as Jimmy Dorsey, Bing Crosby and the Mills Brothers, were filling the radio waves between news reports of the war. Bing Crosby was also to appear in 1944's Academy Award-winning film, "Going My Way."

The emancipation of Poland from the oppression of German forces was slowly taking place as Soviet victories over the German invaders increased. For Poles in Europe and North America, the question arose of whether this would truly be liberating. It seemed as if the Soviet Union was determined not only to defeat the Germans, but to impose itself upon Poland so that it would be politically under Soviet control when the war ended. For now, anyone who wasn't German was a welcome sight in Poland. Steve Palasek was on the move, but not toward the destination he thought he would be going. Promoted to Sergeant, he was moved to the outskirts of San Antonio, the home of the Alamo, to train newer men.

From Steve, Fort Sam Houston, TX, January 4, 1944
– *Well Folks, here I am deep in the heart of Texas, doing my daily dozen being a good soldier. Here's hoping I hear the same from you my soldiers. Seems strange to me to be in such a warm climate at this time of the year. I know that this is a long way from home exactly 1,889 miles. I am about 150 miles from the Mexican border about the same amount from the Gulf of Mexico. The surroundings here are a picture only an artist can paint. The songs they sing about Texas are really true. Thrugh the number of camps I have been in which were mud holes this is the most beautiful. Too far away from home, but the truth I must admit without an exaggeration. San Antonio itself is an old stomping ground of Santa Ana, heres where you see the old missions and churches built way back in 1760. The Alamo which is a mile stone and and has old memories of days and years gone by. Well Stan I am doing a splendid job of my rookies who have been activated into the 724th Rwy Battalion. Fine bunch of boys. The strain they are under the training we as a staff are giving them is the same as the time I was a private. To-day Stan I feel proud of my-self yes and blue in another I will have to wait for my furlough a little longer. Although I have been with the 712th they went overseas my original outfit. I finished my technical training in the Engineers and you want to see a rugged out fit they are it. Work and fight let me tell the cock eyed world they can take it also dish it out. I have trained with many outfits from the casual to the toughest I have survived them all. They tried me everywhere yet I can took it. Today I will and am training men. Teaching them the fundamentals of military life. The principles and main keys to the making of a good soldier. Of course you can figure what kind of job it is with rookies who never had any military experience. Yes, after hours they come to my private room, ask questions just like new men. I raise hell with them lecture to them and help them as much as I can. So that when we, the cadre*

leave them, we want to see our job well done, only to go somewhere else and start on a new batch.

Yes when I get my furlough I will be the happiest man in the world, also will be able to do my work much better. I am working, still you know how it is my mind is wondering around thinking of that furlough.

Well folks I am signing off with my best wishes and regards, God bless you and guide you. I remain one of the seven. Steve

In 1944, the entertainment industry was shifting its direction to propaganda films. The nation was as united as it had ever been in its hatred of the enemy; in support of this emotional wave, the movie studios started to produce a number of films that gave a rather biased view of the war. Walt Disney's studio was in the forefront with live documentaries such as the award-winning "Victory Through Air Power," which presented how the Allies not only could, but would win the war. Other studios followed the same path, adding films that were anti-Axis including short subjects with the Three Stooges and Warner Brothers' Looney Tune cartoons taking satirical aim at Hitler and Japan's leader, Tojo.

The news of Russians arriving in Poland reached Port Washington and, in comparison to German occupation, it was welcome news to those of Polish origin and their families. Alex Palasek went for a physical in January 1944 in hopes of joining the Marines, but he failed to pass the physical due to his nervous fear of the doctors. Instead he began to consider going into the Merchant Marine. Though not actually one of the Armed Forces, the Merchant Marine was an important part of the supply chain to the foreign-based Allied soldiers and sailors. Hundreds of these merchant vessels were lost in the war and many men died in this service to the cause. John Palasek had moved from training in the Pacific near the Americas to the North Atlantic. Stanley Palasek was classified 3-A, according to the draft board, and was not allowed to serve because he had a dependent child — a deferment classification that no longer exists. He was not happy, as he wanted to go into the service like his brothers — in part because he argued often with his young wife, Mary, and he felt they would both be happier if he wasn't there. He was doing important civilian work for the military in the meantime.

Since leaving Press Wireless to work at Sperry Gyroscope, his math and electrical mastery qualified him to be chosen for work on Project MUSE with scientists in the Sperry Labs. The goal of the top-secret Project MUSE was to develop a radio wave system that would allow aircraft to perform blind landings in the dark or in conditions where visibility was nonexistent. Stanley was also anxious for the mail daily, hoping to hear from his brothers and prayed for their safety when he didn't hear from them.

From Steve, Fort Sam Houston, Texas, January 10, 1943 – Hello Folks, I received two letters to-day from you all, for this I say to you thanks a million. The letters were dated Dec. 16 and Jan 6, anyway I know the mail is stuck somewhere along the line. I sure am glad to hear that you all are in tip top shape. I am in the same boat, feeling fine just hoping I get my furlough mighty quick. I have also received a letter from Joe, he is very happy over his new outfit and the branch of service he is in. I get mail from him quite often, I hope he gets all of my mail he sure will have plenty to read when it does catch up to him. As to John, all I had from him was the Christmas greeting, from there I haven't heard since. God bless them both and guide them through thick and thin. For they are doing there best and I am sure they can handle them selves. John no doubt is on the move there fore we must be patient until once again he settles some where. Here I am still in the states and when I move it takes weeks for mail to get on the level again. Where those boys are it may take a month or more.

Speaking of the merry time you all had new years and Christmas, well I sure am glad you had a drink on me. I do wish I was there with you. Still my hopes were shattered. I haven't had a drink all these months but do or die upon my arrival home, I sure will take me one, Providing it don't run out by then. I know it will no doubt knock me for a loop, but who cares. Anyway we shall see when that day arrives. That day will be my Christmas, New Years and a holiday every day.

In this mans army I had a very dull Christmas plus New Years. I had my Christmas dinner in Claiborne La. The next morning I was on the train rolling for Texas. New Years I sat here in my room writing letters thinking about you all, I woke up for *revellie with my head on the letter I didn't finish writing. Yes I admit I was very blue so were good many more in this outfit. But you have to take the good and bad. These kind of dissapointments are natural here in the army.*

This Sunday we non Coms were free to go to town. I for one went alone. As you know Mexicans are all Catholics there fore there are steeples churches and Cathedrals. I at once went into St. Mary's cathedral, where the Arch Bishop was having high mass, plus twelve priests they are called the Oblate fathers. From there I went to San Jose Cathedral, St Anthony's also St. Fernandos Cathedral. In this one I have viewed the bodies of three heroes of Texas, Travis, Davis and Crockett, I read about them, but here I saw them as they lay in there glass caskets. Mexicans gringo's are plenty ful, would cut your throat for a nickel. By the way we have 50 full blooded Indians here in this company plus 100 Mexicans. One Indians name is John Yellow Face the other is George Red Arrow, good many more who have these strange last names. Boy we got something to train, for they are all new men from the induction center. At the same time you carry a pistol to be on guard. Some fun, when you have to do that. Well folks once again I say Adios god bless you thanks for the letters and keep the home fires burning I am signing off with my best wishes and regards to you and your little Family. I remain one of the seven in the ranks your brother and pal. Steve

It seemed apparent to most people that an invasion of Europe by the Allies was on the near horizon. The British continued bombings of Germany and Allied airlifts were dropping radios and ammunition along with some weapons into France and other areas in support of the resistance fighters there. The Sperry X-band system was tested outdoors with airplanes using it to land, and it worked perfectly. This development, to which Stanley was the only engineer assigned, would be a considerable and welcome improvement in aviation for decades to come. For his work, Stanley was promised a raise from his $1 per hour. But his mind was still set on going into the service and away from arguments at home regarding his making so little in his technical career pursuit, rather than making more at manual labor which didn't appeal to Stanley in the least.

Word was finally received from John Palasek in a letter to Alex. He couldn't say where he was, but it was determined that he was in the North Atlantic. A code was set up by letter, that if John used the word "Glass Houses" in his letters, he was in Iceland. Should he use the word "Mansion," he was in the British Isles. Still, mail wasn't coming often enough for a worried family. When Stanley finally received his own letter from his brother John after weeks without one, it lifted his spirits. The stationery was impressively embossed with the U.S. Navy crest in gold.

From John P., January 18, 1944 – *Dear Stanley, I received a letter from you today dated December 16th and I've received quite a few other letters from you. Since they don't come in order they have me pretty mixed up as to which ones to answer. I wish I could write you as often as you write me but I can't answer you letter for letter because of either shortage of writing paper or the want of time to write in. We don't have the conveniences that we had in other places or even the last place I moved from. It seems there is less comfort at each succeeding place we move to. There's no recreation place here or writing room where a guy can sit down without being disturbed and write in comfort more or less. To-date I haven't received your package although I have received mom's packages a few weeks ago. They closed up our small stores so I won't be able to buy anything, no writing paper, no soap, cigarettes or anything for about a month. I have plenty of razor blades and cigarettes but I never was able to buy laundry soap or stationery. I lost my pen someplace too so I wrote Alex to have mom buy me a pen and stationery.*

I still haven't heard from Joe but I'm glad he's contented with his new outfit and that he's well as you say everyone else is at home. I've been in pretty good condition myself too so everything is allright all around I guess. If I repeat myself I hope you'll overlook it. It's pretty hard to make each letter different and I can't go into any discussions about anything as you understand.

I also hope that my not writing often won't discourage you into not writing me. Mail is a very important thing to all of us if not the most important. I guess I said this before too but I can't overemphasize it. Well, I guess I'll sign off now Stanley and see what I can do for amusement tonight. In case your thinking this sheet of paper is nice, it's a sheet I borrowed. So long for the time being Stan. John

American and British troops had landed south of Rome and the possibility of spreading troops too thin across this global conflict had to be avoided. Building up the ranks was the answer. More men would be needed to bring the fighting to a successful end. In mid-January, the draft laws changed as the war intensified. One change that affected the Palasek family as much as many other families was the end of any and all deferments for men under the age of 25. This change signaled the end of Stanley's child-based deferment (he was 23 in the spring of 1944), and rapidly many of his friends were "called up." The Palasek family in the states seemed to be pulling together more as the possibility of being separated by the war was becoming a reality. Their mother went to St. Joseph's Church in the Polish-speaking section of Queens, and had a mass said in honor of her three boys who were away from home. Three of the four brothers at home (Stanley, Alex and William) were now working for Sperry in support of the war efforts. Stanley himself was finding his way back to weekly mass, trying not to get into petty arguments with his wife and caring more about his family and mother than ever before. At night, he'd have a beer before bed and listen to the song "There's a Star Spangled Banner Waving Somewhere" over and over at high volume, much to the chagrin of his downstairs neighbors, Pete and Mary. The 1942 hit by country artist Elton Britt was about a Valhalla awaiting the brave soldiers who wouldn't return. William was showing increasing signs of anxiety at home and at work. Doctors suggested that he had secondary high blood pressure, which was caused by a problem with other organs, but they did not suggest any type of surgeries. They merely suggested he visit a psychologist.

Tensions were rising in the war and in the hearts and minds of people everywhere, particularly for those with loved ones in combat. When the first letter written from the battlefield's front lines was received from Joseph, it was a relief to know he was safe. He was in the Medical Detachment of the 135th Infantry, Company H. But one should not think that being in a Medical Detachment meant he was any further from face-to-face combat. The men who fought in

Italy faced some of the fiercest ground battles of the war. His first letter from Italy tells so much in a few sentences about the mindset that one can develop when faced with the possibility of being killed at any moment by someone who can only be considered a hated enemy, day after day.

From Joe, "Somewhere in Italy," January 26, 1944 –
Hello Stanley, How are you. I hope this letter finds you in the best of health as I am.

I'm sorry I couldn't write sooner but you now how it is up on the front lines. The Jerry's keep us to busy, ducking things they through at us. So a fellow has little time on his hands. And they were giving up plenty of trouble you probly read about it in the papers. Every day. Well while your reading about the news were sweating out another attacked, and making the news. Its a tough raod to some and those dirty rats know there beat but are too damn stubborn.

I was taken to some of the prisoners we captured one day and they were talkin in polish to me. They say there polish but most of the Nazis can speak polish. And they told me different things which I don't believe. For they think if they say there polish they will get a better break. But none of them are no good for they keep shooting till they have no more ammunition then get up with there hands up and yell unarmed. But some of the boys are hasty on the trigger and squeeze the trigger and ask questions latter.

Ive got some souvenirs from a few Jerrys which I hope I don't lose. Well Stanley there isn't much to write for I said about all I can and I hope the censor don't scratch some of it out. For I could tell you things which I now you wouldn't believe, and I myself dont like to write about it for I want to forget everything that goes on every day, and try to see the bright side of the picture but its going to be hard for the war is going on and were fighting it. So I just think I'll cut it short and I'll write as much as I can. Your pal Brother Joe

Chapter 10

The Palaseks were only one month into the year 1944, but the stress and concerns about sons away at war and life during wartime in general were making each day drag on. Wishes and prayers for a rapid end to the war that were brought forth on New Year's Day were not being answered quickly enough. There was an increase in the number of attacks by the Allied forces, which were met by more determined resistance by the Axis powers in Europe and the South Pacific. The U.S. and Britain struggled to make further advances into Italy, being repelled in first attempts to take the strategic location of Anzio on the Western shore. The Soviet Union was continuing to make headway in Poland and the Ukraine. The British RAF bombings of Germany were breaking morale there but only temporarily. In the Pacific, the Marshall Islands headquarters of the Japanese were taken by U.S. troops, but with the vast area of battle there separated by the open sea, advances to other areas under Japanese control were slow.

Fears for Joseph's safety grew among his family in Port Washington. There had not been a letter in a couple of weeks and the news of intense battles in Italy put everyone increasingly on edge. Hearing that the Germans had bombed evacuation hospitals in Italy only caused more alarm, as Joe was in a Medical Detachment. Stanley was expecting to hear from the draft board and had even written several letters asking to go into the service, reformulating his hoped-for assignment slightly to perhaps go in as an engineer in the South Pacific with the Navy. He was reclassified 2-B (working in the defense industry) by the selective service until the beginning of April, when his status would be reviewed again. Even with this news, he prayed daily for the war to end and the family to be reunited as soon as possible. His brothers did what they could to keep in touch with Stan, their family in Port Washington and with each other, as shown by this letter from Joe after he was again hospitalized, to Steve.

From Joe, "Somewhere in Italy," February 19, 1944
– Hello Steve, How are you. I hope this letter finds you in the best of health, and I also hope you've been home on your furlough.

Well Steve how do you like the Engineers. There much better than the Infantry. Its all according what kind of Engineers outfit your in. Right now I don't now whats going on on the lines for I am in a Hospital, recuperating. Well Steve what do you fellows do back in the states. Is it the same old thing, close order drill, extended order and go on the range and take up the kneeling position etc. and all the bull shit. The boys find out when they get here that, that stuff dont do them much good. For a guy is on his own here, I mean when hese on the lines and if you dont use your own sense theres nobody else will use them for you. Military discipline is what a soldier has to have, outside of that if you dont look after your self, its T.S. I guess I'll cut it short now Steve good luck to you and I hope they keep you in the states for the duration, Your Pal Brother Joe

It seemed as if Steve was going to be in the states for the duration of the war, having been shifted here and there but not going abroad. He had trained both in basic procedures and in technical matters until he knew them backward and forward. Now, as a Sergeant, he was training others. John Palasek was shifting from place to place in the British Isles from what his few letters would infer. One week it would be Scotland; the next, Ireland where he also trained, drilled and waited to fight. John Rykowski was in Camp Forrest outside of Tullahoma, Tennessee, learning about and operating the M18 tank destroyer so he would be prepared to fight when the moment arrived. Nicknamed the Hellcat, the M18 was the fastest tank the Allies had in World War Two. The speed and outstanding maneuverability were possible in part because of the light, thin armor protecting the operators of the tank.

Mary's older brother, Adam, a long-limbed man with a receding red curly hairline, had been in the Army for over a year and was also staying in the states for now. Stationed only a few miles away from the house where he was born, he was a Military Policeman at Mitchell Field on Long Island. Then a base of operations for both bombers and fighters, as well as a command center for the Army Air Force (the predecessor to today's Air Force), today it is a part of Nassau Community College and the Nassau Coliseum sports arena. Adam was always on the move as an MP, transferring a prisoner (perhaps a soldier who had gone AWOL) between interment facilities and then on another occasion, standing guard as First Lady Eleanor Roosevelt visited troops in training. One day, upon his return from transporting a prisoner to Massachusetts, Adam managed to stop in to see his sister, Mary, in Port Washington and delivered a gift of a pound of real butter — something most people could hardly imagine possessing.

Meanwhile, February 1944 found Joe Palasek in the center of the action near Cassino, Italy, far from his wife Margaret and small son Joey. It was a frightening place for even the bravest of men, where the fighting never stopped. Being in such a place could bring out both the sweetest of sentiments and the hardest of anger from any man.

From Joe, Italy, February 18, 1944 – *Hello Stanley, How's everything with you. I hope this letter finds you in the best of health and happiness.*

Hows your little boy. I guess him and Joey must be pretty good pals, for he must be quite a boy by now.

Has Steve had his furlough yet. I guess he's quite a soldier by now, and he's lucky to be in the States. For this inferno over here isn't worth the price were paying for it. The wops can have there Italy, the only thing there good for is the hundreds of gallons of wine they make every year. I mean they used to make. The women are not worth a lead nickel they stink? Some of the niggars back home are cleaner than most of these women. I guess I'll sign of now slong for awhile and I'd like to see an increase in your family. Your pal brother Joe.

Marjanna was a loving mother but also a strong-willed woman who had her say and expected others to do as she said. As she got more letters from her sons in the service, both directly and through her sons nearby and at home, she was gaining a better grasp on English (though she preferred not to speak it). But speak it she did, and quite heatedly, when she found out that Margaret, the wife of her soldier son Joe, was not sending candy to her husband in Italy. Marjanna's husband, Stanislaus, always the hard-working, silent partner in raising his family, would stand quietly by in these and many other family matters.

From Joe, Italy, February 27, 1944 – *Hello Stanley, How are you I hope this letter finds you and the family of yours in the best of health. I myself am in pretty good health. I guess I can thank god for that for I am in the hospital, but doing fine.*

I've received the Port News you sent me, which I appreciate very much, but Willie sent me the same paper, I guess I just forgot.

You say in your letter that you want to send me something. Well Stanley if you want to you can send me a box of chocolate candy, and I wrote Margaret to send me some an Willie so if you do send me a box I shure will have plenty of candy to eat. For thats something we cant get over here. Guess we miss all that good stuff thats in the States. But someday maybe we can get back and forget about were we bin and all we saw, and say to our selves that it was only a dream. I guess I'll cut it short now Stanley solong for a while. Your pal Brother, Joe

As March 1944 arrived, situations were still changing weekly in the war. The balance of control in Europe, which had weighed heavily in favor of the Germans and those who sided with them, was shifting. Perhaps in small increments, but with the U.S. joining in Britain's bombing of German cities, the balance was changing. The Nazis were cognizant of the Allies' intent to initiate a major invasion of German-held sectors of Europe, but where and when these campaigns would occur was still unknown. It was not only a question for the Germans, but also for the men who would possibly sacrifice all to make the effort a success. They either fought on in various battles, or waited for orders whether they were overseas or stateside.

The Palasek brothers who worked at Sperry's (Stan, Alex and William) were becoming disillusioned as government contracts decreased and layoffs increased. Stanley commented that it was becoming a haven for draft dodgers under the protection of a deferment for doing defense work. Stanley was not one of those employees. He wanted to go into the service "to have a hand in helping to bring the peace and bring my brothers back and our family together." Even though he wrote that he hated the idea of leaving his "family whom I love dearly. I have nothing but good words for my dear wife, and my baby is a gem."

From Joe, Italy, March 4, 1944 – *Hello Stanley, Just a line from me to you hoping that everyone in your little family is in the best of health. Ive been receiving quite a few letters from you, which I appreciate very much. Yu say in your letters that you keep saying the same thing over again well Stan they sound good to me, but if you ask me something that you would like to now about and as long as its something I can answer maybe that way you wont have no trouble writing. But dont ask me about the weather for thats out or how far we advanced etc. But theres lots of other things I can write which may interest you.*

I have received two letters from John quit some time ago, and I wrote him a few witch I hope he received. As far as giving him my local APO well Stash, That's the only one I have but if he writes to me and put my APO and c/o US Army in stead of c/o P.M. I'll receive them in about 8 days. I received a few from Steve and I also wrote him back. Your pal Brother Joe

In the spring of 1944, Allied troops and the Russians were making headway against the Germans. The battle for Cassino, Italy, was taking its toll on both sides. The Germans had set up what they called "The Gustav Line." This was a line of defense that went from east to west across Italy. The heart of this line, located in Monte Cassino, was a strategic strength for Germany considering that its high hills allowed troops to overlook Allied movements below and to fire upon the enemies. It was important to the Allies to break through, as this was the path to Rome. If Rome could be wrested from the Germans, the liberation of Italy could be successful. Joe Palasek was still in the Cassino region that spring. According to a letter he had sent his mother, he was, "ducking bullets, artillery shells, mortar shells and bombs" and wishing he could get away and forget all he had seen. Even if one wasn't wounded, time in a hospital away from the battle was sometimes given to the men, including Joe, so that they would be rested to fight again.

The RAF bombardment of Berlin had spread to at least 20 cities in Germany and Hitler was becoming concerned about the morale of his people. It was also at this time that the story that inspired the motion picture "The Great Escape," featuring the actor

Steve McQueen, actually occurred. After one year of tunnel digging by over 600 men beneath the prison of the Stalag Luft III war camp outside of Berlin, 76 Allied soldiers escaped from the German camp though 74 were recaptured or killed. The Soviet Union continued to make gains along the Eastern regions that the Germans had occupied. However, Germany was not acting as if it was headed for defeat. Shifting their aim, the Germans took control of Hungary and reinforced their hold on Romania. In the Far East, Japan's invasion of India was having little success against the defense of both Indian and British troops, and a U.S. attack on the Japanese island of Palau destroyed approximately 150 Japanese aircraft, offering more hope to the Allied supporters.

John Palasek was still based in the British Isles near Wales; he was expecting something big to happen soon, and to be a part of it. And even though Steve was yet to leave the States, he too finally got some rest with the granting of a long-awaited furlough for 20 days, which he used to go home. Stan was still anxious to serve, even though letters from his brother Joe warned him not to enlist and that he would regret it. Nonetheless, Stanley's draft status changed to 1A and his deferments came to an end on April 1. Within days he received a form letter from the President that strangely began with the pleasant and cordial word, "Greetings," a word more commonly associated with the beginning of a cheerful message, rather than being given the opportunity to risk one's life in battle

The induction process in 1944 was generally the same as it continued to be for decades after, into the Korean Conflict and Southeast Asian Hostilities. Stan's particular induction letter directed him to the Grand Central Palace, then located in Manhattan at Lexington and 46th Street, close to Grand Central Station — one of the points of embarkation for many from New York who left home to serve. The large beaux-arts building, which filled most of the block, had been New York's location for trade shows and expositions since 1911 and was converted to an induction center during the war. Here, hundreds of young men entered and stripped down to their underwear for the majority of their visit, which consisted of shuffling from doctor to doctor, papers held firmly in hand to be stamped or signed as they proceeded from one exam, test or inoculation to the other. Stanley chronicled his visit on April 11, 1944, in a diary entry as follows:

"*What a day. Wait, wait and wait. Doctor to doctor. Each doctor looked me over and they didn't seem to find anything wrong with me. I am glad that it is over. To pass or not to pass, that is the question. The day has gone by and that question can now be answered. I am in the Navy. I haven't been sworn in but I am accepted.*"

Upon his acceptance, Stanley was given a three-page "Navy Information" flyer. The letterhead featured a smiling civilian to the left side and the same smiling face in a sailor's cap to the right side, flanking the title "Navy Information," and the word "congratulations" in capital letters. The flyer covered many topics that might be on the mind of a new recruit. It explained that he was still a civilian and may "now return home to await further instructions." It went into basic information that would be covered when his service began regarding pay and insurance, but advised him to "bring about $6...to take care of expenses until your first pay day." On page two, there was a section called "WHAT TO WEAR AND WHAT TO BRING." This told the recruit to "Dress neatly but not in your best clothes. Do not bring extra shirts, socks, underwear or pajamas. All civilian clothing must be sent home after uniforms are issued..." The inductee was about to leave his individual style and life as he knew it behind, whether good or bad, and be one amongst many. The recruit was advised to bring a toothbrush, toothpaste or powder, a safety razor and a comb or brush. But the list of what not to bring continued: "Do NOT bring straight razors or electric razors... these cannot be used aboard ship. Do NOT bring cameras, radios... jewelry or valuables. Do NOT bring letters covering your work experience...since you will be interviewed by the classification board at the training station." Stanley had already requested and received such a letter from his employer, Sperry Gyroscope, which spoke glowingly of his abilities and contributions in the electronics field. The letter would have to be left at home, as would the final item on the list: "DO NOT BRING RELATIVES OR FRIENDS to the Recruiting Station. Space is limited and they will not be admitted."

This sentence spurred concerns about his wife and child, and how they would actually be without Stanley at home — though the matter had been argued over many times with Mary in the past year as being for the best. When Stanley returned to work the next day at Sperry, he wrote that he found it odd that whenever anyone, including himself, announced that they were going into the service, everyone there was "so happy for him." What was there to be happy about when a man was being sent to war, he pondered? It would be several weeks until he was called up to serve.

From Steve, Fort Sam Houston, TX, April 1944 –
Hello Folks, How are you, I hope you are as well as I am. By the way Stanley I have received your letter and sure was happy to hear from you all. As I sit here writing this letter I am Sargeant of the guard to-night. Each Sargeant takes a wack at this. I must say this is a beautiful spectacle the change of guard, passing in review, this is quite some ceremony to really carry it out. The men are really picked that had military training. After which I post my guard and sit in a guard house with a gun and bunch of keys. We have here so damn many german and Italian prisoners also Indians and Mexicans one has to pack a gun at all times. [Author's note: The Mexicans and Indians were not prisoners at Fort Sam Houston, but were locals, soldiers and civilian laborers. They were not considered to be trustworthy by the American military in 1944.] *These Mexicans are greasy looking things and hardly speak English, you can't trust none of them. We have full blooded Indians in my Company, brother have we got a job giving these mixed basic* [basic military training]. *Your eyes have to be everywhere. Well folks that is Texas, being so close to the Mexican Border this is our answer. Them damn gringo's sooner stick a knife in you as look at you. I never saw anything like that in my life I could tell you plenty if I were there in person, I will some day. I don't know when I will get my furlough. I made the grade got my promotion now they have the work cut out for me. The 712th which was my outfit the one I left in Clairborne is on there way across the pond. So if I was still a private I would have had my furlough and made the boat. The only way they are giving furloughs that is to us officers is emergency 15 days plus a one day pass to get a start. So far most of the non coms have been home except for a few of us. You see there wires came through the Red Cross, I kid them about it. By saying they must have friends*

working in the Red Cross units back home. I guess they have because I never saw so many emergency cases come up. Oh well, there lucky is all I can say.

By the way Stanley I am enclosing a letter which I have received from our brother John. I want you to read it. He does want reading matter and all the letters the folks back home can write. He is well but wishes he was back in the states. He wants me to guess where he is at. To me it seems he is closer. I receive mail from Joe every few days and I sure do write him in return. It really is a pleasure to hear from our brothers in the lands across the seas. This is no joke but some time this year I expect to go, maybe with this outfit or the next. Of course this is a long way off but it is coming as I have said, I would have been on my way if I was still a private or first class private. I'll be home some day before this comes along.

Well folks I conclude here god bless you all and keep you in the best of health spirit and happiness may this war end so that we may join you all in all the things in life which we have missed. I remain one of the seven. Your brother in the ranks. Steve. Just received a letter from Alex telling me you have your induction papers, I am sorry to hear this because I did hope you could stay out of it, I feel kind of strange about this.

The same day that Stanley received his "Greetings" letter from the President, his wife Mary was overjoyed that her brother, John, came to visit them from Fort Dix in New Jersey where he was being further trained in the operation of tank destroyers. PFC John W. Rykowski looked handsome as ever in his uniform when he came to the apartment. He had a mere 12 hours of leave but his nearest sibling, Mary, was someone he had to spend at least a few hours with, as they had always been so close to each other. He was excited to tell his sister and Stanley about his training and was proud that he was to be a member of the 602nd Tank Destroyer Battalion, whose motto was "Seek-Strike-Destroy." He knew he was going into something big, but could not discuss anything due to a lack of information that he had been given and the need for secrecy regarding the information he had received. He had lost a bit of weight in training; his cheeks were not as full as they appeared on the day early in his training when he had his picture taken. Yet at the young age of 21, his eyes and smile were as bright as ever. As he left, he hugged Stanley and wished that God bless him always. He kissed his two-year-old nephew and godson, Stanley Jr., who he called "Little Buddy" as he slept in his crib. Then John held his sister Mary close, perhaps hiding a tear of his own as she cried and walked him down to the street to send him off on his courageous journey.

Chapter 11

The Allied bombing targets shifted in April of 1944. No longer were the German cities of Berlin and Frankfurt the primary targets; the bombing runs were now aimed at roads and rail lines in German controlled Belgium and France. It was becoming considerably more evident to the world that the Allied forces were making these surgical strikes in preparation for an invasion and that cutting supply and transport lines was imperative. But such scattered destruction left few clues for the Axis powers, which in Europe were now predominantly the Nazis, as to what, where or when an invasion may be attempted, which made exact preparations impossible. The appalling genocide of the Jews in Poland continued and Germany was moving to forcefully transfer Jews in Hungary to Poland for what German commanders called "special treatment." Fighting in the Monte Cassino region of Italy between the American troops (including Joe Palasek) and the Germans seemed like it would never end. The Japanese were beginning to find that their troops were becoming too scattered across Asia and the Pacific. Japanese attempts to invade India were being repelled by the British, and China resisted attacks to its mainland. In the Pacific, American General Douglas MacArthur guided an Allied invasion force of 52,000 men into New Guinea to take its capital of Papua from the Japanese.

Many employees were leaving Sperry for the service or, in the case of older technicians, to Washington or other government facilities for the war effort. Stanley was losing his normal ambition as the corridors and labs emptied. It was all becoming a waiting game for him. All of his desires to serve in the Navy, to leave home, to get away from arguments with his wife, were now diminished by the fact that he would surely be leaving for the service soon, and his concern for his bride and young boy weighed upon his mind. Alex and William Palasek, having become fed up with the fact that they were not likely to advance at Sperry, left the company together. Alex still hoped to join the Merchant Marine if he could not get into the Armed Forces, and took a job in an automobile repair garage in Port Washington for the time being. Willie, having failed his military physical due to displays of anxiety and twitching, was hoping to land a job at the Post Office. Nothing was available there and after a brief time working at one of the yacht clubs, he became caddy master at the Plandome Country Club, which his father had helped construct several years earlier. John Rykowski was stationed in New Jersey with his battalion. Once a week he was to receive 12 hours of leave, but no more, as the call to ship overseas could come at any moment. Whenever possible, he would visit his sister, Mary, for a few precious hours before taking the two trains back to his base. When he visited on April 6, 1944, Stanley noted in his journal regarding John: "He looks fine but there is no doubt that he is worried and who wouldn't be, after all who knows what the future holds." And again, there were warm hugs, kisses and a walk to the station just below their apartment window to wave goodbye as John boarded the train. The visits were welcomed but the farewells were always painful.

    Five days later, on April 11, 1944, Stanley again reported to Grand Central Palace in New York City for a final physical along with his two friends, Eddie and Bernie. At the end of the long day he was given an 8" x 5" piece of paper from the Selective Service System indicating by a check mark in a box and a rubber-stamped signature on the bottom, that he was "Physically fit, acceptable by Navy." His friends were also accepted into the service. The war was rapidly intensifying, and more men were needed. In the front window or on the front door of most every home where a loved one was away in service to his country, there hung a white banner with blue and red trim and a blue star for each family member serving in the military. A smaller gold star would be placed upon the white one, should they be killed. The sad, silent tales of white and gold stars were increasing as each day passed.

    As far back as the 1860s and the "War Between The States," the use of railroads has been a significant part of military operations. Whether they were destroyed to stop troop carriers and supplies or being serviced to get a train from point A to B in order to transport the same goods that were being stopped elsewhere, railroads were vital. Military Railway Services were established in the U.S. in the 1860s and, after a time of peace, were reinstated during both World Wars for the same purposes. With few (if any) servicemen trained in the laying of tracks, their components or the operation of trains, battalions within the Army's Railway Operations were sponsored by domestic rail operators such as the Union Pacific, Illinois Central and Reading Railroads so soldiers could be trained by older, experienced railroad men. This training in the states consisted of the assembly and operation of tracks between military camps. Having spent his time in the service in various camps to be trained in supply and technical engineering, Steve now found himself as a Sergeant in one of these battalions.

From Steve, 724th Railway Operating Battalion, Camp Shelby, MS, April 16, 1944 – Dear Stanley, Received your letter for which I wish to thank you. Well Stanley I see by your letter that you to have joined the ranks, that you are one of us, Uncle Sams defense work. About to give the boys a hand in this terrible struggle. I sure was quite anxious awaiting the news as to how you made out. I did have that sneaky feeling that you were in pretty good condition. Well you made brother you are going to start a new life and a new venture. Stanley, you mentioned a furlough, I sure would like to see you before you leave for duty. I don't know just how much time you have left. I am afraid not enough. See the rest of my outfit is getting there furloughs and I can't get in on this deal. But one thing I do know that in time I will try to at least get me a short leave, before we head for the Port of Embarkation. You see this outfit already has an apo number [Author's note: postal address in the U.S. for troops that are overseas] which means we are one step closer to that banana boat.

    My staff sergeants rating is due me any time now. So it won't be long now that I can see that I'll be wearing that rocker underneath the three I already have, without the T. [Author's note: He would no longer be a technical Sergeant once he became a staff Sergeant.] I see one thing they really have drained Port of all the able bodied men. I was hoping in a way that somehow you might *stay out, although I did know how you felt about all this mess. I and the rest of us felt the same way about this situation, war is hell, but here we are, the four of us now. One more star in the banner.*

Here in Camp Shelby it is so damn hot, the moment you get your clothes on your all wet. The temperature sores of to 115 which is very warm. I am sun burned to hell and the mosquitos help a lot. Everything is in full bloom but burning up from the heat. I guess I'll cut it short here and Stanley may god bless you and guide you on your new venture. Have faith, hope and I am sure you will win we all shall win. Good luck sailor I do hope I may see you before you go away. I remain your brother and pal. Steve

As important as defeating the Japanese continued to be for the United States and its Allies, Europe and the defeat of the Nazis had become the primary focus of the war. While MacArthur was assembling a base in recently-liberated New Guinea in order to proceed with attacks on the Japanese, it seemed an afterthought compared to what was happening in Europe. Over 3.5 million Allied servicemen, of which over one-third were from the U.S. (including John Palasek), had been brought together in the United Kingdom. Heavy bombings of Germany and occupied France increased and drills on landings of troop carriers were held on the south shores of England.

Joe Palasek sent a letter to his wife, Margaret, to let her know he was out of the recuperation unit of the hospital and waiting for a new platoon. Having experienced the horrors of war for several months, he wouldn't wish what he was going through on anyone, particularly his own brother.

From Joe, Italy, April 23, 1944 *– Hello Stanley, How is everything with you. I hope this letter finds you Mary and your little Battler in the best of health. In one of your letters you said you have until April then you are going in the service, but since that letter I haven't heard from you. I sure would like to now how you made out and what your in the Army, Navy etc.*

I hope you didn't pass your physical, for you don't have to get in the service, but I guess you want to go, so I wish you lots of luck, and if your in the Army stay out of the infantry. There isn't much to write so solong for a while god Bless you and maybe someday we all will get together again. Your Brother, Joe

As an inevitable attack on the European mainland was becoming increasingly imminent, Germany's general Rommel was hastily making preparations. The Germans erected massive angle iron spikes tightly along the northern coast of Europe from the Netherlands, across France to Normandy in order to deter Allied landing craft and military vehicles from entering Europe from the sea. Trenches and bunkers were being erected and heavily armed along the shoreline. The German commanders still did not have insight as to precisely where an invasion would occur as May arrived. The placement of their Panzer tanks in order to be most effective was still a concern for them. Tank divisions were being separated and therefore weakened in an effort to cover more potential invasion sites.

Stanley and Mary, still struggling with life together in a small apartment on Main Street, realized they couldn't afford to continue renting their apartment on a sailor's pay. They moved most of their belongings to a friend's house and put larger pieces of their simple household furniture in storage for $5 a month. But after only two days, they agreed that their new arrangement of having two families with small children sharing a house with one kitchen and one bathroom would not work for Mary and the baby. The couple agreed that it would be best to sleep in their apartment for now and to again move their few possessions to Stanley's mother's home on School Street when Stanley eventually left for the Navy. Every day, as his call up to serve got closer, Stanley realized more and more how much he loved and would miss his wife and child. Mary expressed her unhappiness that she no longer would have even the small apartment they called home, and likewise her displeasure with living under someone else's roof. To her, still only 19 years old with a two-year-old child, life was simply unfair and she resented it. As the spring weather arrived, Stanley tried to fully appreciate the warmth of the sun, the blooming flowers, the fresh air and green grass — simple things he feared that he would not have a chance to enjoy in the near future. Many days were spent at Jones Beach by the Atlantic shore of Long Island with his Sperry coworkers, setting up the defense systems they had developed for Project MUSE. The glorious views of the crashing surf and white sands were regularly interrupted by the sight of warplanes practicing low above the water, thus forcing the reality of life and work during wartime to invade his daydreams of happier times.

***From Joe, Italy, May 1, 1944** – Hello Stanley, How are you. I guess everything is going pretty fine with you and judging by your letters you say you are disgusted with civilian life. Take my advice Stanley and stay home with your wife and baby for once you get in the service you can't get out till this mess is over. And once you get over here your only going to duck bullets, artillery, mortars etc. and your only gambling with your life. So I think it's much better arguing with your wife, then getting yourself into the scrap. For if they wanted you they would have taken you long ago so stay where your at nd you'll never have to worry about bullets etc. Your pal Brother, Joe*

  The Allied forces assaulted the Germans from several directions as May progressed. The Russians had seized control of the Crimean peninsula from them and were pressing toward the north. In Monte Cassino, Joe Palasek's infantry division continued to be repelled by the Germans but the Allied forces no longer consisted only of Americans and British soldiers in this region. Brigades of soldiers from India, Poland, French Morocco and Canada united in battle as they attacked the German forces in Italy from various sides. Finally, on May 18, 1944, the Allies outflanked the Germans. With French Moroccan troops moving through the hills toward the enemy at surprising speed, the last of the German troops could no longer resist and those who did not flee under the cover of darkness were taken captive. The Polish brigades proceeded into the village, which was no longer under the watchful eyes or guns of the Germans, and raised the Polish flag over Monte Cassino. They then proceeded to open up Germany's Gustav Line in the Italian mountains as well as a path to Rome.
  Days were passing slower than usual for all of the Palaseks in mid-May 1944. For Steve in Mississippi, training classes that earned him an extra $5 a day were helping to make the time pass as he

waited and wondered if he would soon be sent to a pier to ship overseas. For Joe, the end of his hellish fight in the mountains of Italy was over. He knew that he wasn't going home soon and that there were many battles with their own nightmare inducing scenes yet to come, but for the moment, he could breathe easily while generals methodically planned his future. John Palasek was still in Wales, training and nervously passing every long day with the knowledge that something big was coming and he was a narrow body of water from where it would begin. Stanley was preparing to leave both his job and his family, unsure of what the future would be for any of them. The long, slow days seemed at the same time to be passing too quickly when he rested his head at night and counted them down. And for every family and friend still in the states, each day dragged in hopes that tomorrow there would be a letter from their soldier saying they were okay. The cold and snow of a long hard winter had passed and the weather was changing, bringing more flowers and greenery for all to enjoy. The world was also about to change for each of them in ways that no forecaster could predict.

Chapter 12

On May 17, 1944, Stanley left work at Sperry's for the final time. He said his goodbyes and went drinking with the few men there who he considered to be friends. Having passed up a farewell party for himself and two others at the stately Garden City Hotel, he was quietly given a travel case and a few words of encouragement from one of his mentors in the lab where he had worked, along with the offer that he was always welcome to return. This was not in his plan, nor on his mind. For the next seven days he made the most of civilian life and spent time with his family and Mary's family. He went to the Town Dock and fished for the small bluefish known as snappers, played golf with Willie at Plandome Country Club and took Mary shopping in New York City where she bought $150 worth of clothing for herself. This extravagance made her happy, knowing clothing was not going to be an issue while her husband was in the Navy. The day before Stan was to report, Willie brought Joe's wife, Margaret, and eight quarts of beer to the School Street house. Margaret brought nine dozen local hard-shell clams, which they steamed in two large pots and devoured, washing them down with the beers.

When Stanley's induction day finally arrived on May 25, 1944, he reported to the local draft board in Port Washington before taking the railroad to 383 Madison Avenue in New York City. There, he filled out form after form for hours. Being given the opportunity, he was able to take the "Eddy Test," which could offer him a chance to be assigned to the Navy's Electronics Training Program, but he was discouraged when they suddenly halted the test as he was only halfway through the questions. All of his skills in electronics might now be overlooked and he would have to go into the Navy beginning at the bottom like most men. He was next sent to Penn Station, then a grand structure fronted by massive columns and large concrete statues of eagles across the top of the 7th Avenue façade. He entered the main hall of the station, which was filled with sunlight that poured in through the glass ceilings, and went to the designated meeting area on the concourse. Here, he was issued train tickets and received cigarettes, candy, gum and apples from the Red Cross representatives who were there. A man named Mr. Gleason from the Holy Name Society handed Stanley and the other Catholic men a prayer book and a medal of Saint Christopher, the patron saint of travelers. A sailor escorted Stanley's group to the recruitment station in the terminal, where he was instructed to register for a room at the YMCA and given three days of liberty (rather than the mere nine hours most men received) while the results of the "Eddy Test" were reviewed and his destination was determined. Rather than stay in the New York YMCA, he returned to his mother's home for the three days.

On Monday, May 29, 1944, Stan's brother Alex reported to Sheepshead Bay in Brooklyn where he was to finally fulfill his desire to join the Merchant Marines. It wasn't "The Marines," but it was a start. Stan's bride, Mary, had taken a job at Kent's Dry Cleaners in nearby Manhasset to help make ends meet. Stanley returned alone to Manhattan that night, after three days of liberty with his family not knowing where he would be sent. After seeing many tears shed by families at the station, the roll was called. The men were then told that they had 45 minutes before the train left, so several, including Stan, dashed up the stairs to the Horn and Hardart automat on the opposite corner of 34th Street, across from Macy's, to get some food for the ride. Then they headed to "a gin mill," as Stan would say, for some final drinks at the bar. Back in Penn Station, after another call of the roll, the men were boarded on what Stanley called in his journal, "the filthiest train of coaches that were ever put together on any track." The seats, floor, windows and ceiling were covered in black soot. At 10:20 that evening, Stanley's train pulled out of Penn Station into the darkness of the tunnel under the Hudson River and into the night through New Jersey. His destination on the overnight ride was Sampson Navy Base. Formerly farm land overlooking Seneca Lake, one of New York's Finger Lakes, the area had been converted to a Naval training center in 1942 and named for Rear Admiral William T. Sampson, from nearby Palmyra, New York, a hero of the Battle of Santiago during the Spanish-American War.

As the night wore on, sleeping in the filthy train seats was impossible and the soot from the engines was infiltrating the men's eyes and ears, turning their white shirts to grey. They began to look and feel like the coal miners of Pennsylvania that they were riding past. The bright light of molten steel from the factories, which would be turned into the tools of war, glowed through the darkness. Daybreak brought views of lakes in New York's southern tier and a smile to many as the chilly, foggy air became a fresh breeze for the travelers. Around 10 a.m., the train pulled into Sampson and came to a halt.

Stanley and the men were marched to the reception center for their first Navy meal: an apple, a small glass of milk and a bologna sandwich. Next was a physical, which consisted of walking past the doctors who were not about to reject anyone at this point unless there was an obvious reason. The men also got to take a shower, which helped to remove the soot from the train ride, and received three inoculations. After being huddled off in a truck to the barracks with their gear and blankets, the men met their Commanding Officer and began several days of lectures and exercises. The daily grind of being woken up at 5:30 in the morning to drill, run and march was something much less than exhilarating, but obviously necessary.

Within two weeks, Stanley was complaining of stomach cramps and was sent to the dispensary for medication. A couple of days later, still suffering, he was sent to the hospital where he underwent a psychological interview. Stanley explained that six years earlier, while performing one of his many jobs as a veterinarian's assistant, he was bitten by a rabid dog and underwent treatment, which then consisted of 13 very painful inoculations to his abdomen. He explained that since then, he had been treated for stomach pains a couple of times. He also admitted to the Navy doctors that he became excited too quickly and the stomach pains often followed. Stanley was sent to the base hospital and after a couple of days, he was recommended for discharge based upon the fact that his condition existed prior to his being drafted and should have exempted him. Being sent home took several more days, which were spent in the hospital amongst patients who Stanley felt were obviously in need of treatment, but were ignored by staff who would say their ailments were all in their imagination.

On June 19, after only 21 days in the Navy, Stanley was sent home with an honorable discharge. He gathered his belongings and signed the necessary papers before he boarded a truck with his bag and a few weeks' pay, along with five other men, to go to the Geneva, New York train station. There, he had a meal and a beer, sent a telegram to his wife and went to a movie before the train left at 10:50 p.m. After two train rides, he was back in Port Washington before 10 a.m. the next morning. He stopped at his mother's house, then went to the draft board office and was reclassified, from 1-A to 1-C, honorably discharged. He called Sperry Gyroscope and they told him he could have his job back. It was necessary to support his family, but not something that was done without some deep regrets. His Navy career was officially over, but not his service to his country. For not only was he returning to work for a defense contractor that had already made great technological contributions to the military; he was also going to be able to support his brothers in the service by writing letters they desperately wanted from home and serving as the repository for the thoughts they put on paper, wherever the war took them.

Chapter 13

Earlier in the spring of 1944, the three leaders of the Allied powers met in Tehran to discuss a plan to invade and liberate

Europe. There was hesitation about including Joseph Stalin in these talks. He was a ruthless man who seemed to have his own agenda for the Soviet Union to control territories where their forces had defeated those of Germany. However, considering that the Russian Army had made significantly more gains against German-held territories than the other Allied forces and managed to repel attacks on Stalingrad, it was necessary to continue to consider Stalin an ally. Their discussion turned to the concept of a massive invasion of Europe that would be staged in the United Kingdom and would enter Europe primarily by sea along the French coastline. Winston Churchill was against the notion. Twenty-nine years earlier, Churchill was the First Lord of the Admiralty during WW I. He had presented a controversial plan for a massive troop invasion of the area east of Germany in order to prevent Moscow from being taken over by German armies. Under his direction, the invasion was attempted at Gallipoli, which was then a part of the Ottoman Empire. The invasion failed and 56,000 men died as a result of Churchill's decision. The prospect of an even greater defeat in 1944 weighed heavily on Churchill. In exchange for Stalin's promise to the United States to fight against Japan's invasion of China, Roosevelt and Stalin overruled Churchill and the wheels were set in motion for an invasion.

  The Allies had liberated Rome by entering the country from the south by the end of May. It seemed as if everyone on earth knew an invasion of Europe from the north would follow. Very few actually knew what form it would take, and even fewer knew exactly where or when it would begin. Adolf Hitler attempted to anticipate Allied movements. His Nazi military had taken considerable losses in the past months along the Russian front and in Italy, but his grip was still tight over much of Europe. He believed Germany would eventually reach its goal of domination and continued on as if his success was inevitable. He grievously erred in his strategy that spring.

  Near the cliffs of Dover, England, German reconnaissance planes had photographed a massive Allied military buildup. Hundreds of tanks, troop carriers and airplanes were accumulating adjacent to large barracks on the coast. The nearest point across the English Channel was the German-held city of Calais in France.

German intelligence learned the Allied base was under the command of General George Patton, the first man to command a tank battalion in WW I and an integral part of the initial invasion of Sicily in 1943. At the same time, German intelligence discovered that a massive Allied Army was preparing for an attack on German-held Norway from Scotland. Hitler insisted that the much-expected invasions would take place in Norway and Calais, and instructed his generals to shift troops and weaponry in order to prepare a defense against attacks in these regions.

The Allied plan, code-named Operation Bodyguard, was working as intended. The massive buildup of weapons on the English coast near Dover was indeed commanded by General Patton. The number of soldiers under his command was minimal, as few men were actually needed to assemble and shift the positions of decoy planes, tanks and trucks that were designed by Hollywood studios and made of lightweight materials such as plywood or inflatable. Tanks could be lifted by two soldiers and appear from the air to be moving. The massive British Army being assembled in Scotland to attack Norway was also a well-played ruse. The Allies broadcast realistic but false radio communications regarding troop movements with the intention of being intercepted by the Germans. Additionally, captured and "turned" Germans were used as double agents to report to German commanders how an army was being established in Scotland to attack Norway. These and other diversionary tactics resulted in the Germans trying to defend the entire northern coast of mainland Europe and stretching their defenses.

On June 6, 1944, many Americans were leaving movie theaters where they watched Bing Crosby in the musical "Going My Way" or preparing for bed. It was already the early hours before the dawn of the next day across the Atlantic. After months of preparation and several days of delays due to weather, the Allied forces, over 150,000 strong from over a dozen nations, began the largest invasion of WW II by crossing the English channel — not toward Calais, but to the French coast near Normandy. The lives of those who were on that shoreline, and those that followed by sea and air — as well as countless others who were directly or indirectly involved — would never be the same.

From Steve, Camp Shelby, MS, June 12, 1944 – Dear Stanley, I thank you ever so much for the first letter I received upon my return here to Camp Shelby. Before I continue I must say I am perspiring a mile a minute, for the heat is really unbearable.

Well Stanley things are really pointing for that step closer to the boys over there. We already have received our new issue of clothing and equipment plus good many changes due to this new change in program. They took away all our summer uniforms we have nothing left but the winter stuff, which means bundle up brother its going to be slightly breezy.

It really doesn't make much difference, I hope we get out of here, for this is only a hell hole the devil himself wouldn't accept. I guess a guy has to take good with the bad, you can't take the cake and eat it. I had to send my license, all papers pictures that may identify me plus give away my outfit. Yes we are getting rid of many items receiving new, at the same time packing crating and reviewing all we ever knew. We are very busy from dawn till night. The men, well some can take it others brood. I'll tell you the truth none of us feels at ease because we don't know much yet we realize we are going. Some cuss there luck, others rave to hurry up with it, lets get it over with quick.

I can only say one thing and that is to trust in the good lord almighty for he alone can help us through thick and thin. We attended high mass, for our intention our guidance whereupon we received the blessing and good luck where ever we may be. Leaders of men as we were addressed by the priest, have faith, help and assist your men, be kind have courage to go on as our comrades our buddies have done a wonderful job for us for all our loved ones. God help us wherever we may be. The Captain stated kill or be killed. I guess I better change the subject. Getting back to furlough, I enjoyed all my time with you, I counted on greater things still at times they don't work out. Some day folks we shall get together as Joe wrote me, we shall have a rally without end, joy and something real to celebrate, freedom, Victory peace forever after.

With a good luck, god bless you all my best wishes and regards to you Stan and all the family. Say an extra prayer now and then. Be good. I remain your brother and Pal. Steve

Young Alex Palasek was now in the mix, stationed at the Sheepshead Bay, Maritime Service Training Station in Brooklyn as an apprentice seaman. Established shortly after the attack on Pearl Harbor on the grounds of an old amusement park and opened in December 1942, it was the largest training facility for merchant seaman in the nation (it later became the location of Kingsborough Community College). Here, men were taught the basics of merchant seamanship, from ship maintenance to knot tying to operating a galley in order to feed the crew. Workouts included climbing rigging and "Jacob's Ladder," a rope ladder that would flip the climber upside down if used incorrectly. Self-defense arts were a daily part of the seaman's life. According to the base publication, *The Helm*, training also covered less common matters such as survival techniques and what to do if captured, as well as the hazards of getting an all-too-permanent tattoo that one's loved ones may not appreciate someday, such as a woman's name. Still not having reached 18 years of age, Alex wrote home to his brother, Stan, that he needed him to explain to their mother a matter she might not easily grasp. A notarized letter was needed, signed by mother Palasek, which would allow Alex to go to sea. Upon receipt of the letter, Alex would be considered a boson's mate, first class.

Stanley was back at Sperry, in the same lab that he had left not long ago, continuing work on the final stages of Project MUSE. He was also busy trying to find a new place for his small family to live in, as being in the house his mother was renting wasn't working out well. He hoped to find a small house of his own to rent, but real estate agents came back to him empty handed. Finding an affordable car would also help with his commute to work, but on a salary of $1 per hour, that could not be his most urgent quest. Finding a new job was, to Stanley, a more imperative pursuit. Adding to the day-to-day stresses were reports in the newspapers and on the streets of Port Washington of the terrible battles in Europe and in the South Pacific. He was troubled to hear that his neighbors, the Mazur family had lost Ernest, one of their sons, in France; he and Mary both had family and other friends there. The sudden lack of mail due to the intensity of the war made life that much harder for him and everyone in the states. A letter from nearby was as welcome as one from far away.

From Alex, Sheepshead Bay, NY, June 14, 1944 –
Dear Stan, I have been here 16 days now, and man what drill we have, and we have an obstacle course here that really gives you the business. We got two more shots yesterday, they gave us pills to take with them, we had to stand at attention for a little while and six guy's passed out cold as a cucumber. So far we had seven shots we have two more to go.

Today we had to go through the obstacle course, climb Jacob's ladders, ropes hand over hand, climb cargo nets, we were shown wrestling grips how to break them, boxing for 3 rounds. I feel darn good except I'm a little tired. The food here is very good except that sometimes you don't get enough. Today I went to confession and am going to communion tomorrow at 5:00 P.M.

We had lifeboat training today. So far I have had two hours of lifeboat drill, we have to have 28 hours of lifeboat drill before we take a test for our lifeboat ticket. Have you heard from John, Joe or Steve? Well, its getting so I haven't anything more to write so solong and God Bless You. Your Brother, Alex

As the Allies were making their way slowly into France, the Germans were introducing their newest weapon: the V-1 guided bomb (or as the Allies termed it, the "buzz bomb" due to the sound it made in flight). Using an autopilot system for guidance, these bombs were delivered from a launch ramp or aircraft at a significant distance from their intended targets, resulting in a lower risk of attack on the German aircraft that were launching them. The bombs were often inaccurate in their targeting but were yet one more thing to fear. The continuing slaughter of Jews by the Nazis was not deterred by the Allied invasion. Hundreds of Jews from the Greek island of Corfu were rounded up by Nazi troops and sent to the mainland, where they were put on freight trains as if they were soulless cattle and delivered to the Auschwitz death camps far away in Poland. In the South Pacific, American troops continued to move closer to Japan by defeating the Japanese soldiers holding the Mariana Islands. One of the largest Japanese armies to invade India was defeated by Indian and Allied troops after a three-month siege. Still, an unrelenting army of approximately 200,000 Japanese soldiers continued to march into the Chinese interior.

Steve Palasek finally managed what he believed to be the impossible by getting a seven-day furlough, explaining that his daughter, Regina, was ill; at the time, a sick child was the only way he could temporarily return home. In reality, it was his wife, Stephanie, who was ill. Her fear of her beloved Steve's inevitable assignment to a war zone overseas resulted in her losing weight and constantly feeling tired. Seeing Steve was all that she desired. Being back home also gave Steve a few days to attend his daughter's first communion and to see his parents and brothers. Stanley in particular was happy to see Steve and spent an evening going from "gin mill to gin mill," getting "brewed up" until the early morning hours more than once. The furlough ended far too quickly for Steve, Stephanie and Regina, but Steve knew that "his men" depended upon him and he was not going to let them down.

Day after day, Americans tried to keep in touch with events in the war, as so many of them had family members on the active battlefields. Every day, one would fear that they might receive a letter from the U.S. War Department containing the saddest of news regarding a loved one. Escaping to the movies during that very hot summer in the east to see Humphrey Bogart's film "Passage to Marseilles" in an air-cooled theater was a possibility for those who had the spare cash. For some, distancing themselves from the news for a few hours of entertainment turned to disaster as the traveling Barnum and Bailey Circus, held under a tent coated in waterproof paraffin wax, gave way to an unexplained fire during a Connecticut performance. The disaster killed more than 150 of the 7,000 guests in attendance.

At this point, any good news was more than welcome. The victories in the war's battles were not enough to bring joy to everyone, not when the lives of loved ones were at risk.

From Steve, Camp Shelby, MS, July 25, 1944 – *Dear Stanley, Received your letter to-day, for which I say thanks a million. Each time I write you may be the last time for a while. Because each day each hour is now closer to our D-day. We are just idling here awaiting orders if you get what I mean. I'm a little blue but I guess I'll get over it. I only do hope we get around home territory to stay a while so that once again I may see you all. All this* *week is devoted to masses for our intention also solemn devoted prayers. This hanging around sure gets into my hair. Every one seems so tense I guess its only natural. Another thing its so hot I guess I'll be glad to go anywhere. Anyway we can't win it by sitting here sweating in Camp Shelby. To help the situation I got three more needles and these damn near knocked me on my can.*

I think we have a real McCoy outfit. One that can really take it, also dish it out when the time comes. We shall see in due time. Don't worry we brothers can take care of our selves come what may. So far god almighty has guided all of us and taken care so that we may be real soldiers. Besides Stanley I guess I know quite a few tricks after one years training and passing my little knowledge to the ones who have gone before me and those who shall now go with me. I am to lead these boys by platoons through thick and thin. It will be my responsibility as to their care and protection. I guess you know me, I can handle myself.

You mentioned in the letter to me Stan about two off our home town boys being killed in France. God have mercy on there souls, But you see some must die, some can go on no matter what. One must rely on his own common sense. His coolness in order to think and control himself. Baptism of fire which is taught every soldier. Also the subject Kill or be killed. That is the motto that is either you or him. There is so much one must study not just to memorize but to actually put this into use in the field of operations.

I guess I have covered all I know lord knows where I'll be in a few days. Hoping hope on top of hope. So God bless you and our home, be good and take care, keep your chin up, for it won't be long before we get to-gether again. Remaining your pal and brother. Steve

As Allied forces grew in strength, expanding the areas that they controlled, both the war in Europe and the continuing conflict in the Pacific intensified. More and more men were having to face the battles head on around the globe. Few of these young men, including most of the Palasek boys and Mary Rykowski's brothers, had ever travelled farther than 25 miles from their homes prior to 1941. As the distance from home and loved ones increased, so would the danger.

Chapter 14

Popular songs in the 1940s did not appear and disappear as quickly as they do in the 21st century. It would take weeks or months for a new song to be released, played on the radio, and heard at dances and personal appearances by the band or singer. Some songs would appear, disappear disappointingly and then reappear to great acclaim a year or so later when the timing was better or it was used in a motion picture. One of the more popular songs of the time was penned by Johnny Mercer and recorded by the vocal group, The Pied Pipers. The song, "Accentuate the Positive," told the listener to do just that and to eliminate the negative and not to mess with mister in-between.

For many people, the time to do just that had come in the summer of 1944. Newspaper articles told of the advances that the Allies were making in Europe and the Pacific. Radio reports from the likes of Edward R. Murrow and Walter Cronkite brought those at home a graphic description of the war's realities, often with the sounds of a battle in the background, yet these announcers and reporters tried whenever possible to bring hope to the listener. Newsreels that were shown before motion pictures were beginning to show smiling Allied soldiers walking into European cities that were long held by the Nazis, as flag-waving locals cheered them on. This accentuation of the positive encouraged a nation that desperately needed to have its spirits lifted. Talk on the street was turning to the notion that this could all end sooner than later, on both the European and Pacific fronts. For many, the hard times, some of the hardest they would ever face, lurked around the edge of a calendar's page.

The realities of August 1944 were that the Allies were firmly established in Europe and moving cautiously forward. Field Marshall Bernard Montgomery, the British commander who had previous success in North Africa, was frustratingly slow in advancing the Allied troops into Europe. The first Army of the United States, under the leadership of American Field Marshall Omar Bradley, and the third Army under General Patton were soon to join with the British forces in hope that a combined leadership and strategy would make considerably more progress. In southern Europe, many of the Allied troops who had fought diligently to liberate Rome and most of southern Italy were being shifted to the invasion of France. In an attempt to slow those Allied troops who remained in Italy, the Germans destroyed much of Florence — including all the bridges across the Arno River except the Ponte Vecchio. Hitler mistakenly believed there was precious art hidden there. The Japanese were losing control of Guam in the Marianas Islands, isolating the Japanese military there from the rest of their forces. General MacArthur hoped this would soon be used as a stepping-stone by the United States to recover control of the Philippines and move toward an invasion of Japan.

Stanley and Mary Palasek were still living with Stanley's parents in the rented house on School Street as August began with high hopes of finding a place of their own again. As with so many other American families, the number of brothers and sons who were not only away from home, but headed to foreign lands, was mounting daily. Joseph Palasek was one of the soldiers who were to remain in Italy after many of his comrades were moved to the north of France. He continued as a member of the 4th Field Hospital Unit. The unit was charged with immediately treating casualties of battle when evacuation to a standing military hospital was not possible. The enlisted men of this corps not only assisted in the care of the injured, but also as Joe's letters explained, faced the enemy in battle where they were stationed. Steve Palasek's extended time sweltering in southern training camps was coming to an end. Having worked his way up to Staff Sergeant and a training officer, it was now time for him to put both his training, and that of his men, to work. Steve was given 12 hours of leave on his way past Long Island to say farewell to his family before heading to Camp Shanks, a port of Embarkation (POE) in upstate New York. From there, he and his men were on their way to Europe.

Alex Palasek was completing his basic training for the Merchant Marine and was anxious to go overseas. Although Alex's deepest wish was to be a part of the Navy, he was now a part of a service that predated both the Navy and the Army. With fewer regulations than the Navy, the Merchant Marines were often considered to be a lesser service in the eyes of many Americans. Among the Merchant Marines themselves was a freer spirit than in other branches of the service, but no less of a desire to serve. Their men were also in as much danger as anyone else, suffering more casualties during the war than any other branch at sea. The first servicemen to die during the raid on Pearl Harbor were Merchant Marines aboard the SS Cynthia Olsen, when the vessel was attacked and sunk hundreds of miles off of Hawaii's shore by a Japanese submarine. Alex may have been wishing to be a part of the Navy, yet his service in the Merchant Marine would be no less important or daring.

John Palasek had been in Wales, both at a Navy base and finally aboard a ship as a sailor. Now he was on the move. Though he was unable to directly say in his closely-monitored letters exactly where he was, clues let his brothers know he was headed for the Mediterranean. Being a short strait of water away from the largest attack on Europe to date when D-Day occurred he was sure he would end up fighting along the coast of northern Europe once the invasion began. Instead, the ship he boarded was bound for North Africa, where he again found himself waiting to be ordered into a battle situation.

From John P., Tunis, Tunisia, August 8, 1944 – *Dear Stanley, Well, I finally received some mail. Twelve letters to be exact. Four of them from you. I hadn't been expecting mail so it was a pleasant surprise to me. You'll notice a new address I have and I was told to use it while I am here. I am still in the same place as when I first wrote you on my arrival here. I don't know whether or not mail from the states is censored but as long as you've been writing none of your mail has been so you needn't worry about mentioning the weather and things that are going on in the states. I'm sure no one will object.*

I read Steve's letter that you enclosed and I can understand his feelings about shoving off but that is something not unusual and everyone feels pretty much the same when that time comes. After a while, you get used to being away and since you know you can't go home you just don't think about it. At least that is the way it is with me. I guess that's all Stanley. I'll have to sign off now and see what I can do with a letter to Joe. I'll write again soon and keep you posted on any doings. John

From John P., Tunis, Tunisia, August 12, 1944 – Dear Stanley, I don't know exactly what to write about except that I am still in North Africa. In that letter you enclosed from Steve he mentioned an accident [Author's note: their brother] Carl had. I wish you'd let me know something about it because it's a mystery to me as to what happened. Carl never writes me so I don't know how or what he's doing. Quite a while ago I'd written Stephanie and I guess she's too busy to bother about writing. Nice bunch of relatives I've got anyway. I don't really give a hoot very much except that its enlightening to know what a small world some people live in.

I often wonder whatever became of my pal Armand. The last I heard from him he was about to go into the army. I guess I'll have to drop him a line one of these days and find out. Maybe the little jerk got married instead.

Judging by that letter of Steve's I guess he must be on his way by this time or maybe he's already there. The way he wrote me when I was in Wales I thought he was about to shove off any day. That's why I didn't write him, instead I waited to receive a new address.

I haven't had any liberty in twenty eight days but I'm supposed to get Tuesday off. It's a long ways to this particular liberty town and I'm kind of curious to see it. I'll let you know what kind of a time I have when I go. I guess that's all for now and don't forget to keep writing. Palasek, J.P. John

By mid-August, the news continued to bring reasons to be hopeful as well as news of incidents to crush the human spirit. The American troops had recaptured Guam, therefore effectively regaining control of the Marianas Islands from Japan making it possible to re-establish Allied air bases there that would be capable of striking Tokyo. Fifteen days later, on August 25, it was announced that Paris had been liberated from the Germans, and Allied armies were parading down the Parisian Boulevards. Much of the credit for the victory belonged to the French Resistance, who lost almost as many people in their ranks as the number of Germans they killed. As General Charles DeGaulle returned to the city, the streets continued to be a ground for skirmishes between Germans, many in the form of snipers, and the liberated French. With these victories and ongoing skirmishes came knowledge. It was clear that much more fighting would have to go on throughout Europe to truly cease Germany's control, and that many more lives would be lost accomplishing this goal. Additional scenes of Nazi horrors came to light as the Allies moved into territories that Germany formerly controlled. One of the most disturbing discoveries was of the largest Nazi concentration camp yet in Majdanek, Poland, where about a million Jews were recently gassed, cremated, and their ashes sent to Germany to fertilize farms — a sobering reminder to everyone that this war would not be over until the enemy surrendered completely.

 The combination of hopes and fears of the Palaseks and Rykowskis included the vast scale of the war and its influence on their daily lives, as well as changes one faced that either uplifted or hampered dreams. Stanley and Mary were excited about moving into a place of their own again with their two-year-old son. By coincidence, a larger five-room apartment was available in the same building they had left on Main Street only months earlier. Mary was thrilled about the concept of more space, a familiar location and no longer living with her in-laws. Stanley was glad as well, hoping this move would make their marriage happier, although it also meant purchasing more furniture to fill a larger living area. More positive news made Stanley smile when he heard from a company he had previously been associated with, Press Wireless. At this time, the company was setting up radio communications between Normandy and the United States in Baldwin, New York. Stanley was ecstatic; his tasks since returning to Sperry Gyroscope after his brief Navy tour were now done by technicians, rather than engineers like him, and his days were long and dull. However, when he asked his superiors for a release, they repeatedly explained that he was much too valuable to let go, turning his joy to bitterness.

 The concerns at home were compounded by news that 56 children in the county had contracted polio. This crippling disease would not have any hope of prevention for another eight years, and required its victims to live with various stages of paralysis requiring braces, wheelchairs or even a lifetime in an iron lung. Since small children were most susceptible to this disease, Stanley worriedly read the dark reports on this outbreak.

Mary's parents, Theodora and Adolph Rykowski, were concerned for their own sons. Theodora cleaned houses to help with the costs of the home she and her husband were fortunate enough to own on Roslyn's Powerhouse Road, then a primary road between Long Island and New York City. They also had a small shed by the side of the road where their children would sell tobacco, snacks and beverages to travelers. Adolph was a maintenance man on one of the Gold Coast estates who was known to drink away much of his income. They came to America a few years before Stanley and Marjanna Palasek and had their tenth child, their fourth daughter, in 1935. Their eldest son, Chester, was in his thirties when war broke out, but their other boys went on to the service. Now they, too, waited to see where life would take their sons. Adam, tall and curly haired, was serving as a Military Policeman stateside, protecting dignitaries as well as rounding up and escorting servicemen who were absent without leave (AWOL). It is almost surprising that he and his younger brother by seven years, Eddie, never crossed paths, as the wiry and somewhat wily Eddie was not on base as assigned more than once. Frank, a muscular young man who had recently started his own family, had every intention to join the Navy. Instead, he served in the Coast Guard Reserve, as his teeth were not good enough for classification as 1-A by the draft board. His Coast Guard group was instrumental in detecting and helping to stop a group of German saboteurs who had landed on Long Island's south shore with the intent to destroy American power plants and military manufacturers in 1942. John Rykowski was in Europe with Company "C" of the 602nd Tank Battalion in Patton's Third Army. The Rykowskis' youngest son Alexander (better known as "Ollie") signed up for the Navy in the spring of 1944. His wit and smile hid any concerns he might have held inside about serving in the military. He knew what his country needed and would proudly do whatever was necessary. It seemed that it was only a matter of time before Adam and Ollie would also go overseas. They each received the customary days of leave, and young sailor Ollie welcomed the liberty to go home and set straight affairs and family matters prior to being sent to war.

    Contact with friends and with family back home continued to be important to all of these servicemen. Reading letters from home was as essential as sending them. To know that someone cared about them and knew their thoughts kept those people close in spirit. When an enlisted man's assigned battalion or location of assignment was changed, his APO or military address in the United States (through which mail was distributed worldwide) would change as well. Not wanting to lose touch for a moment, a soldier or sailor would immediately write home with his new address as soon as it was available. John Rykowski made sure everyone had his new APO when he shipped off for Europe. In the heat of a battlefront, where secrecy was necessary and the ability to concentrate on danger was of prime importance, mail could not always be guaranteed delivery.

An August 12 V-Mail sent by Stanley to Mary's brother John was returned as undeliverable. Stanley wrote that he knew John was in England. Stanley wished him well and God's blessings, and assured John that Stanley Jr. and Mary were well. Hearing anything back from John would take weeks, if he received the letter at all, as John continued to be on the move with his aggressive commanders. Nine days after Stanley's V-Mail was sent and three days before it was returned, John's battalion was moved south to Portland on the south shore of England, a base where many of the troops from the D-Day invasion left for France just weeks before. For four days, the men of the 602nd TD rode across the English Channel aboard an LST (Landing Ship: Tank) and came across to Omaha Beach, where they went ashore with their M18 Hellcat tanks. Since the D-Day battles were long over and the beach was safe, the 602nd battalion moved on to the nearby town of Formigny, France, which had been liberated only one month earlier. Eventually, John sent a few words in a letter to tell his parents that they should let others know he was in France, doing well, and if at all possible, could they send him some cigars? A small, colorized photo of him was included. Looking a bit thinner since his first photo in the Army, and posed in front of a mural of a lake in his dress uniform, he seemed to be managing a smile for the family back home. From there, the battalion moved quickly into St. Hellaire and Rigny-Le-Ferrow, areas of France that could be considered as safe refuges prior to attacking the Germans.

The Allies were continuing to edge their way northward through Italy. The fighting in these hilly regions was considerably difficult. Achievements by the Allies now outnumbered setbacks by a significant margin, but movement forward was labored. Moments between battles were treasured times, including those moments for Joe Palasek along the western coast of Italy.

From Joe, Italy, August 13, 1944 – Hello Stanley, How is everything with you. I hope every one is in good health and happy. For thats the only way to be these days. Smile and the hell with worrying. For things are tough all over.

I guess Steve must be in Virginia or on his way over. I do wish him, Alex and Johnny [Palasek] all the luck in the world and may god guide them where ever they are or go.

Here it is another Sunday, and hot as hell for we dont get enough rain and its really hot. So I think I'll go swimming this after noon. For the waves are high as hell and it's a good way to spend the afternoon. There isn't much to write about. God bless you and keep you in good health and happiness at all times, always your pal. Joe

Alex Palasek, still a Merchant Mariner, was on his way to the west of the United States. His parents, particularly his mother, were distressed that the war had lasted so long that it was still necessary for their youngest child to be in the service. After his last day of leave at home and a five-day train ride from New York, Alex arrived some 3,000 miles from Long Island. His residence for the time would be a converted factory at 1000 Geary Street, on the corner of Polk and Geary Streets in San Francisco.

From Alex, San Francisco, CA, August 17, 1944 – Dear Stan, Here I am in San Francisco and boy is this place a hole. It's strictly a Navy man's town a maritime man is mud under the people's feet. How is Port still warm? Well it's cold as a son of a gun out here we've been wearing pea coats, and sweaters, honest its cold as hell, the sun has finally come out, for a few hours.

Well it won't be too long and I'll be pulling out. My name is nearing the top of the shipping list. Boy some of the states we cut through are real nice, especially Denver Colorado. Right now I'm broke and what a hell of a place to be when you are, we won't get paid till we ship out.

How is everyone at home? I hope they are well, hope Johnny, Joe & Steve are alright. How's mom & pop. Boy what a ride we left New York Friday at 6:45 pm and got here Wednesday at 10:30 am. When ever I get ready to come back to New York I'm not going by train I'm taking a plane back, It cost's a $1.10 for a parachute and if you don't use it you get it back, that's by and Army bomber.

This place we are living in is a dump compared to the hotel we had in N.Y. I mean it this is a four story building where they used to make the Pierce Arrow car so you can imagine the dump. We haven't got a darn thing to do here except sit and wait, so I guess I'll sign off, so solong and God Bless You. I'll see you some time in the future which I hope ain't too soon. Your Brother, Alex.

Earlier in March 1942, a group of entertainers in New York City came up with a novel idea for servicemen poised to be shipped overseas. It was the Stage Door Canteen, a venue for servicemen to enjoy free food, soft drinks, cigarettes, dancing and entertainment by local and popular talent. Open seven nights per week, it would not be unusual in New York to see actress Helen Hayes serving sandwiches or clearing tables. The concept spread to Boston, Newark, Los Angeles and other cities, including San Francisco. Though the fame of the performers may not have been as notable in Newark, the happiness it might bring a servicemen headed to war could be a star-studded moment.

From Alex, San Francisco, CA, August 20, 1944 – Hi *Stan: How is things at home. I'm still here in Frisco and I'm restricted to the base for shipping out. I haven't had a liberty now for two day's so my time is getting short here in the U.S.A. I'm no. 4 man on the shipping list. Everybody here is plenty anxious, we can't leave this building except for chow, which we eat in a restaurant. They give you a 50¢ meal ticket and the food ain't too bad it's not enough that's the whole trouble.*

You can't have any fun here in Frisco, they have a stage door canteen we are allowed in but that's a dump, mostly navy, marines and army are there, so you can't do anything but sit like a bump on a log. They have an amusement place here it is the same as Coney

Island only much smaller you can see all of it out of the corner of your eye, that's a gyp joint. I'm dam glad my time is close so I can leave this hole. Denver Colorado was the nicest place that we stopped at and had fun. The people treat you darn nice, and the town is not too big but its pretty.

The past two days we have been sitting around and waiting for our name to be called on the p.a. system, some of our gang have already left most of the engine men anyway. Have you heard from John, Joe or Steve, by the way is Steve across yet? Well solong I'll see you someday. How's mom & pop and everyone? Solong your Brother, Alex

Chapter 15

As the final days of steamy hot August 1944 burned away, the war in Europe began to reach a level of intensity never before seen in history. The Germans, having left Florence and the Arno River with only one passable bridge before shifting north away from the Allies, stripped trees and foliage from mountainsides and valleys through the Apennines of Italy virtually from coast to coast. In place of the greenery, they constructed thousands of fortified bunkers and observation posts in an effort to stop the Allied invasion more effectively than they had in the now bloodied hills near Cassino. With the French Mediterranean coast liberated and the reigns of French governance over Paris now in the hands of the Free French, the Allies pushed on into northeastern France and Belgium from the west, south and north. Colonel Peter Kopcsak, a former all-American football player, was the Commanding Officer of the 602nd Tank Destroyer (T.D.) Battalion under the leadership of General Patton and his Third Army. The logs of this battalion, in which PFC John Rykowski served, offered brief daily summaries of the group's movements beginning with their assembly in New Jersey to their fighting in Europe. By August 29, the 602nd was establishing itself in the region of Eure-et-Loir, between the Loire and Eure Rivers in the north of France. Company "C" of the 602nd T.D., commanded by Lieutenant Robert E. Graham, established a secure perimeter around the headquarters with John operating one of the defending tank destroyers.

Alex Palasek sent a brief note back to his family from the other side of San Francisco Bay. He was in Oakland and aboard the S.S. Robert Fulton, a cargo ship built just a few years earlier. To the best of Alex's knowledge, he was bound for Hawaii. Called "Ugly Ducklings" by President Roosevelt for their utilitarian appearance, but more officially known as Liberty Ships, these vessels carried much of the cargo overseas to support the American troops. In addition to the Merchant Marines on board who made up the ship's crew and operated the ship, there was a small detachment of servicemen known as the U.S. Navy Armed Guard that manned the modest number of artillery guns on board. Unbeknownst to Alex as he boarded the Robert Fulton, it had been refitted with newer weapons and had minor repairs while in dry dock a year earlier. That dry dock was the same Sun Shipbuilding Company, of Chester, Pennsylvania, where his older brother John had worked before he went into the Navy.

Even during the time of greatest conflict of the war, there were moments of relief for the Palasek boys. Joe was moved away from the battlefields on leave for a few days and was able to visit Rome and the Vatican, which had not been severely damaged, saving its beauty and history. Sending a note to his mother with a few pictures, he told of how incredible St. Peter's Basilica was, but also plainly stated that the next thing he wished to see was his wife and child, Margaret and Joey. John Palasek was also attempting to enjoy a few days of liberty close to his North African base, which allowed him to sleep as much as he liked and enjoy a few beers each day — something he had not had since his arrival in Africa. Stanley received a Merchant Marine pin from Alex in the mail as well as another returned letter that he'd sent to Mary's brother John, which mentioned the hope that Steve Palasek and John Rykowski might cross paths in France. Steve had arrived in France by ship, mentioning in his letter to his mother that he was doing well after a voyage which included "plenty of activities" to keep the men occupied and their worried spirits up as they headed to battle for the first time. His first V-mail from France let his brother know that being so far from home meant mail from there was all the more important.

From Steve, France, September, 1944 – *Dear Stanley, Well here I am back to my pen while I have a moment to spare. Feeling fine hoping this letter as always may find your brood in best of health and cheer. I haven't received any mail from anyone as yet, although I haven't given up. You see, the [mail] service here under war conditions is slow, a guy just has to have patience. I am counting on mail for I sure would like to hear from all of you, I haven't got much to say, situation remains unchanged I am quite busy at all hours of the day. I wrote Stephie of my first chat with a polish gent stranded here and his story is exactly of what you know doubt read in your daily papers. I was glad to found a person I could parley with. The weather here is cool and rainy at this time. I haven't heard from any of our brothers through out the world but I am waiting. I write you all as much as time permits. God bless you all, my best wishes and regards to all the family. Be good and I'll be seeing you some day. Remaining your brother and Pal, Steve*

Steve's next letter from France came after a small deluge of mail finally got through to him in France, obviously lifting his spirits and increasing the length of his reply. Yet after months of training, the sights and experiences of war's realities can affect one's frame of mind, even that of a leader.

From Steve, France, September 19, 1944 – *Dear Stanley: I don't know how to thank you for ten letters I have received from you. This surely made me feel good sort of picked up speed on the morale end of it. You sure do write very interesting letters and I do appreciate them. Happy to hear about all our brothers getting along so well throughout the world. I was wondering where Alex was I shall scribble a few lines as I already have, I know he will receive the letters some day because I sent them on the old address.*

I am sorry Stan that I am in no position to write you in return as often as I have back in the states. Things are quite different here there fore you all must somehow forgive me. From the day of my leaving the states to my arrival somewhere in France, work was cut out for me. All I have ever picked up in training back in the states is being put into action here. I haven't seen much of

England, I really don't know as to whether I told you this or not, but I only stayed a short while in England plus a train ride to the place where I took off for France. Since then I have travelled a long ways. Won't be long now before we march through Berlin. I do wish to say I'll take the states any day. I can't speak French I just about get along. Not that I give a damn but to ask for direction one must at least try. I don't trust any of these people due to Fritzy living here so darn long. Life is really tough here and I am not exaggerating one single bit. I wish I was permitted to write the things I want well it would make your hair stand up. I surely had more than enough and judge that from Joe's letters at the time he was in action. I tell you at times I can't even think straight. You get mad blow your top, still this does not change anything. The scene remains the same. Some towns here are in good shape, then again, well you figure this out. War is hell only leaves ruins, poverty to all who are enveloped in its fangs.

The food is good and bad, some time you get lots of rest than again your without. Nothing is definite or one can say, here I am to stay, it might be a building or you might use mother earth for a bed; Everything goes here. I will admit no one is happy here or anywhere this side of the ocean. The main idea is to get this over with and damn quick.

Get back to where I come from and live again, carry on where I left off. At the rate things are going one can never tell we may be home soon. Let's hope so in god we trust. The weather here has been hampering operation, its cold and misty at all times.

Here Stan I must cut this letter short because I have only a moment to spare god bless you all my best wishes and regards to you and family. Remaining always your pal and Brother. Steve

In September 1944, the Allies had taken the fighting in Europe not only to German-occupied nations such as the Netherlands, France and Belgium, but into the German homeland itself. The battles in these areas did not come without a cost. British and Polish Allies, under the direction of British Field Marshall Montgomery, entered the Dutch region of Arnhem with 10,000 men unprepared for what was to be more than a week of fighting in the rain without sufficient supplies. The Germans took more than half of the troops as prisoners, and approximately 1,200 were killed. The Russians were making significant headway from the east against German occupied regions. And even though the Japanese were slowly eliminated from many islands in the Pacific, which they had held, the fighting for these territories continued to be fierce. At a meeting between Churchill and Roosevelt in Quebec, Churchill called Japan "an evil and barbarous nation" and vowed to do whatever possible to fight against Japan in congress with the Americans. The Prime Minister also expressed concern over the Soviet Union's influence upon the countries it liberated, exchanging freedom from the Nazis for allegiance to the U.S.S.R.

On September 8, John Rykowski and Company "C" of the 602nd Tank Destroyer Division had moved from guarding the bivouac that was used as battalion headquarters to the hills above the small village of Goviller in the northeast of France. The next day, September 9, they were assigned to cover and hold a bridge some 25 kilometers east, across the Madon River in support of the 35th infantry. Battalion leader Peter Kopcsak noted that Company "C" made contact with the Germans near the village of Roville-devant-Bayon; "contact" being the word he chose to describe being in a battle. Losses were listed as two enlisted men being killed, and one seriously wounded along with the destruction of a half-ton truck and an M-18 tank destroyer. Although company "C" was to successfully take out a machine gun nest by a single soldier with an M-1 rifle, the German artillery was overpowering and the Company had to withdraw. In only four more days, the Battalion had successfully crossed the Moselle River and would eventually enter Belgium and Germany.

The 602nd Tank Destroyer Battalion Commander's journal included an "In Memoriam" to the 12 members who were killed in action. The entry for September 9, 1944 merely mentions that two were killed in action in France, names unknown. A dedication was also included in the journal which read: "To those Officers and men of the 602 Tank Destroyer Battalion who have made the supreme sacrifice and have laid down their lives in defense of those ideals that we hold most dear so that we may live in peace, we dedicate this short history with a deep respect and a truly humble spirit."

On the night of Thursday, September 21, the war struck its deepest cut since it began into the hearts of the Rykowski and Palasek families. The next day's entry in Stan Palasek's journal reads as follows:

"The war has stabbed at us and sunk its claws into our hearts. Last night Mary's mother received a telegram from the War Dept. saying Johnny (Mary's brother) was killed in action in France on Sept. 9. This is hard to believe. He just landed in France a month ago and he didn't mention being in battle. He asked for cigars and said he was in a quiet spot. God but its horrible, so young, strong and happy. I pray to god that there is some mistake. There must be a mistake how dreadful to think of such a thing. If it is so, may god rest his soul. He was a good fellow if there ever was one. He always asked about Buddy of whom he was godfather [Author's note: Stanley Palasek, Jr., Mary and Stan's son]. At home he was the best, always helping his mom, giving her all that he made. He hadn't an enemy in the world. He was a good hearted happy fellow. Oh god I pray that there is a mistake. It must be a mistake. He was the favorite of Mary's mom."

Stanley wrote in remembrance of his brother in-law, PFC John Rykowski, that "he hadn't an enemy in the world." But that was in the world that he, his family and his friends grew up in on Long Island, New York. When he volunteered to leave that small world to fight in the larger one, he suddenly had many thousands of enemies, all of them dressed in grey uniforms, and none who knew his name, his smile or his kind heart.

The telegram that Theadora Rykowski had received on the evening of September 21 was a brief, standardized message. Sent from Washington, D.C., it simply stated, "THE SECRETARY OF WAR DESIRES ME TO EXPRESS HIS DEEP REGRET THAT YOUR SON PRIVATE FIRST CLASS JOHN W RYKOWSKI WAS KILLED IN ACTION ON NINE SEPTEMBER IN FRANCE THE ADJUDENT GENERAL." After several weeks, two members of an honor guard came to the Rykowski home bearing the American flag that was used at young John's burial, but the soldiers did not know where he was interred.

Now, one of the white stars on the banner hung in the window on Powerhouse Road was to have a smaller gold star placed in the center of it. With the war far from over and several sons in or headed to dangerous parts of the world, everyone in the saddened Rykowski and Palasek families prayed that gold would never again be added to their windows.

Chapter 16

For Stan, Mary and their families, September 1944 turned into a time of reflection, of returning to family visits on weekends and to church on Sundays. One afternoon, two soldiers from the War Department knocked on the door at the Rykowskis' Powerhouse Road home. John's mother Theodora feared the worst for her other sons as she greeted the men. They explained that they were there to follow up on the telegram that was sent earlier in the month regarding John. Asking the men what had happened to her son, they could offer her few details at that time. Little had been reported officially, and sensitivity continued to surround discussions with civilians about all of the fine points during the height of the war. It was explained to Mrs. Rykowski that she had the option of having young John's remains returned to be buried near his home. The two men delicately explained that much of the cost would have to be carried by her if he were to be buried in the local Catholic cemetery, Holy Rood, and that the destruction of John's tank left little of her boy to be recognized. With tearful remorse, Theodora chose to leave John's interment to the Army in Europe.

Millions of boys were still serving in the Armed Forces in Europe, Africa and the South Pacific. Every day, many of them viewed their final dawn far from home. Those were other families' sons, brothers, and friends, and those losses not only affected their families but also those who knew them. The grim reality that the war played no favorites and brazenly dared to take one of your own family members hurt down to one's soul. To ease those aching hearts, a new desire seemed to take hold across the nation: to write more letters to those in the service, to pray for them more often, and even to start buying Christmas presents early with the belief that they would receive them on time if shipped promptly. Everyone back home was under a new stress due to a familiar loss, particularly Willie Palasek, who more than ever needed the comfort of his mother and his brother Stan. The fact that there were fewer letters arriving from battle zones overseas that September did not make things easier.

      The duties and requirements that servicemen performed were changing. In Europe, the fighting wasn't over; some of the hardest battles were yet to arise. There was also the need to prevent regions and villages that were recovered from the Nazis from being forced back into German control. In areas of Italy and France, Allied troops scoured hamlets and cities, ready to fight any forces that may be left behind. Army engineers, such as Steve Palasek, were tasked with reclaiming chateaus in France that had housed German military and operations centers. In October, a promise to the South Pacific was fulfilled when General MacArthur returned to the shores of the Philippines, just as he famously declared he would back in 1942. Fighting the Japanese there would still be a considerable undertaking, but MacArthur called for the people of the Philippines to rally with him. In Europe, it seemed as if every victory for the Allies that October brought a loss at the hands of the German forces somewhere else on that continent. With the German line across Italy broken, hopes of easier Allied movements north into Europe proved to be only hopes as the fierce fighting persisted. These slow advances were countered by the Polish Army, which lost more than 15,000 men and an estimated 200,000 civilians to German bombers during a failed uprising against the Germans in Warsaw. Yet, with most of France liberated by October, hopes for an end to the war grew. In the United States, meetings were held to discuss a potential organization of the Allied states to be known as the United Nations.

*   **From Steve, France, October 1, 1944** – Dear Stanley, May this letter find you all, in best of health and spirit as I am to at times. Why I say that, well a fellow sort of gets on edge every now and then, I guess you can understand the picture here is quite different. There is but one thing in all our minds to get this mess over with and hurry back home. As days go by I am really getting fed up on all this stuff let me tell the world. These countries are beautiful as far as scenery is concerned. What I can't see is the people who can't seem to mind there business, work there lands, try to better them selves live up to standards as a nations proud of all*

they have, instead of scheming, planning this sort of thing as is to-day, Hell on earth destruction and ruin. They have there political rallies, party splits, hatred war among them selves. How the hell can this be a united nation pulling to-gether working hand in hand. All this and more is beyond me. To-day the paper hangar [Author's note: a reference to Adolf Hitler and his troops based upon Hitler's supposed early line of work as a house painter and wall paper installer] he to is very much surprised for the first time as our steam roller is crushing all the obstacles he has thrown before us on his own grounds. Well the devil will soon have him. His fight now is fruitless and he knows it nut to make things look tough we fight for every inch of ground, all well and good two can play at the same game. The weather throughout here had been cool and rainy this doesn't stop our boys from keeping on the G.I. ball. Slow but sure we are going ahead at all times.

I haven't heard much from home, until I do well well I'll have to keep guessing at lots of things. I haven't had any mail from Stephanie, I know she writes, I am blaming no one, the trouble is my mail is bogged down some along the line. As yet things haven't quite evened out. Mail as all us brothers realize here over seas is ammunition, which bolsters a guys morale helps him all the way around, in no matter what kind of situation may come his way. That's the soldiers news paper his greatest head line a word from home.

Well the day will come around when we won't have to write any letters, But talk to each other at one of our family reunions. Yesir that will be a great day when the Army and Navy gets together. Remaining always your Pal and brother, Steve

Joe did get a letter through to Steve who, in turn and in keeping with his words regarding the importance of mail to a serviceman, wrote to his brothers Joe, Alex and John often. When mail from Stanley finally reached Steve in France, it brought with it the startling news of Mary's brother being killed in battle. Letters from the war were becoming more important since John Rykowski's death, as they were an assurance that a loved one was doing well as he wrote. But they were never a guarantee that that would be the case once the letter was sent home.

From Steve, France, October 3, 1944 – Dear Stan, Here I am once again, scribbling a few lines to inform you that I am to date feeling fine just getting along. I have received your few lines which have deeply touched me. I am sorry to hear about Johnny, Mary's brother, may his soul rest in peace. I sympathize with you in the hour of distress, Here's hoping that god give your wifey the strength and health to carry on where he left off, Johnny. He was a swell kid and a darn good soldier, gave his best for his country and loved ones. No one knows who goes next, for the going is slow and hard. We are all in it, carrying on where others left off. You gripe, you curse your luck, then again your at ease taking it on the chin. I only will say this much, to go through all I have to date, to witness all this destruction and pulverization of cities towns and village, the children and the great majority of people, homeless, not knowing where there next meal is coming from, If I only did one great deed over here, I know my time was well spent regardless of what the conditions were. For I do know that while I am here no harm will come to my dear ones back in the states. That if I pull out in one piece I will only have a faint memory of all this hell which has brought only grief and sorrow to many a home. A job that has been done well so as to not have a repeater such as we had after the last war.

    Fritzy as we know is really tough and don't let anyone tell you otherwise. He is now being kicked around on his own soil. How long he can take it no one knows although it's a gain yard by yard he fights on. I have slept under open skies in abandoned buildings a college and now a one time mansion where some big shot lived. We have followed the paper hangars trail, he also has lived here, all ear marks show it. I have been constantly on the go. This letter I have just received is the first one in ages. I haven't had a letter from my wife as yet. I have been writing every one as much as time permitted. Back in the states I used to write very often, here the scene has completely changed. I am sorry I can't name cities or towns do to the strict censorship but the day shall come when we don't have to write letters.

    I hope by the time this letter reaches you, it may find your wife Mary in best of health and spirit. Tell her she must be a soldier, *you all must be for I realize this may come to the unexpected, we must fight on, preserve and take care of ourselves, to the best of our ability. God bless you and guide you through thick and thin, keep in step with the millions who are with you fighting on to victory and the safe return to our homes, so help us god. I remain your Pal and brother. Steve*

As October waned, the loss of PFC John Rykowski was still on the minds of the families when the return of one last letter that Mary had sent to her brother reminded her of war's cruel reality. The fact that her brother Ollie was now shipping over to Hawaii only added to the stress. At almost the same time, a brief V-mail arrived at the Palasek home on School Street. It was from John Palasek. He had spent months waiting to get into the Navy. Then, after induction and training, he had sailed on the Queen Mary to the United Kingdom, where he spent months waiting and preparing to be a part of the invasion of Europe — but he was shipped to North Africa instead. Not having seen a hostile shot fired, he was now heading back to the states on a Coast Guard vessel for 30 days of leave before going back to the Navy. It raised Stanley's hopes that his other brothers and the Rykowski boys may not be far behind. With further hopes of leaving Sperry where he was doing little, Stan bought a used 1934 Plymouth figuring that he may need it to get to a potential new job. Getting gas for it would be another matter. Gasoline continued to be a tightly rationed item, though most anyone could get a mileage ration book and a sticker on their windshield with the letter "B" that allowed the driver four gallons of gas per week. Government warnings were issued that vehicles were not to be used for pleasure trips. Stanley was faced with a pile of paperwork in an attempt to secure an "A" sticker based upon his work in the defense field. This would grant him eight gallons of gas per week. By the middle of the month of October, Stanley's efforts finally resulted in a new job at Press Wireless in Baldwin Harbor on the South Shore of Long Island. Here, he would be one of many radio operators monitoring radio transmissions from reporters around the globe whose stories would be relayed and used in both reporting on the war to the public and as an information source for the government.

Chapter 17

There is an old axiom, sometimes credited to comments made during the second-term campaign of President Abraham Lincoln in the height of his own terrible war: "It is best not to swap horses in the middle of a stream." Today, the President of the United States is limited to two terms based on the 22nd amendment to the Constitution. In 1944, three years prior to that amendment's ratification, it appeared as if the President could be elected to a fourth term. The nation was seeing a turning tide in the war, particularly in Europe where several of Adolf Hitler's leaders had recently plotted to have him assassinated. Much of Europe was being taken back from German control and Allied soldiers were closing in on the center of Germany. There was genuine hope for change on the other side of the Atlantic. Employment, following the worst depression America had ever experienced, was in full swing thanks to jobs supporting the war. Would a change in leadership be necessary or wise? The Republicans nominated Thomas Dewey, the mustachioed Governor of New York, to run for President against the incumbent Democrat, Franklin Roosevelt, claiming that Roosevelt's failing health could lead to difficulties running the country during such a critical time. Roosevelt put forward every effort to show the nation that he was well, including touring the country and often riding through cities while waving from an open limousine. Dewey campaigned hard and was well-liked, particularly in the Northeast and Central regions of the country, and was within nine percentage points of Roosevelt in the popular vote that November election day. But the American Electoral College system gave Roosevelt his fourth term in office by overwhelming numbers.

In the Pacific war, a colossal naval battle between the United States and Japan occurred in the waters near the Philippines. More than 280 ships were involved, with the Allied fleet destroying 28 Japanese warships including the last of the Japanese aircraft carriers; meanwhile, fewer than 10 Allied ships were lost. Numerous bombing runs of unprecedented proportions took place concurrently in Singapore in order to successfully destroy much of the Japanese-controlled seaport there and, more importantly, Japan's principal fuel supply. In Europe, Patton's third Army, including the 602nd Tank

Destroyer Battalion, finally progressed across the Moselle River close to the German frontier. The Germans were not about to relinquish pressure and they introduced the V-2 rocket to their arsenal. Capable of traveling at speeds too great to be stopped by Allied defenses, the explosive rockets were sent into England to inflict severe damage from afar. One day, an attack by four of these rockets, which traveled to an altitude over 60 miles at a speed exceeding 3,600 miles per hour, destroyed 2,000 homes in Croydon, a town on the south side of London. This was only a small part of the continuing German offensive. As autumn transitioned to winter, snow began to fall in the higher regions of Italy where numerous German battalions continued to hold their ground against the Allied offensive. Unable to maneuver easily in the snow, Allied tanks held fast and troops trained for future battles.

From Joe, Italy, November 5, 1944 – *Dear Stanley, Thanks for the mail I've been getting from you. You say you got yourself a car I'll bet you paid plenty for it. But I guess if I was there Id do the same.*

Things around here are the same. Are planes are blasting the hell out of them supermen. And they roar over our heads ever day out side of that Stanley their isn't much to write about. I just wish they would send me home. Wish you and Mary and your little battler luck and every thing that goes with it. Your pal, Joe

Stanley was pleased with his new job (as was his wife), and further happiness was had as he and Willie were enjoying the fact that their brother John was around — when he could be found. When John was not out on his own or with other longtime friends, and Willie and Stanley were not working, the three of them would make the rounds. A meal at Stanley's or dinner at their mom's was bookended by numerous visits to various bars in Port Washington, as well as nearby pubs in Manhasset and Roslyn to drink beer until the early morning hours. Days for the brothers to be together were being marked off the calendar, so they enjoyed their time together knowing that soon, only letters would connect them with John.

Prior to the war, New Guinea consisted of territorial islands under the governments of the Netherlands and the United Kingdom.

The United Kingdom placed much of the territory that it possessed under the control of nearby Australia. The Japanese rapidly and successfully invaded these islands in 1942 and many of the South Pacific war's hardest-fought battles took place here on the shores and in the jungles. Operation Cartwheel was a combined Allied effort to remove the Japanese forces from these islands. Under the leadership of General MacArthur and Britain's Admiral Halsey, Cartwheel was instituted as a joint effort to force the Japanese troops out systematically. Some of the most intense fighting in the South Pacific occurred during the months long battle of Tulagi, later and more familiarly known as Guadacanal, where Allied death tolls were great as a result of conflicts and jungle diseases. In 1944, Cartwheel had established a resilient foothold for the Allies. The battles raged as there were still numerous areas of the islands that were occupied by the Japanese. Support for the Japanese troops came from warships. Much of the support for the Allied ground troops came from the Merchant Marine supply vessels from both the United States and Australia. The Merchant Marine vessels had little fighting chance against Japanese warships patrolling the waters and were destroyed all too often. Crews would attempt to escape the sinking ships in lifeboats that were then pursued by the Japanese, and many of the seamen were killed.

From Alex, New Guinea, November 9, 1944 – *Dear Stan, I received two letters from you today I also got the stamp's for which I appreciate very much. So Johnny is home that's good at least he'll be home for the Holidays. How's Mary & Stanley Jr. How's mom and pop and Willie.*

Say tell John I wrote to him but now that he is home I don't know if he'll get my letters. He told me in a letter that sometimes things may get a lil dull so I should take a drink a little maybe, if you can get anything stronger than water down here you'll be lucky.

If you want to know some thing I'm out here and since I've left the states I haven't been ashore as yet, I can see the land but that's all. There are natives down here, and I haven't seen a woman at all, not that I personally care to. Things do get kind of dull I've done some reading, I've read about every book and magazine I could get a hold of that's on our ship. If you have an old Port New's around could you send it or tell mom to, it don't make no difference how old it is. So far I'm all right I'm pretty well occupied, I haven't been homesick, though my buddy who went through the school with me was, and I know from what I saw of that I won't get sick cause though there isn't any thing down here I'm enjoying myself. It won't be long and I'll be eighteen and old man cox will be looking for me if anything comes from the draft board take care of it for me if possible, I guess I'll have to stay with this outfit since the Navy or Marines won't take me. Well as new's is getting short I'll close so long and God Bless all of you. Your Brother and Pal, Alex

    P.S. I don't know when I'll be back there is scuttlebutt that we may be back by Jan. or maybe March.

    P.S. Who the hell is president now we can hear the elections over the radio but it sound's like a bunch of blabble. Is this Press Wireless N.B.C.? Solong

The recent Allied campaign into Aachen, Germany was anything but rapid. It proudly stood as the first successful incursion into Germany. Following along in the tracks of the front line troops was Steve Palasek and his division, establishing Allied posts and converting German posts to the needs of the Allies.

From Steve, Western Germany, November 13, 1944 – *Dear Stan, Writing you a few lines in answer to your letter for which I say thanks a million. You must pardon me for not writing to you, although I see you really understand, I am very busy. Yes Stan, we have a lull, then again off I go, like a bat out of hell. The weather is really bad and freezing. I don't believe we will ever see the sun shine, nothing but dark clouds.*

    I know John is home as you told me, how is he doing. Yes he is trying to have a grand time, make the best of his thirty day stay, I see you are right there helping him along. Well boys, I do wish I were there, join you in all that fun. I guess Joe and I have to wait till this is over with. So take it easy, take care of our sailor and have one on me. Some day we will really have a hot time in the old town. I know the town is empty, but I know John can be shown. Its tough to be away so long, then try to match with the good old civilian, I myself will need assistance in adjusting my-self, I can feel it, after all this kind of life. Well Stan, you guessed I'll admit to my where abouts, you seem to have a charm the way you got down to things. This is not much of a letter, you must pardon me, but my time is short so god bless you all be good and don't do anything I wouldn't do. I remain your pal and brother, Steve

President Roosevelt, in a proclamation he issued, reminded Americans that in this "year of liberation, which has seen so many millions freed from tyrannical rule, it is fitting that we give thanks with special fervor to our Heavenly Father for the mercies we have received individually and as a nation and for the blessings He has restored, through the victories of our arms and those of our allies, to His children in other lands." He further declared November 23 as a national day of Thanksgiving.

With rationing making many everyday items difficult to obtain, November 1944 brought a mad dash by civilians who were hoping to purchase a turkey for Thanksgiving. Difficult to find, but representing the desire to continue necessary traditions, families watched the newspapers and listened to radio reports of turkeys being sold nearby as well as rumors from others regarding where a turkey might be found. Often, these expeditions went without reward. Mary and Stanley were not fortunate enough to find a turkey that year and after Stanley got home from work that Thanksgiving day, they shared a humble dinner of roasted chicken as they had on lesser days when they were fortunate enough to have a bird on their table. They were grateful and safe in their apartment that evening.

From Joe, Italy, November 23, 1944 *– Dear Stanley, Just a few lines hoping that you, Mary and your little battler had a nice Thanksgiving dinner. I also hope everything with you is fine. If you can Stanley send me a picture of you Mary, an little Stanley. I would like to have on of Willie, to, also of pop and mom.*

Things around here are the same as always you now by the papers whats new. Another thing which I always forget you and every one always get the funny papers. Tell Margie to save them and every once on a while send me them all. Your pal, Joe

With November ending, so was John Palasek's well-worn home leave. At dawn on the Sunday following Thanksgiving, Stanley drove his brother John to Lido Beach on the south shore of Long Island in the "jalopy" in which he had just installed a new fan belt, with fervent hopes that it wouldn't fail them on the 30-minute trip. Here at the Naval Personnel Redistribution Center, barracks became a young man's home for a short time while he waited for his next wartime destination. With much of the fighting in Europe centered on attacking German strongholds by land and air, it seemed most probable that a sailor like John was headed for the South Pacific where Alex was already stationed.

Chapter 18

December 1944 dashed in with robust winds, frigid temperatures in the 20s and snow in the village of Port Washington, New York. The two ponds that lay across Shore Road from Manhasset Bay, Baxter's Pond and the Mill Pond, froze over quickly much to the enjoyment of a few ice skaters. Such conditions were not favorable for keeping Stanley's used car running and so it again surrendered, this time to the cold. But Stan kept a balanced perspective as he wrote in his journal, "what the heck am I kicking about, look at the boys in the trenches, they are the ones that have a right to kick."

Christmas decorations were going up in the town and in shop windows as simple, sparse green balsam trees began to fill previously empty lots about the town, soon to be taken home and decorated. Tree ornaments would again be simple this year; balls of glass nearly as thin as paper, painted with stripes of primary colors with a beige paper loop inserted in the top. The boys in the trenches or at sea needed the glass and metal more than the Christmas trees. Judy Garland's voice was heard often on the radio, suggesting that everyone should "have yourself a merry little Christmas." But as many sons, brothers and friends were not home, and some of those never would be again, the words were a haunting, empty wish to some families.

Three months after her son John was killed in action, Theadora Rykowski received a package from the office of the

President of the United States. Enclosed were a certificate recognizing that John was killed in action in Europe, and a presentation box containing the Purple Heart. This medallion on a purple ribbon bore the profile of George Washington, who established the honor while Commander-in-Chief of the Continental Army in 1782. Theodora showed it to her family, and then put it safely away out of view. It could never replace the boy she loved and lost.

In Europe, Allied ground troops were pressing further into German soil and Russians were moving across the Danube River into German controlled-Hungary. The term "Allies" was becoming less applicable to the relationship between the Soviet Union and the nations with which it was aligned. It seemed obvious that the U.S.S.R. intended to control the future of the nations it redeemed from Germany. The Russian liberation of Hungary in 1944 was just one of several such provocative moves.

Germany was now on the receiving end of the heaviest bombardments to date by U.S. and RAF attacks, as over 1,000 bombers dropped their explosive payloads in a single day. Though the Japanese battle fleet was greatly diminished in recent months, the danger faced by Allied vessels in the South Pacific was by no means reduced. The Japanese kamikaze forces were attacking Allied ships daily, although their effectiveness was limited to actually hitting the targeted vessels one quarter of the time and sinking ships much less often thanks to continuously improving Allied defenses and technology.

From Joe, Italy, December 8, 1944 – *Dear Stanley, Thanks for the mail I've been getting from you. How is every thing with you and your little family. I sure wish you all have a Merry Christmas and a Happy New year. You said in your letter about the guys bringing back lugars [Author's note: The Luger was a German semi-automatic pistol used by German soldiers] etc with them. I don't know how they do it, but no one is alowed to take fire arms back with them our send them through the mail for if I could I would have sent you two Lugars I had when I was in my old outfit. So you see Stanley I don't now how they got them back to the states. Thats all for now Stanley your pal always, Joe*

When it came to electronic technology for the home in 1944, the television was still an uncommon luxury. Though it had been introduced at the New York World's Fair in Flushing in 1939, broadcast operations were set aside due to the war and radio continued to rule the airwaves, both for information and entertainment. News, stories (both humorous and dramatic), and music often came live into one's home thanks to radio. Soldiers also listened in, when a radio was available. In one attempt to demoralize the Allied troops in the South Pacific, a sultry voiced woman who went by the name of Tokyo Rose came to prominence. This American woman of Japanese parentage sympathized with the Japanese, and she would send her siren call across the airwaves to the soldiers, telling them that their girlfriends and wives were being unfaithful to them in their absence.

With the Allied troops moving into western portions of Germany, so followed Steve Palasek and his battalion. Level-headed in his words, through all the difficulties of training and being shipped overseas to do "what this man must," the strain of matters was beginning to affect him: The never-ending cold rain and ever-present mud, and seeing the captured enemy being sent across the Atlantic to prisons in the states close to where he dreamed to be were factors that added daily to Steve's mounting frustrations.

***From Steve, Western Germany, December 14, 1944** – Dear Stan: I guess its about time I wrote you a letter. Maybe you thought I have forgotten you, I really haven't. The trouble is I am forever on the go, the lord only knows where do we go from here. Yes Stan, I am quite sure I'll be under way again for better or worse. I as yet haven't received any packages although I know the mail is jammed up somewhere due to the oncoming holidays. The only package I received was from mom. Guess what there were ciggarrettes in it, boy that is something we are not getting either due to some mix up I guess.*

I wish to say thanks a million for informing my wife of my where abouts, She was puzzled and I couldn't tell her directly. Censorship is one thing a guy can't buck, if he does he sure will learn otherwise in short order. Right now I am very busy believe you me.

I have some job trying to catch forty winks now and then, I get disgusted, gripe, cranky and nervous, this sort of life will get you in time regardless of when it may be. Some times I feel like a nervous wreck. Boy I wished I were back in gods country, it is all I keep thinking of. You can't help it especially when you idle a moment or two.

General mud is sure raising cane around here, for over two months it does nothing but rain. You get used to it, at least I have and I don't give a damn anymore.

By the way I had a letter from Alex and he seems happy preparing for a trip back to the states. He did have quite a trip with a few incidents which he couldn't mention in his letter, saving it for a later date. He still has that urge to get in the scrap. I have written him quite a letter which will give him an idea what this sort of thing is like.

Stan you should see these so called B_____ of supermen being herded like cattle every day. Where the hell they are coming from is beyond me. What burns me up is they feed them clothe them pay them give them a nice ride back to the states. Think of the expense keeping these rats I would love to fill them chuck full of lead and dump them overboard in mid ocean. Its to bad they have rules which we must go by in these cases. There is no justice is what I say. I am sure our boys are not being treated as well as they are. I have talked to all kinds of soldiers, Frenchmen, Slovaks, Belgians and the Polish and brother the stories they tell would make your hair stand up.

I just received a letter from Joe and he feels fine, taking life easy and stated that when this is over the beer in the states will surely catch hell, I think he is right. Did you hear from John, or is he still at Lido Beach. I for one hope he never has to take off for that miserable Pacific.

Well folks with best wishes and regards to all, God bless you and guide you, I am signing off here, your pal and brother. Steve

Steve was huddled away from the chilled rain and fog that blanketed the northern and central regions of Europe that December as he wrote home. His brigade and other Allied troops were inching their way into Germany, and the German war machine continued to devise both offensive goals and plans to defend the homeland from further invasion. The Nazis decided that retaking once-held territories in Belgium and capturing the strategic port of Antwerp would be a step toward re-establishing supremacy in Europe. The hilly and forested Ardennes in Belgium were occupied by the Allies, who felt confident that German artillery could not maneuver through the hills and dense woods. The Germans realized the Allies' air supremacy was greatly diminished due to the unrelenting fog. Taking advantage of these conditions, one of the largest land battles of the war took place in the Ardennes that December. The infiltrating German artillery went through the midpoint of the Allied defense lines toward central Belgium; when viewed on a map, the German attack formed a bulge in the Allied positions. Thus, the clash became known as the "Battle of the Bulge," and it was one of the bloodiest battles in the war with over 19,000 of the approximately 600,000 involved Allied soldiers killed. On December 22, the rejuvenated Germans insisted that the Americans surrender the region, to which U.S. Brigadier General Anthony McCauliffe famously replied, "Nuts!" The following day, clearer weather allowed Allied planes to inflict tremendous damage on the German army from above; a few days later, Patton's 3rd Army arrived. The terrain's winding rivers through the forests also worked to the Allied advantage. This was the case in the tiny Ally-controlled hamlet of Bastogne, Belgium, where a hilltop fortress at the bend of the river valley that had defended the region repeatedly since the days of the Roman Empire was once again impassable to the enemy.

  On December 19, Stanley Palasek was finally moving on to a new job. His days of driving 30 miles round-trip in a car that was anything but dependable were replaced by a one-hour commute to Manhattan on the Long Island Rail Road, which was literally steps from the back door of the Nielsen Building where he lived. He had a job at WCBW, which at that time was the Columbia Broadcasting System (CBS) television station for the New York area. He began working for WCBW at the top of the Chrysler Building, where the transmitter for the TV station was located. He was to maintain the transmitter and make the on-air announcement that would "sign the station on" before its few hours of programs aired. It was the start of almost 40 years in the television industry for Stan. While Stan was busy working on some of the most advanced technology at home, his brothers abroad were left wanting for much simpler luxuries.

From Joe, Italy, December 22, 1944 – *Dear Stanley, How is everything with you. I hope this letter finds you, Mary and your Big boy in the best of health and also had a swell christmas. I sent you a picture of myself witch I hope you received, you can see that Im gaining a lot of weight about one ninety five or more pounds.*

Stanley if Margaret hasn't gotten the flashlight I asked her to send me I would like you to tell her what kind I mean, the Army light, the kind you can fasten on your belt. There isn't much to write about so until we meet again, Ill say solong for awhile. god bless you all and keep you in the best of health. Joe

In Europe, one of the fiercest battles was over and the Germans were again being moved out of Belgium. The Allies had to press onward into Germany to halt the struggle against the Nazis. As the U.S. troops marched deeper into Germany, the Nazis dressed men as American soldiers and sent them into Allied-held territories. Their plan to infiltrate U.S. lines was quickly exposed, and the spies were summarily executed for espionage. New suspicions of additional Japanese kamikaze attacks in the South Pacific were becoming a reality, which resulted in increased apprehensions there and at home. Unknown to many, U.S. military planes were running secret test bombing runs over the area of the Great Salt Lake with hopes that a new weapon could be implemented, if necessary.

On the last page of his 1944 journal, Stanley wrote of the difficult times, the hardships they all faced and the yearning for his brothers' safe return home. He also wrote, *"My prayer for the coming year is that this awful war come to an end and soon so all our boys can come back to their loved ones and I pray to god that the end of this war will spell the end of all wars, so our children 20 years from now will not have to go through it again."*

Chapter 19

At the dawn of 1945, most Americans and countless others around the globe struggled with lasting questions. How much longer could this war possibly go on? How many more boys would have to say farewell to their mothers, and how many would never return? Could the fighting get even worse than it had been in the Ardennes? How long could the Germans and the Japanese last against an Allied force that was up to the task of defeating the enemy, though the enemy resurfaced again and again without surrender? Wasn't there something that could be done, dramatic final actions on both the European and Pacific fronts, with such a force that the enemy would have no choice but to resign? These same questions concerned everyone in the Palasek family, as well as other, more personal ones. Where would the boys be going next, and how much danger would they face? And looking back on the loss of Stanley's young brother-in-law, would either of the families lose someone else before there was peace? The small joys of Christmas and New Year's Eve were over; the real world, with all its struggles and potential evils, would not change simply because calendars had done so.

From Steve, France, January 12, 1945 – *Dear Stan, Received a letter from you to-day which you have written me the night before Christmas. By your words I judge your Christmas was not like the ones we used to know. Well folks I am sorry to hear this, but we in the service felt the same as you. We said a silent prayer for the dear ones back home, For all our families. I know the feeling. I imagined how mom and dad felt. But please do me a favor tell them I am allright, carrying on with my duties to the best of my ability. I guess you can understand. I am feeling fine, the snow is very heavy and the going is rough and tough. I have been writing you and William, everyone quite regular, please be a little patient, I won't fail any one. The mail situation is bad. Out going mail especially due to transportation which is being used for more important lines. I can't write mom very often in Polish it takes lots of trouble to get the letter through. Tell mom please do not worry. I conclude here with the best wishes and God bless you all, thanks a* *million for the package. Be good, lets march to gether keep in step. I remain your Pal and Brother thinking of you always, Steve*

Steve's brother, Joe, was stationed less than 700 miles southeast of France. He remained encamped in the cold and snow of the Italian hills in order to maintain the Allied hold on the region and prevent it from being taken by the Axis troops that might remain there. The standard uniform and supplies that the soldiers in Europe were issued were basic, suitable for most days of the year. Extra items to keep warm, though simple in the minds of many, were precious commodities to most soldiers in the field.

From Joe, Italy, January 16, 1945 – *Dear Stanley, How is everything with you and your little Stanley. I hope this letter finds you all in the very best of health. I sure hope you try to get me those caps I spoke of in one of my letters to you. Ask Margaret for the money. You know what kind I mean. I received a letter from Alex and I'm happy to hear that he is well and will be coming home soon. You said that Mary's brother Adam is in the infantry he sure got a bad break for the combat.*

By the way Stanley how is Mary you never tell me in your letters about her. For you have a swell wife and I like Mary a lot. She don't mind no one's business but her own and she is a very quiet girl. If you don't mind Stanley send me a picture of Mary an your little guy. I would like to know what my sister in law looks like. Also, don't forget Stanley you'll do me a big favor if you tell Margaret, or get those caps yourself please. Don't forget Stanley, you Pal an Brother always, Joe

When January 1945 arrived, it had been approximately five years since Warsaw was forced to succumb to the control of Nazi Germany. Now Soviet commander Marshall Zhukov aggressively moved his heavily-armored troops into Poland until they both surrounded and breeched the perimeter of Warsaw. He then directed Polish troops to enter the city and seize it from the Germans. Thus, the first European capitol to have fallen to the Nazis was no longer under their control. With this Russian-led "liberation," the expectations and fears previously brought forward by British Prime

Minister Winston Churchill were becoming an unfortunate reality. The Soviet Union was now in control, and began rounding up members of the Polish Home Army who might cause unrest, resistance or display preferences toward the London government rather than Communism. This cold European winter was to last for years beyond the eventual arrival of spring.

In Port Washington, Stanley was enjoying his new job in the television industry, which was still in its commercial infancy. Stanley was hearing rumors that the simple grey broadcasts of TV programs were far from the dreams for television's future. The idea of sending pictures to homes in color was an idea as old as the concept of television itself, but a working system had yet to be developed. Four years earlier, CBS had developed plans for a semi-mechanical system for color television but these were set aside at the demand of the War Production Board as it was not essential to the war efforts. When Stanley heard stirrings that the color television efforts were to be renewed, he offered his engineering knowledge to the product development team and was given the opportunity to help develop the system.

Not only were several of Stanley's brothers away in service to their country, but Eddie Kasper — a good friend through most of his youth — was also in the Army. As they were growing up together, Eddie and Stanley would play their guitars at home or in local establishments and go hunting for rabbits in the woods by the Port Washington sand pits. Stanley had hoped when he was going into the service months ago that his friend, Eddie, would go into the Navy with him. Instead, Eddie went into the Army. He was sent first to Fort Dix in New Jersey, and was soon after stationed in Europe. Stanley wrote to his friend on occasion to bring him up to date on Port Washington events, and sometimes received a response.

From Eddie Kasper, "Somewhere in Germany," January 26, 1945 – *Dear Stan, Received your letter today and was glad to hear from you. I'm on the front line now and have a few minutes to write. boy its really hell here and no place for a civilian because we mow down anything in front of us. I have a german pistol, its called a luger, what a pistol. I bet you would like to have it. It comes in handy where I am but when I get home I'll show it to* *you. Well boy I never thought I'd see war but here I am creeping and crawling. I'm all shaken up and jumpy it really knocks the hell out of a guy. be good and I'll be waiting for a few lines from you. your pal, Eddie*

The Russian Army (or The Red Army, as it was rapidly becoming known as due to its strong Communist leadership) was now well into Poland and pressing on to Berlin from the east. With mutual belief that the war would soon end, the Treaty of Yalta was signed between the "big three" nations of the Allied forces: the United States, Great Britain and the Soviet Union. The pact established the plan for the division of Europe, particularly Germany, and the Soviet intentions to govern Poland and Yugoslavia when the war eventually ended. The city of Dresden, a railway transit center for the Germans which had seen little of the effects of the war, was devastated when the Allies sent waves of bombers with explosives and incendiary shells across the skies. The destruction of Dresden took over 50,000 lives; it was opposed by the United States, which saw the campaign as an act of terrorism. The Soviet Union insisted that it was necessary in order to destroy the morale of the Germans. The Russian troops, moving close to the small German village of Peenemunde, forced the Germans to evacuate the V-2 rocket laboratory in that village; at the time, it was headed by Dr. Werner Von Braun, who would one day become a household name to all Americans who cheered on the "space race" of the 1950s and 1960s. In the Pacific, the Allies under the leadership of General MacArthur were now well into the Philippines. They liberated Manila from Japanese control and moved as forcefully and rapidly as conditions allowed through the other Philippine islands.

John Palasek joined the Navy in the first year of the war. He had been sent across the Atlantic to Wales prior to the D-Day invasion but rather than participate in the massive invasion, he sailed to North Africa after it had been secured earlier in the war. Subsequent to his time in Africa, he was back in the United States without hearing one shot fired in aggression. After spending several weeks on the south shore of Long Island waiting for new orders, he was sent on the long train ride westward to California, the staging area for the war in the Pacific. There, he would await his next assignment.

From John P., San Diego, CA, February 21, 1945 –
Dear Stanley, I got paid Monday and had me a little liberty after staying in a week and I had a pretty good time with the boys. The week after this I'm supposed to get a seventy two [Author's note: three-day leave] so we hope to go to L.A. and see what Hollywood looks like. That is of course if I'm still here. I haven't any idea when I'm going to San Bruno [Author's note: the Navy staging area for sailors going to the South Pacific] but the longer its put off the better.

The way I gather it now the outfit I'm in is a mobile repair unit. I don't know if you've ever seen them or not but the amphibs have big trucks which contain shiplifter shops, equipment, etc. These trucks roll out of SST's onto the beach and repair damage done to landing craft. Interesting work, eh wot? Phooey! The buddies of mine who are now in San Bruno are in a PT repair outfit. I had a letter from one of them and he sent me ten bucks he owed me from Lido and I expect to get another one shortly from another guy who owes me thirty so I shouldn't go broke before next payday.

Well, here I am at the bottom again and I don't think I could fill up another page so I'll knock off here. John

As John wrote this letter in San Diego, four days of the most intense fighting in the Pacific campaign were reaching a crescendo on the tiny island of Iwo Jima. A strategic island with four airports, Iwo Jima boasted flat, open volcanic beaches where Allied soldiers were pinned to the ground by Japanese guns for days as they perilously landed on its shores. Although much of Iwo Jima still had to be taken for the Allies to make use of the airfields, the historic raising of the American flag on Mount Suribachi on the fourth day of the invasion was an iconic moment for Allied soldiers and those praying for their victory.

Mary Palasek's younger brother, Ollie, was in the Navy stewards' branch at this time. This division aboard ship was primarily made up of black sailors who tended to food and cabin service under the direction of white sailors. They were all equally trained to fight, should a battle ensue. A brief letter from Ollie arrived, written on stationery with the American Red Cross header upon it.

From Ollie Rykowski, "Somewhere in Orient," February 16, 1945 *–Dear Stanley, Mary, and Buddy: Just a few lines you folks to let you know that I received your letters today and was really glad to receive them. I really enjoy your letters because they give me the latest dope around home and that's what a guy always wants to here about out here.*

Well this trip is really give me a never for getting experience of this war. I have been to many interesting and famous and popular place out here. Sorry I can't write about them because of the censors. I guess Alex or what ever they call him is telling you about live aboard ship and it isn't bad, especially in the stewards department. How is mom making out by the letters shes O.K. and sorry to hear about Adam overseas. Well see mom often and give her a helping hand when she needs it I'll repay you someday. Well words are getting lesser so I'll sign of praying that everything home is safe and may I return home fast and safely. Your kid brother, Ollie

Stan's brothers Alex and John, as well as Mary's brother Ollie, were all sailors in different branches of the service. John was currently experiencing the war more in the fashion of Frank Sinatra and Gene Kelly in that year's musical, "Anchors Aweigh," while Alex and Ollie faced challenging times in the heat of the South Pacific. Americans were keeping their hopes high as more positive news was reaching the daily papers and the radio stations, which broadcast updates in between songs by the popular Andrews Sisters and Bing Crosby. And though the winter's cold was bitter that February on Long Island, it was a warm promise to all to hear that one German city after another was being either decimated or invaded by the Allies, including Cologne and Remagen.

From Steve, a Chateau in France, February 25, 1945 *– Dear Stan, Hello everybody. The mail situation is still slow, both to and from. V-mail is the quickest but some how never appeals to* me. I need more room when I write. Not that I have more to say, because you understand the real news I can't tell at the present time, due to strict censorship. So old man winter is still raising cane in Gods country. I could just imagine. Well it is quite a change here, farmers have already started palnting, tilling there lands those that have a shack still standing. Its getting warm and spring is really in the air.

I am felling fine Stan just taking things as they come. We have quite a break live in this enormous building, for the time being, while doing so, I have put my set of engineers tools to use. By installing showers and baths for the boys and making our selves comfortable for how long I don't know. Right now I am the water works engineer. We had some real eggs for breakfast, pancakes cereal for a change.

What comes next I don't know. In the army there are many suprises. Anyway I can say it is quiet here and no fear of Fritzie molesting us, we are far from this. Some change Still a guy can't feel at home nervous as hell, well I guess its all in the game. There is no place like home. Tough ball game folks, still in the ninth inning and we are still at bat. Although you can see are score is getting better every day.

Speaking of decorations, well all I have is the E.T.O. Ribbon [Author's note: European Campaign Ribbon] and have received the bronze star, for participation in some free for alls. I guess you can figure the lay of the land. You don't receive those every day. Just any body can't have them. Oh! Yes a good conduct ribbon I am entitled to wear also an overseas stripe which goes on your sleeve like a hash mark. I guess that explains everything answers a question. Its past six months that I am here now across the pond. Boy when I stop to think of it my nerves tingle. Time sure is going by fast. How I wish I were back to where I came from.

Alex I know also had quite an experience I am wondering as to what he will do, I do hope he stays out of the army. This is a tough old grind. A sailor's life is tough but much cleaner.

Well Stan I guess this covers about all I know. Be good and take care of your self and your family. God bless you. I remain your Pal and brother. Steve

Stanley read this letter with significant feelings of regret. Though he had asked Steve about any military decorations he had received, it was merely his curiosity that made him ask. He wanted to know what was given out to the men who were fighting in Europe. Reading how proud Steve was of his well-deserved medals and ribbons brought Stan's thoughts to those of jealousy, thinking that he himself might have been awarded those honors (or more) had he been able to stay in the Navy for any significant amount of time; but that opportunity had passed, and his empty feelings would have to be set aside. His brothers' safe return was more important. His spirits were lifted as good news arrived: Alex was on his way back to the states after his time in the South Pacific with the Merchant Marine. All jealousies aside, it was a time to look forward to being with his younger brother again.

Chapter 20

Concerns continued to mount in the U.S. Congress and the U.K. Parliament, due to outside attitudes concerning the recent annihilation of Dresden by Allied bombers. The Germans claimed it was a terror bombing that had unnecessarily taken many innocent lives, and British churches began to question whether such an action had been needed. Nonetheless, the Allied assault across the German borders continued. Wesel, Dusseldorf, Cologne, Bonn and Remagen — all major German cities that sit along the Rhine River — were simultaneously under attack by the Allies. The Rhine had become the final line on the map that Hitler insisted could not be crossed by the Allies at any cost; all bridges across it were destroyed by the Germans to hold back their Allied enemies. All bridges except one: the bridge at Remagen. As the Allies approached, the Germans attempted to destroy the bridge while under fire. Two detonation attempts failed; when a Nazi soldier successfully ignited the fuse on the bridge by hand, the explosion proved too weak to collapse the durable bridge. After seeing that the bridge still stood, Allied General Omar Bradley, commander of the 12th Army, exclaimed, "Hot dog! Shove everything you can across it!" And so the Allied soldiers proceeded across the Rhine.

Meanwhile, in the South Pacific, the Allies were setting up airfields in the recently-captured Marianas Islands, which greatly reduced the distance between Allied air bases and Japan. U.S. B-29 Superfortress bombers made regular runs on Tokyo. In a raid similar to the one that destroyed Dresden, incendiary bombs leveled 16 square miles of the industrial area of the city and killed over 80,000 people. Military strength, both in arms and explosive power, grew exponentially. The Allies lost over 13,000 soldiers while capturing smaller islands and areas of the Philippines from Japan by the use of land troops, and hoped that such massive bombings would bring Japan's surrender without having to send troops to that nation's soil.

***From John P., San Diego, CA, March 10, 1945** – Dear Stanley, Some of the boys were about to leave today for Port Hueneme [Author's note: a naval assignment location in Ventura County] but the draft was cancelled till we get a little more synthetic training but we're liable to shove out anytime. The chief here put a few of us in for second class a week ago and he was told that he should have put it in before the first of the month and we would have got it. Oh well, it's the same story always as far as that goes and in my opinion he shouldn't have even mentioned it because some of the boys were disappointed and I can't say that I blame them. But so much for that.*

Last week I had a 72 and went to L.A. This little guys cousin we went to visit put us up in his apartment. Saturday night he took us to a night club in Hollywood and we had a steak dinner and I was drinking vodka Collins all evening which turned out to be a pretty fair drink. The joint had a ten dollar cover charge just to give you an idea what the prices were. Sunday morning the cousin took us sightseeing in his car and showed us all the major studios Hollywood canteen, San Fernando Valley, Beverly hills etc. We had a pretty good time and none of us got drunk which is something for the record. We went up to a planetarium overlooking the city and it sure was a sight.

Tomorrow I hope to go to Mexico and I'll tell you about that when I get back. I don't think I'll drink any tequila because I had some in a bar in Dago one night and it sure is dynamite. I guess I'll just see what I can see.

I sent you another picture which I hope you got. The other one I sent mom was taken in a town named National City near here while we happy chappies were in the midst of our extra-curricular activities and any resemblance to persons living or dead is purely coincidental.

I guess this'll do for now so I'll log out and get into my dress canvas for a little of what old Patrick Henry argued for. I hope the weather is looking a little like spring around your way. It sure is nice here and I've got a good tan already. –John

In between his seemingly frequent liberty times, John Palasek was usually placed on watch duty on base while awaiting orders and participating in "synthetic training." Such training is done under conditions similar to actual battle; in the 21st century, much of this training involves computer simulation with less potential harm to the soldier should he blunder. In WW II, such training was a significantly more dangerous exercise that often included the use of gas masks while in training chambers and obstacle courses in pools with oil burning upon its surface.

From John P., San Diego, CA, March 13, 1945 – *Dear Stanley, Yesterday I started in some more synthetic training which I had at least a half dozen times before. We had abandon ship drill yesterday afternoon and the way you get it here its quite a little work out. You start out by swimming 150 feet across the pool and then jump off a 20 ft platform with a lifejacket on, swim the short way across the pool and climb 30 ft up a landing net and soon as you get up you come down a single line and into the water again and swim about 75 ft to a life raft which you swim under when you reach it and that ends it. All this is done non-stop in a pool 150' x 50' which is a good sized swimming hole. I'm on watch right now 8 to 12 in the A.M. so I'll miss the gas chamber this morning but I'll have to go through that same swimming junk in the afternoon. Ah me, what a life. This program is scheduled to April 10th which of course doesn't necessarily mean I'll be here that long.*

I went to Tijuana, Mexico Sunday with Hause, and we had a look see. It costs a buck for a cab from here to the border then a navy bus gets you the rest of the short way. It's just another Tunis with out the smell what with gin mills on one side of the street and souvenir shops on the other with cat houses in the rear. All we did was find us a gin mill and drank beer and had a steak dinner. Those guitar playing troubadors are o.k. if you like that kind of music and I do. I guess you can get most anything over the border including electric irons, american smokes or a dose of clap. I sent a few cheesy postcards which should get there in a month. The Mexicans are never in a hurry to do things like we are.

From what I read in your letter I guess you really tied one on for yourself last Saturday. Keep it up only don't overdo it. After all somebody's got to uphold the tradition of the tribe and now that I'm 100% good since I quit the mantle of responsibility can fall on your shoulders. By the way Stanley, when you were down Giacobbe's [Author's note: a Port Washington bar] did the old lady mention that Palma was getting mail from me? Before I left, friend Palma asked me to drop a line so I did and so she did and as long as she feels like writing I guess there's no harm in my telling her a few sea stories. When I was over seas Mary Donnel used to write me often and send me packages and at one time I got a 32 page letter from her which proved something or other. I heard from her a week ago too and I guess she was kind of peeved because I didn't stop and say good bye or something. Anyway I was in Giacobbe's getting me a package on which I don't regret. I don't know what all this proves except that maybe I'm a wolf in ship's clothing but I guess there's no harm in keeping 'em all happy –haw! I get a kick out of bull____ing with the twidgets anyway. I'm too far away for anyone to tell me where to get off at if I hurt their feelings. So much for that crap which only started as a question.

Oh yes, here's the piece de resistance and if I hear it again I'll scream so help me or bat somebody with an oar – We were recommended for second class again and the warrant swears we'll get it by the first of the month. All this is bullshit to me because this makes the umpteenth time its happened and the second time at this base, besides being Easter Sunday, April 1st is also all fools day. Boy, if I got all the rates I was recommended for I'd be an admiral by this time. All this is plain unadulterated bullshit to me and I pass it on to you as such. Anyway it helps fill up the page.

Tomorrow I go to that chicken shit fire fighting or target practice or something. We've got a lot of boots in our outfit to contend with. This is the shits *@*!?

Ho hum – guess I'll knock off and hit the sack so I can get up for church in the A.M. Tomorrow is Sunday and I got liberty all day and all night but no shekels to go anywhere since Monday the eagle shits. I guess I'll get some sack duty all day. If I'm going to be a commando I gotta train – Yeah, me and superman! Hope you don't object to my vulgar langwidge. I'm getting like Donald Duck, got two web feet and don't give a _____ dam. John

Though the Allies destroyed the German V-2 rocket labs and damaged those firing bases, not all of the existing rockets and fuel were destroyed. In mid-March 1945, London was again violently struck by these weapons as they were fired from the site of a racecourse near The Hague. To the east, Russian troops were now within 40 miles of Berlin and continued their fight toward the city, which was now the ultimate goal in Europe for the Allies. With much of Germany's infrastructure damaged or destroyed, Adolf Hitler ordered a "scorched earth" policy, wherein all buildings, transport, and even food supplies would be laid to waste should Germany lose the war. The Allies in Europe were now preparing for new strategies to further halt the Nazis in their unceasing efforts to win a war most people on the outside (and even within Germany) felt was to be inevitably lost. More contemporary and precisely designed equipment was brought into Italy with the intention of eliminating the Germans in the Po River Valley by force. General Montgomery had crossed the Rhine River in Germany, American forces were pressing forward from the west, and the Russians were poised to attack Berlin from the East.

From Joe, Italy, March 24, 1945 – *Dear Stanley, Just a few lines hoping you, Mary and your little battler are all in the best of health. I feel pretty good myself but lonesome as hell for Margaret and Joey.*

You say your little guy is three years old. Boy time sure does fly. I hope he had a nice birthday. god bless him I sure wont recognize him when I see him I dont think Ill know my kid either for I guess he must have grew a little also.

I get awful blue at times and them dirty Bastards of a crew the Nazis are lestning to meaning Hitler the Bitch and the rest of them Id like to get a hold of the maniacs. Joe

Before, during and after prohibition, the making of wine (sometimes fortified to high alcohol levels) was not uncommon in people's homes, particularly if buying wine was beyond one's financial means or the homemade batch produced a strength beyond that allowed by the law. There were many Italian households among the immigrant families who settled in Port Washington during the early part of the 20th century; a few of them brought along the basic skills from their homeland to make and bottle their own wine, often from grapes grown in their own backyards. Although he favored beer and whiskey, Stanley did not refuse an offer of homemade wine in exchange for his help from neighboring families in need of his electrical expertise.

Hopes for the war's conclusion among Americans were getting higher, based upon the mounting pressure and advancement of the Allies into Germany. Many workers in war-related manufacturing industries saw these advances as a sign that better times were near for the nation, some Americans began to look for jobs in industries that would continue in peacetime. Some workers were discouraged by curfews set by their employers, such as Grumman's defense plant in Port Washington, in an effort to assure that their workers would be properly rested for each day's work. Discouraged by the new work rules, groups of workers refused to agree to the terms as an infringement of their personal liberties; they were often fired in favor of workers who were more conciliatory. These trends led to shortages of workers at plants that supplied the still-necessary implements of war. Battles in the South Pacific did not appear to be as close to a conclusion as in Europe. Like it or not, the need for war materials, the shortage of staples for civilians, and the inconvenience of war would not let up just because some victories had been won.

From John P., San Diego, CA, March 25, 1945 – Dear Stanley, Right now I am on watch sitting in the sun so its as good a time as any for scribbling. I guess you must be doing pretty well with the guzzling since you've acquired all that wine. I'm not a drinking man anymore myself as I told you before and you probably don't believe. But if I could get some good Bock beer like they used to have on the east coast, I guess I'd have a few. The beer they pass off as beer in these parts is strictly crap and not worth the price they want for it.

As you can see I am still in the same place but I guess it won't be long now. Some of these outfits like I'm in fly to pearl Harbor and ship out from there. I hear this is one of those beach battalion outfits where you ship all unnecessary gear home before shoving out. I'll soon find out. I guess a guy can't go on missing all the major invasions like I've been doing in the E.T.O. [Author's note: European Theater of Operations] Speaking of the E.T.O., I got an Easter card from Steve. In the letter he mentioned that star you wrote me about. He said the whole outfit was awarded it for taking part in the offensive. As I get it it's not like the bronze star medal which is a high award and altogether different. The bronze star he's talking about is one which goes on the E.T.O. ribbon and a man doesn't have to be in actual combat to get it. It's awarded for support of operations also. All these ribbons and awards are pretty confusing if you don't understand them.

I hope Alex gets what he wants but I hope he doesn't land in an outfit like I'm in, a cross between army and navy. I guess when we get on one of those beaches were destined for we'll live with the army and eat K. rations which are pretty savory-if you're starving.

If, as and when we get to that commando training, the scuttlebutt has it that they dish out a little embarkation leave and I hope its right. I wouldn't mind. The only breaks I ever get is a hot roll in a crap game once in a while and I quit that business too so I'm not getting any.

There is a captured German film out which is being shown to the public entitled "The Enemy Strikes." [Author's note: this film is available on the Internet as of this writing.] It deals with the German breakthrough and shows some gory scenes of our dead and Germans smoking our camel cigarettes etc. It's being shown and narrated with the idea of awakening the defense workers to the fact that the war isn't over by any means so that they'll stay on the job and not look for a peacetime job till it is over. If you ever get the chance you ought to see it. I think they ought to release all these restricted pictures to the public and maybe they'll understand its not all a question of time and a half and the mighty dollar and rye high.

Well, I guess I'll bring this to a screeching halt for the time being. Hope the weather is good and have some Bock for me. –John

At the same time in Europe, John's brother — who was spending some of the best years of his life facing some of the worst scenarios of any war — sarcastically commented on defense factory workers back home who had complaints and could not possibly relate to what actually being in a war was truly like.

From Joe, Italy, March 29, 1945 *– Dear Stanley, How is everything with you, Mary and your little boy. You say in your letter that the defense plant just about cleaned house, well I guess theirs those wise guys who now what war is, and are fighting a good fight over the radio. Also those poor defense workers cant stay out so late since they past that curfew. I really feel sorry for those poor boys for twelve oclock isnt enough time to get drunk, then their working so hard and getting paid so little it must be tough on those hard working guys. I just like to see one shoot his mouth of to me when I get back there. he sure will have a good fight on his hands, your pal Joe*

Chapter 21

Stan Palasek was fond of many musical genres including the operettas of Gilbert and Sullivan. In one of his favorites, The Mikado, a lyric states that, "The flowers that bloom in the spring, tra la, breathe promise of merry sunshine… we welcome the hope that they bring." The lyric juxtaposes optimism with the less hopeful line, "The flowers that bloom in the spring, tra la, have nothing to do with the case," which Stan often would quote. So it seemed for those engaged in this war that the promises of spring's flowers were empty ones. Despite the somber mood of the day, spring was beginning to embrace Port Washington, New York in April of 1945 as grass was green, and crocuses, daffodils and dogwood trees were coming into full bloom.

Hopes were taking root and budding, particularly with the invasion of Okinawa by the Allies. The landings on this strategic island, close to the south of Japan, were met with almost no resistance from the Japanese; they had moved inland, away from the massive invasion by over a half of a million Allied troops. Here, the Allies could construct airfields for bombers and barracks where troops could prepare for an invasion of nearby Japan.

President Franklin Roosevelt, suffering from the effects of polio and other maladies, often struggled with the routine aspects of governing since the commencement of his fourth term. Roosevelt and Churchill shared geo-political concerns regarding the Soviet Union's potential control over liberated nations in Europe. These leaders knew early on that they would have to make concessions to Stalin — and they had made allowances that they felt were necessary at the conference in Yalta. Stalin was clearly going to forcefully go beyond these limitations by controlling as much of Eastern Europe as he possibly could after the war, by any means necessary. They realized they would have to deal with the results of Stalin's ideals later in order to win the war if they sought to risk fewer of their own soldiers' lives in the attack on Berlin, particularly when the Russians were poised to march through Berlin's eastern threshold.

On April 12, 1945, President Roosevelt died of a cerebral hemorrhage in Warm Springs, Georgia, while resting and preparing for the opening of the United Nations. Vice President Harry Truman, a WW I veteran, county judge, U.S. Senator and former haberdasher from Missouri, had only two face-to-face meetings with Roosevelt since their inauguration. Truman's leadership qualities had been recognized in battle, and he was chosen with confidence over William O. Douglas to be Roosevelt's fourth and final running mate. It was now Truman's task to finish what his predecessor had begun.

Far away from and little affected by the events in Washington, the American forces in Europe fought on without missing a beat. Well known today, but less so when in action during WW II, were the "Tuskegee Airmen." These African-American pilots were trained at the base in Tuskegee, Alabama, and consisted of both the 332nd

fighter group and the 477th bomber squadron. At the 1944 battle of Rimini along the Adriatic coast of Italy, these airmen joined with Canadian and Greek forces to push the Germans from their position on the so-called "Gothic Line." The liberated airfield in eastern Italy became a base for the Tuskegee Airmen to escort B-17 and B-24 bombers in their P-47 and P-51 fighters. These pilots successfully downed over 100 enemy planes in air to air combat and destroyed numerous German and Italian planes on the ground.

From Joe, Eastern Italy, April 17, 1945 – *Dear Stanley, How are you I hope this letter finds you Mary, and your big little guy in the best of health. I received the pictures Alex sent me and you really are putting on weight. You sure look good. So does Carl. Things around here are about the same, when I have off I go to some of these air ports and watch our fighters and bombers take of for were surrounded with air ports lot of the pilots are colored. I mean the fighter pilots, their damn god too. I don't like the way they buzz our camp for they really fly low. Outside of that Stanley it's the same every day. until this mess is over with. Your pal always, Joe*

A few weeks earlier, Alex Palasek had returned home after his tour with the Merchant Marine. His time in the comfort of home and family was brief as he had to report to Fort Dix in New Jersey, a name that was familiar to him as it had once been the training and dispatch site for the Civilian Conservation Corps (more commonly known as the CCC) where some of his brothers had labored. Now it was a basic training site for the Army. His stay at Fort Dix was brief. He was soon on a train ride similar to the one his brother Stan experienced, with soot from the engine filling the coach, but he was traveling in the opposite direction. Alex was headed south to Camp Croft in South Carolina. This red clay training site, which had been a home to peach and cotton farmers, was now the infantry replacement training center. Alex had been assigned to the 35th battalion of the Infantry Training Regiment (ITB), where he would be prepared to fight in whatever capacity he seemed most qualified. Having already served and seen the war first hand, the trepidations Alex had when he first went to enlist in the Marines were long forgotten.

From Alex, Camp Croft, SC, April 21, 1945 – Dear Stan, Today is Sunday and I just came back from church so I have the day to my self now so I decided to drop you a line. I'm feeling fine and hope this letter finds you the same. Tomorrow we start training real hard, harder than we ever have. We have to run for about 3 miles, infiltration course that's crawling under machine gun fire but that comes a little later.

Most of the fellow's here are married in our company all except 6 of us. There are about 260 of us and boy are there are a bunch of cry babies they been in the army about two weeks and they are crying about furloughs. We had a long run and hike yesterday you should see the guys fall out I'm holding my own so far.

Tell mom to send me the allotment paper I sent home for her to sign or she won't get her allotment. How is Steve, John, and Joe I wrote to them yesterday. Also tell Willie to please send all my mail to me. Take care of your self and your little family. God bless all of you. Your Brother, Alex

One of the forward infantries moving into Germany in 1945 was the 330th, in which Mary Palasek's brother Adam was a staff sergeant. He had suffered the freezing cold winter, fighting in the Ardennes where his wet clothing would turn to ice. But it was the duty of the infantry to make the path and villages safe from the enemy for the heavier artillery and tanks to follow. Over 700 of their ranks were killed in action and almost 3,000 wounded as they fought onward, fatigued and freezing. Once across the Rhine, the 330th moved rapidly in order to take control of towns before the Germans could set up their highly efficient defenses. Fighting intensified and battles were fought day and night into April, with the goal of forcing a German retreat. The 330th fought across every terrain, including fields, forests and eventually the highest mountain range in Germany: the Harz Mountains. Here, atop the steep rock peaks the Germans were attempting to reorganize.

From Adam R., Germany, April 22, 1945 – Dear Sis, Yes I have been a little neglectful in writing to you. Trying to write to most every one with so little time allotted for writing is quite difficult.

I have been traveling fast and have gone a long way into Germany. For almost two weeks we were away from civilization and no one could write a line. Well we finally got back for a spell so that we could wash and shave. Everything is still the best that can be expected over here. I am still in good health although a little tired.

How are you and the family making out? Are they keeping Stanley busy at his new job? I'll bet my boy Stash is getting to be a big man now. Thanks for the News. Give my regards to everyone good luck & God Bless you all. Your Brother, Adam

In late April 1945, as the spring weather in Europe improved, so did the position of the Allied forces. Vienna was no longer in German control and Austria would not be placed under the Soviet Union's authority as the nation had resisted the Nazis throughout the war to the best of their ability. The combined Allied forces in Italy, with renewed vigor, had moved farther north across the now fading, imaginary lines set by the German forces, bringing the surrender of the Germans in Italy. Adolf Hitler, in his bunker below Berlin with Eva Braun, refused to concede defeat, declaring that any retreating soldier should be shot. He insisted that should all be lost, the Nazis' industrial, transportation and military installations should be destroyed rather than be handed over to the enemies. But the enemy was destroying many of these assets without the aid of the Germans by bombing the Nazis' planes, ships and depots incessantly. Adolf Hitler did not live to see his inglorious defeat; he committed suicide in his bunker as the Russian forces bombarded Berlin on the way to the Reichstag, the Nazi headquarters. In northern Italy, near Lake Como, Benito Mussolini — still on the run since his arrest and escape, with hopes of one last charge — was stopped on the road dressed in a German uniform. After being interrogated, Mussolini recognized that all was lost and asked to be shot in the chest. The Communist partisans who stopped him complied, then strung "Il Duce's" corpse upside down in the square to be mocked by the citizenry in the warm spring air.

Chapter 22

    Stanley Palasek's promise to himself the previous year, to attend church more often, had fallen by the wayside — as do many resolutions. He attended mass on Christmas Eve, Palm Sunday and Easter, along with a handful of other Sundays, but long hours at work and other interests kept him from regular attendance. Sunday, May 6, 1945, he was standing shoulder-to-shoulder with other men and women beside the wooden confessional booth at the rear of the crowded St. Peter's of Alcantara church for seven o'clock mass. All of the pews were filled with likeminded worshippers who had come to pray that the rumors from Europe were true. Two days later, on his way to work, Stanley picked up a copy of the *New York Daily News* from a corner newsstand in Manhattan. He smiled as he walked through the city streets with it under his arm. The headline read, "It's Over In Europe." On May 7, 1945, in the city of Reims, France, General Alfred Jodl of the German high command had met with American leaders and signed an agreement to surrender all forces on land, sea and air that were under German command. The war in Europe was finally over. There were celebrations in the streets of England, America and towns throughout Europe, as well as many raised drinks in the gin mills of Port Washington.

    The day brought a considerably quieter joy to soldiers in Europe. They were cheerful that the fighting was ending there, but recognized that it may be some time before they could return to their homes. The possibility loomed that they would be sent to fight on the other side of the world, where men were still dying by the hundreds and thousands, and more were in training stateside to go to battle against Japan. Often, a soldier's destination from Europe was determined by his Advanced Service Rating Score; factors such as time in service, time overseas, battle stars and awards, as well as dependents back home under the age of 18 were considered to decide a soldier's fate.

    From Joe, Termoli, Italy, May 14, 1945 *– Dear Stanley, Thanks for the mail I've been getting from you. I'm happy to know that you and your little family are all in the best of health.*

I myself feel fine, but now that the war is over I sure would like to go back to the states for awhile, if the rumors are true, that are flying around here that's were we supposed to go. I guess you've heard about the point system which they are going to let the guys out. I myself have only 80 points five short of going out. For being in combat, and getting a few stars etc. Helped me a little also being limited service might get me out.
    There isn't much more to write about solong for awhile. Always a pal Joe

    From Steve, Compiegne, France, May 15, 1945 – *Dear Stan, I have received your letter this day, thanks ever so much. I am glad to hear that you are all well and just marking time with us in the service, here where all hostilities have ceased, here where now we are guessing and hoping for some break in this chain. The war for most of us is serving god and country is merely half over. Yes we took a deep breath and smiled a little, without the cheers. Until Japan is knocked down to her knees there seems to be no feeling, just a job well done. I cannot say that I am going home, because I don't know, neither can I say I am going to the Pacific. Many such units as ours will go there no doubt about it. But to date there is hardly a rumor. So we really haven't got one started. We do know some such units will go to the Pacific, some directly, others via the states furloughs and then on the road to Mandalay. Believe you me when things get organized Japan will receive a better dose than what Germany did and she is now an ash pile. I sure do hope this unit can manage to at least stop in the states. You see we are getting new men replacements in other words brother we need them.*
    I haven't written any one this passed week because I was on a mission in Paris, after completion we received passes to explore this Capitol city which makes France. I first took in all the historical buildings, rode the subways, which are as modern as New York. The city is beautiful, its high ways water displays such as they had at the world's fair. I went to the Arc de Triomphe, Eiffel Tower, the opera plus a few good American shows. I ate my meals at the Allied Red Cross which furnishes accommodates all troops on pass. Cabarets night life goes on as it would on Broadway. I really was surprised and how this was my first time, I thought I was home

except for the lingo. The reason I tell you all this is because today censorship was lifted. I can seal my own envelope and say what I damn please, what a relief. I know I'll be lost when I get back to Gods country after this ordeal. Now the idea is to keep the fingers crossed and hope for the best.

I am now located in Compiegne, in this Chateau or mansion in English. Prisoners do the work of cleaning the building even K.P. [Author's note: an abreviaton for "Kitchen Patrol", generally helping the cooks] I play ball twice a week. I believe we are getting a new type shoulder patch, instead of the star. They call us the Blue Star Commandos. One thing during the hot time we never knew where the front lines were like the infantry until we smacked right into them. The Jerries bombed our bridges strafed our men I am telling you I never knew what a German looked like real close until I saw a dead one, they were good ones. I used see pictures of the S & S troops the Wermacht, the Grenadiers and the Nazi Luftewaffe But never thought I would ever be here to witness and aid in winning this war. I laugh to see these bastards, scrub our floors, snap to attention when I walk by.

I believe Joe will be on his way home soon, I do hope so, he wrote me and claimed they might. He for one deserves a trip home. John wrote me and stated he expects to leave soon. I must say so long for a while, I guess I covered just about all there is for the time being, until my next letter, God bless you all, my best wishes and regards and I'll be seeing you, we all shall meet again shortly. Your Pal & Brother Steve

In Europe, the Allies focused on regaining order and establishing control in the countries that had been torn asunder both physically and politically. The news in the Pacific was anything but peaceful. It had been over six weeks since the Allies landed in Okinawa with little resistance. Subsequent to that first invasion, the Japanese proceeded to defend the island forcefully. There were over 20,000 Allied casualties, far surpassing those of the struggle for Iwo Jima. The Allied troops were gaining ground at the plodding rate of approximately 100 yards per day. Allied submarines were successfully taking a toll on the Japanese fleet and air attacks on Japanese factories and strategic targets near Tokyo were causing pronounced damage, yet it was on the shores and hills of this small island where the battles were most intense. Bombers and warships could not win here. The need for men skilled with handheld weapons and prepared to face eternity was vital.

From Alex, Camp Croft, SC, May 15, 1945 – *Dear Stan, How are you, hope this letter finds you in the best of health. Tell Willie I got the hanger's also the $10.00 tell mom thanks I'll pay her back as soon as I get paid. Boy we had quite a few tough days, digging foxholes in boiling hot sun, then a few hours of bayonet practice. I never knew there was so much drill to a bayonet. I got a 95 on my M1 rifle written test. This Monday coming we go out on the range for a solid week steady firing. Also we have a few night problems coming so if we get 4 hour's sleep you're lucky. You should see the positions we fire from they tell us when we feel the most uncomfortable, when our back starts to ache, and our arms go numb we're in the right position.*

I hope Joe comes home he deserves to also Steve. I guess thats all for now solong and God Bless You. Your Pal and Brother, Alex

From John P., San Diego, CA, May 28, 1945 – *Dear Stanley, I appreciate yours and William's generosity in wanting to finance my trip home if I got a leave but I don't think I could get one. I'd certainly like to get home even if only for a few days but it seems you have to have a good reason to get a leave. Like your mother in law kicking the bucket or wife having a kid or business to be straightened out. Since I don't fall into either category I guess I'm S.O.L. They don't appreciate the fact that a guy has 30 days leave in two years but still these guys who've been in the states all the time can get leaves every so often the poor homesick bastards. This stateside duty is rough on them so I guess they rate a rest at home every so often. As I see it the next leave I get will be when the war is over and that's a helluva long ways off yet.*

I certainly hope Joe get discharged when he gets home, he certainly rates it. I hope Steve gets home before going to the Pacific but I wouldn't bet on it. I guess they'll make up their minds when I'll leave here one of these days. I might just as well be overseas since I can't get a leave and if I keep staying here I'll always have that to bitch about. I guess that's all I have for now. I'll let you know as soon as I'm about to make a dry run or otherwise so don't get the idea I skipped out if you don't hear from me regularly. John

With his brothers Joe, Steve, John and Alex either in a mending Europe or stateside, Stanley, his brother Willie and his parents were no longer as anxious about the Palasek boys' fate or how many letters they received from them for the time being. Even Mary's brother Adam was in a now more placid Europe. For now, the only one of the two families who might be directly in harm's way was Mary's brother Ollie, who rarely wrote from where he remained in the precarious Pacific conflict.

Chapter 23

In 1942 in England, singer Vera Lynn recorded the song, "The White Cliffs of Dover" to lift the spirits of Britain during a most horrific time. The song promised that there would be bluebirds over the white cliffs of Dover, England. Without saying so in the actual lyrics, these bluebirds would one day, perhaps tomorrow, replace the German bombers that regularly flew over these cliffs, which stood tall along England's southern shore. There would be peace and the children who had been sent from London to stay safely at sponsors' homes in the countryside during the war would once again sleep in their own beds. Three years later, the promises of that melody were at last coming true, except for the bluebirds which are not found in England.

To call the events following the end of the war in Europe "spring cleaning" would be appropriate considering the season when they began, but the efforts required were significantly more challenging than simply cleaning a few windows and airing out the rugs. Those simpler spring cleaning tasks were keeping Mary Palasek busy, along with trips down Central Drive to the pond in Baxter Estates where her young boy, Stanley, could feed the ducks and Mary could relax while her husband was at work in Manhattan. The tensions and quarrels at the apartment when husband and wife were together had lessened, but by no means disappeared. Even the larger two-bedroom unit they lived in seemed to be too small in comparison to what Mary dreamed of enjoying. Perhaps a house of their own, with a yard where young Stanley and a brother or sister could safely play, would be possible one day; Mary would daydream by the pond, on a bench under the trees. Stanley found that a few extra drinks at home after work to be his preferred escape from the pressures of life in the apartment. His concerns over where his brothers were, and when they would be home (if at all), were cropping up again as well.

In Europe, the civilians who had left their homes in fear now yearned to return to those cities that had been brutally damaged by war and restore them to a semblance of what they once had been. Bringing order to life and government was part of the plan. In late May, the Allied commanders drew up papers in Berlin to divide Germany into four sectors controlled by the U.S., England, the Soviet Union and France. In the U.K., German prisoners of war were put to work cleaning up rubble and repairing the damage inflicted by their own shells.

The battles in Asia continued with no evidence that the Japanese would be willing to concede defeat. Allied forces continuously bombed the cities and industrial areas of Japan's mainland in hope that it would force surrender. To the contrary, the Japanese kamikaze attacks on Allied vessels increased. The battle for control of Okinawa, with its brutal land battles between infantries, was showing few signs of coming to a conclusion.

The last of the able-bodied Palasek boys to go into the service was Carl, the loner and son who wanted to live as he wished, with no one else influencing his choices and little regard for his family's circumstances. But in the spring of 1945 he was called up to the U.S. Army and sent to Fort Dix before being sent to sunny Florida's Camp Blanding, named for General Albert Blanding. Training would take place both at the camp near the St. Johns River and, on occasion, along the oceanfront area further east. Although the similarly sandy shores of Okinawa were being slowly secured, the cost was great and this infantry replacement center was where Carl found himself among others who were called to reinforce the Pacific forces.

From Carl, Camp Blanding, FL, June 10, 1945 – *Dear Stanley, Received your letter figger I'd answer it as I have all day* off today its Sunday. Don't have anything in particular to do. We are in the rainy season now in fact its raining like hell even now. It's sure hard to keep clothes dry we manage to get a wet ass every day. Damn this place to hell if it ain't Hot then its wet Boy if they ever send us to some other state & I never see the south again it will be too soon. Oh well we go into our 4th week of this training starting tomorrow the whole course is a cycle of 17 weeks After this we'll have 13 weeks to go after that we hope to get 10 days home I hope. They put me in company D for Dog. Tomorrow we go out on the damn rifle range what Hell Hole that is we get out of bed at 4: oclock when all respectable people are still in bed come in at 9 oclock at nite & start cleaning rifles. Boy it gets you so that it just ain't no fun even to look at a gun. None of us like to fire a gun because you just have that much more work cleaning the damn thing if there was no penalty I'd thro the blasted thing away. The sand here is so fine that you have to take the rifle apart every piece of it to clean it out. Oh what the hell its only 14 wks more after that they can go pound salt up their fannies. Well I guess I've thrown enough Bull for the time being I'll get thru this O.K. might see you in the fall sometime if I'm lucky so long & good luck, Carl

From John P., San Diego, CA, June 14, 1945 – Dear Stanley, I received your letter today so I'll see what I can put together for an answer. So you've been out tying one on again. I think everybody should blow his top a little every so often. I do it myself every now and then but it's pretty expensive around here. The beer is twenty cents a bottle and up. The bottle is the usual size and the beer is so green you can't get a head on it. All they sell is lousy bottled beer and you can drink it till the cows come home and stay sober but the next day you get all kinds of pains. I'll take limey beer any day over this crap.

Now about that code business: Substituting names of people for places is ok if you can dig up enough names. The latitude and longitude idea is alright but it wouldn't pass the censor. We use the names for correspondence and it won't be such a give away for the censor.

Each week that comes up I expect to start packing my gear but so far I'm still waiting. I'm anxious to get the rest of the training over. Anyway the eight months I've been in the states went by pretty fast. More so when you're constantly expecting to haul ass.

I hear Steve is guarding prisoners so it doesn't appear that he'll be heading home so quick. I hope that it's right about Joe being on his way. Guess I'll knock off for now meantime keep in drinking condition for when Joe gets home so I'll be able to keep up with him. John

One week later, the battle for the island of Okinawa — a mere 400 miles from Japan — came to a bloody end. The Allies were victorious but not without an enormous loss of lives. Over 12,000 American soldiers were killed and over 36,000 were missing or wounded during the months of fighting. For the Japanese, it was more like a battle to the death. After more than 9,000 Japanese soldiers died fighting in just the final three days, less than one-third of that number were left to surrender. Hundreds of others took their own lives rather than face the humiliation of defeat, many by diving off cliffs to the rocks below. The Japanese force of some 30,000 men on Okinawa was finally overpowered. For those like John and Alex Palasek, training became more intense and letters fewer as President Truman considered invading Japan. To do so, in light of the resistance that the Japanese had mounted to date, would possibly result in the death of another quarter-million brave young men. The odds of surviving such an invasion would not be in any soldier's favor.

After weeks without word from any of his brothers, Stanley anxiously wrote to Camp Croft to determine the location and status of Alex. He received a reply from William McCray, the chaplain of the base, which said: "The soldiers are kept very busy, and it is easy to put off writing. He is getting along all right I believe." This did little to ease Stanley's concerns, but more good news was soon to arrive in the mail from the north of France where things were getting better for Steve.

From Steve, Tergnier, France, June 20, 1945 – *Dear Stan, Received your letter this day and am I glad to hear from you and how. For one reason that you have received the money I sent and the favor you are doing me. I like the way you chose the flowers*

the card and the wording of it I am really satisfied. You asked me what you should do with the extra money. Well just have a drink on me on that day which is my wedding anniversary. Or have a drink with pop, I appreciate the favor. Only I ask once more when this day nears please check with the florist to make sure the flowers get there. My wife gets $140 a month since I boosted my allotment, I still receive $25 per month any addition I play poker in spare time and this I have plenty.

All I am doing is wasting valuable time waiting for a boat. When that will come I don't know exactly, But we are scheduled for the states, I hope those orders don't change. We now have American beer here in the Chateau. I can't take much of those suds for some reason or another. The bar we built would cost in the states at least 5,000 dollars, it's out of Bakelite.

Tomorrow I am leaving on a seven day pass down to Southern France, called the Riviera in peace time, rich man's paradise or The Florida of France because it is never cold there. I am going to a city called Nice on the border of Italy. I wrote Joe and boy I would like to meet him there. The place is operated by the Red Cross for enlisted men only, no brass allowed. I am glad of that. The best meals, hotels, swimming, golf every kind of sport you can think of.

Stan I am still trying to find that town where Mary's brother is buried, eventually I will find it. I found graves of men from New York. I have toured many of the cemeteries France is noted for that. I am proud of Alex and I know his break is coming soon. I had a letter from Joe and believe me he seems disgusted.

With best wishes and regards to all, God bless you and thanks a million. Your Pal & Brother Steve

Peace had come to Europe and reparations were continuing. Yet peace had not come to the Far East. Troops continued to fight while awaiting replacement and reinforcement by newly trained boys in the states or by transfer from Europe. The potential for even more intense combat in Japan lingered over each of these young men's souls. On July 17, 1945, a brief message was sent by President Truman to Prime Minister Churchill, simply stating, "Babies satisfactorily born." The secret behind this message was not to last long. The message's concealed subject matter was to result in mistrust by the Soviets at Potsdam Treaty meetings. The Manhattan Project — the same secret project that Stan Palasek had been interviewed for several years ago based upon his engineering knowledge, and which he declined rather than move to Tennessee — had come to fruition. America had successfully tested an atomic bomb. Upon seeing the test in the New Mexico desert, the project's architect, Professor Robert Oppenheimer, recited a quotation from the Hindu writings, the Bhagavad Gita: "I am become death, destroyer of worlds."

Chapter 24

Not all new technologies introduced for the first time in 1945 were as ominous as the atomic bomb. Although not publicly announced until the following year, the Electronic Numerical Integrator and Computer, or ENIAC, became operational in Philadelphia and was the first electronic computer for general calculations. The same microwaves that Stanley had been working with at Sperry in order to allow safer landings of aircraft in bad conditions were now being put to use at the Raytheon company in Massachusetts to heat and cook food. This would become the microwave oven, America's favorite way to make popcorn. And a little-known breakfast cereal called Cheerioats, which consisted of small circles of oat grain, changed its name and became Cheerios.

From above Japan, rather than bombs, thousands of leaflets were released demanding an unconditional surrender by Japan to the Allied forces with the threatened alternative being total annihilation. Japan refused to comply, citing uncertainty of what would happen to its monarchy upon admission of defeat and Moscow's procrastination to Japan's request to mediate surrender. Not very distant from Japan's shores, General MacArthur was building up an invasion force of at least 650,000 Allied soldiers. In England, the populace voted out the Torrey government in favor of a Labor-led government, thereby forcing Winston Churchill — the Prime Minister who had held the nation together through the worst of times — to resign.

Home in Port Washington, Stanley was spending most of his free time painting the house on School Street that his mother and father had bought with the help of allotment money from their sons in the service. The boys came first in Marjanna and Stanley's hearts and they let their boys know to stop forwarding their military pay if they needed money, or merely ask and they would send what they could to help.

From John P., San Diego, CA, July 26, 1945 – *Dear Stanley, I received your letter today and thanks for writing. I notice you often mention that if I need any money, Mom will send it and here's the way I look at it. When I made out the allotment and bonds it wasn't for the purpose of saving money for myself. If I could help out more, I would. I'll be only too glad to do my share.*

I've been broke so many times since I'm in this lash-up that its become a regular habit with me. That's because I shoot crap and what I lose is mine and I go on my merry way and don't get in debt by borrowing. Which is also one reason I wouldn't ask Mom or anyone else for a single penny. Because I'd only get into a crap game and probably lose it. This is between me you and the lamppost and I hope you don't mention the subject again-period.

I had a letter from Carl and he said the dentist was busy with him. Steve wrote me all about the gin mill they're setting up for themselves and they expect to have American draught beer soon as its finished. I hope he and Joe do get home soon anyway and Alex gets home about the same time also so you can have a good house warming.

By the way, did you see the Navy's point system in the papers? Looks like there's no hopes for anybody getting out unless they're old and feeble. I see where the papers are printing that surrender crap like they used to about Germany and everybody thought different. Personally I don't take any stock in the papers because they won't know shit from shinola and they only print what the War Dept. lets them print. There's no doubt about it though that Japan is getting a hell of a pasting and is due for a lot more. Bet there won't be much left of it by the time they're ready to throw in the towel.

Well Stanley I guess I'll quit here before I go on and on raving about this and that all of which doesn't have much effect on the price of oil in Borneo. I do hope it could be finished before Carl or Alex ever get on a banana boat anyway. How's the hooch work with the paint? John

On July 28, the people of New York City and the nation were stunned when a B-25 bomber traveling from Massachusetts to New York's LaGuardia airport in extremely dense fog struck the 79th floor of the Empire State Building. Being a Saturday morning, few were working in the Catholic War Relief Services office where the plane made impact and its fuel burst into flames. Three crew and eleven office workers were sadly killed, but the integrity of the structure and its construction withstood the incident.

From Alex, Camp Croft, SC, August 2, 1945 - *Dear Stan, Received your letter yesterday and I was sure glad to hear from you. How's mom pop and everybody? As for me I'm okay just a bit tired sleeping on the ground is pretty rugged. Last night we caught a 4 ½ foot cotton mouth snake, also a lot of lizards that scare hell out of us when were asleep they run across our legs or face. One fellow got into his tent and layed down he felt something move he lifted his blanket and found a snake all coiled up it struck but he dropped the blanket on it I never saw a guy haul ass so fast in all my life.*

This Friday we move 12 more miles out, this country is pretty its hilly and green, mountains, but its dirty. The "chiggers" something like a tick really bite the hell out of us. Tell mom thanks a lot I received the shoes. I got paid yesterday and I'll just have enough dough to make it home by the skin of my teeth. It costs us $17.00 to go home I got paid $20.00. I'll probably see you around the 25th of August solong God Bless all of you Your Pal and Brother "Alex"

From Steve, Tergnier, France, August 3, 1945 – *Dear Stan, Thanks ever so much for sending me Carl's address because I misplaced the one you gave me. I will write him a few lines just for fun. After all I do like to write at the same time keep contact with all my brothers.*

As for my-self I am feeling fine and hoping to get home soon. I may be disappointed if things keep going the way they are. The reason is they started redeploying men here out of my unit direct to the Pacific and the army of occupation [in Germany]. The ones that will be left will finally get home. To date I am safe, sipping American beer three nights a week. If I have to go direct to the Pacific it will be the greatest heart breaker to me and how. I'll then just give up and hope for the worst. Other wise Stan there is nothing new around here, I am tired of this dive and just raring to get home to gods country where I belong. So with best wishes and regards I am signing off here. Your Pal & Brother Steve

War as mankind had known it changed forever just three days after this letter from Steve was posted. The United States' B-29 bomber, nicknamed Enola Gay after the mother of its pilot, Paul Tibbets, literally erased three quarters of the city of Hiroshima, Japan from the face of the earth in mere seconds, along with approximately 100,000 of its inhabitants. The act's necessity was much debated, as were its justification and moral magnitude. Destroyed in the process were military supply depots and a Japanese military command center. Receiving no report of Japan's intention to surrender, three days later a second atomic bomb was dropped over the seaport city of Nagasaki, where much of the Japanese naval force had been manufactured and harbored. American engineers estimated that the next bomb could be ready by the middle of August.

Mary's brother Adam took time to write to her. With his younger sister's 21st birthday days away, it brought a smile to her face to read his words. Now a Sergeant in the 330th Infantry, he was nearly as far to the east in Bavaria as was possible. Their sister, Sophie, was less than pleased as she had recently heard that her husband, Steve Holick, had been drafted.

From Adam R., Deching, Rohrnbach, Germany, August 11, 1945 – *Dear Sis, I received your most waited for letter of July 31. I always like receiving mail from anyone who chooses to write and I try to answer them as promptly as possible.*

I had three days pass in Paris which was well spent for I had a swell time. When I was returning I met some boys from Johnny's old company who knew as a buddie and they gave me some information. Upon my return to the company I received a letter from his former CO this letter was a answer to the one I sent him. It was a very nice letter. I forward the letter to Evelyn so that if she wants to she can let mom see it. If you see her in the mean time ask to see the letter.

I am glad to hear that Stanley is getting on in his work and that he likes it. Tell him to keep up the good work.

I did read about the crash [Author's note: He is referring to the crash at the Empire State Building] in the Stars & Stripes, which is an Army paper. That must have been some crash. I often wonder why we didn't have more crashes being so close to LaGuardia field.

The engineer was finally caught in the great net, the draft. It looks like he will either be in the Medics or truck driving. The once I feel sorry for is Sophie. She is the one who is suffering. What she should try and do is try to get a few rooms in Roslyn so she will be near people that she knows.

We are supposed to go home sometime in November. The new turn in the Pacific war may change things in this theater so all of the boys are sitting around with crossed fingers. So long for now sis. Give my regards to everyone. Say hello to both little and big Stanley. Good Luck & God bless you all. Your Brother, Adam

As Adam mentions, he had written a letter to the commander of the 602nd battalion of the Third Army after meeting some of his late brother John's fellow battalion members in Germany. Within weeks, he had a reply from his brother in arms.

From Capt. Samuel C. Walker, Co. "C" 602 T.D. Bn. –
Dear Sir; In answer to your letter dated June 29, 1945.

Your brother's destroyer was in position on the edge of a woods over looking Bayonne [sic] France and the Moselle river. The destroyer was brought under fire and in an attempt to withdraw was hit. Your brothers' death was instantaneous and he did not suffer.

Needless to say we all felt his death and it caused a void in this organization which has been never filled. Your brother was known and respected by every member of this Command. His grave is in the U.S. Military Cemetery, Champegneul, France.

This organization is located near Mainburg, Germany and if you so desire you are welcome to visit with any of your brothers' friends. Hoping that nothing but luck follows in your footsteps in the future. I remain, Samuel C. Walker, Capt FA

Adam's personal letter brought happiness to Mary. But the one he soon forwarded from Captain Walker failed to do so, and he expected this to be the case. Any comforting thoughts of John from the Captain were lost on the Rykowski family back in Roslyn. Months after the stabbing pain of John's death, weeks of grieving were followed by those of healing and acceptance; upon reading the letter from his captain, the wound was reopened. Though Captain Walker was nothing less than sincerely compassionate in his words, the hurt of the loss and the knowledge that their brother, Theadora and Adolph's son, was laid to rest far from where any one of them could possibly visit added to their anguish. John's grave was in a village that no one could even find on a map. Johnny would not be coming home again, and it hurt.

Chapter 25

By August 14, 1945, WW II was over. Devastated by the effects of two nuclear bombs, Japan's Emperor Hirohito unconditionally surrendered. Thousands of people outside of the royal palace in Tokyo wept as they heard the news, and many felt they had personally failed their nation. On remote islands such as Guam, Japanese soldiers refused to believe the war was over well after this date had passed, insisting that they would only accept the surrender if their direct commanders told them it was so. Many of those commanders had already left or been killed; to this day, there are legends that some Japanese soldiers grew old in forgotten areas for decades, not knowing the war had ended.

Immediately upon the defeat of Japan, Vietnam — which had been under the control of France, but was internally divided by differences in whether a Communist government would be best — struggled through the brief but historic August Revolution. Within a month, North Vietnam would gain self-rule under Ho Chi Minh in

Hanoi and separate from the southern territories that wished to stay aligned with France after Japan lost control.

The next day, August 15, could not possibly be an ordinary Wednesday. It was Mary Palasek's 21st birthday and it would be celebrated well — not only by Mary and her family, but by people all over the world for another reason. In Washington, D.C., crowds chanted the name of President Truman. The Federal government was to be closed for the next two days. Across the globe, people cheered in the streets (although rain dampened things in London). Celebration was also the case in New York, where taxi horns and ship whistles resounded among the joyful voices of those in Times Square. Even in Port Washington, the noise in the streets lingered as Stanley returned home from work to his small apartment by the railroad station. There, his brothers Willie and Alex greeted him; in a stroke of luck, Alex was home for two weeks on leave. Also present to join in the combined celebration of Mary's birthday and the end of the war were her older sister, Evelyn, with her husband, Al, and their daughter, Evie. Margaret and Stephanie, the wives of Joe and Steve (respectively), took the last seats in the apartment. For the younger men, the floor provided adequate seating in the cramped living area. Stan brought home a bottle of Champagne, but it would hardly fulfill the needs of the small crowd on a day like this; he went up Main Street to buy enough booze to swallow most of his pay for that week. But it didn't matter; there was joy to be had and an air of merriment to revel in. Before long, though, Evelyn gave a look to Mary, who sat quietly and nodded knowingly to her sister. Evelyn, always ready to speak her mind, asserted "What about Johnny?" The room went silent.

Stanley set aside his camera and made sure everyone's glass was full, even Alex and young Evie, who sipped a Hoffman ginger ale. He instructed everyone to wait a second. Raising his refilled glass of Canadian Club whiskey and ginger ale, he said, "Here's to Johnny. May God bless his soul." Tears were shed for the moment, but they couldn't dilute the alcohol and spirit of the day. Finally, well after the midnight hour had struck, Alex and Willie (the last of the guests) made their way down the stairs to walk back to School Street together. After putting her young boy to sleep and cleaning up all evidence of the celebration, Mary went to bed and shed one last tear for Johnny as she fell asleep close to Stan.

Chapter 26

Though the news in Asia and Europe told of an end to combat, it did not bring everyone home on the next available transport. Nor did it mean that basic training for those newer draftees was over.

From John P., San Diego, CA, August 19, 1945 – *Dear Stanley, I just decided to write you a letter now that the war is over, or did you know. I'm glad it is but I just finished reading the paper about the Navy's point system and according to that I might just as well forget about a lot of things I intended to do when I get out because it doesn't look like I'll be out for many moons to come. I may find myself in Japan yet and get to be so Asiatic you won't even know me. I could kind of reconcile myself if I got a little leave at least so I could get home and maybe see Joe, Steve and everybody else.*

Oh well I guess I never would amount to much anyway so I might as well do a good job of it since I'll probably be too damned old to have any incentive when I get out. Maybe I should have married some old sea hag and I could have had ten points. Judging by that point system a single guy just doesn't count. I guess it's the guys with kids that need all the breaks even if their old lady did draw a big allotment from the govt for several years and drawdown a salary in a defense plant amounting to about ten times as much as she was worth. All this sounds like a little bitching on my part and it is but that's what's on my mind and I might as well be truthful about it. I'll get over that though I guess and anyway I can thank God I'm alive and kicking and in pretty good health which means something to me at least. If anyone mentions four freedoms to me as long as I'm in this Navy, I'll bat him over the head.

Since the war finished we've been on a holiday routine. Plenty of liberty for everybody and nothing to do but muster in the morning and lie around in the sack which is good duty and suits me fine. I'm just plain disgusted and maybe it's just a passing mood but that's the way it is right now. At least while the war was on there was a purpose behind my being here even though everything wasn't always peaches and cream and the fact that we all had a job to do was consolation. But now that its over there's no sense to my being in the Navy because I'm only wasting time and if they don't lower the point system I guess I'll have a lot of it to waste. If Joe comes home and you send me a telegram they might give me a leave and I could go to Red Cross and borrow money for passage. But then, I'm probably just having a pipe dream so if I were you I wouldn't bet that I would get a leave even if everybody came home.

Friday is payday and I guess I'll go to L.A. with my buddy and we'll get crocked drinking to our future in the Navy. By the way Stanley, see if you can get some film some place now that the war is over. I'm going to try in L.A. Well Stanley, I guess that's enough of my troubles and you probably have enough of your own. I did forget to say that I certainly am glad the fighting is over so Steve, Carl and Alex never have to worry about getting their pants shot off. I used to think about that quite a lot and I guess that'll be off my mind now. If any of them do go over for occupation it won't be too bad, I don't think, outside of being there and putting in time.

I wish I could end by saying I'll be home for Christmas but even that is fantastic so if mom asks when I'll be home you can tell her I don't have the slightest idea. I guess that'll end this pretty lousy letter. If you don't hear from me for some time the reason'll be that there's also lately nothing to write about so don't think I flew the coop. John

The post-war world was shaping up to be as difficult for civilians in war-torn countries as it was during the conflict. The economies of most European nations were damaged as badly as many of the structures that once stood. The people of England, having been supplied with food and necessities for the home by the U.S. under the Lend-Lease Act, faced drastic cutbacks in these commodities due to Truman's decision to end Roosevelt's generous policy. Everywhere one looked in Europe, displaced families gathered what little they still had with hopes of returning home or possibly starting anew where they stood.

From Joe, 47th Field Hospital, Senigallia, Italy, September 1, 1945 – *Dear Stanley, How are you, I hope you Mary and your little trooper are in the best of health and may be with god's help we all will be together again shortly.*

I haven't wrote in a long time for one thing there isn't nothing to write about. I just got back from Austria and being back here in Southern Italy is no good for its always hot as hell, and just like the South in any country rotten. It was swell being up north for up toward Switzerland the snow was so deep the GI buses couldn't get through the Alp Mtns.

We were wearing heavy close and at night it shour was good sleeping but here all you do is sweat like hell. I hope we get out of here soon. I'm sick of Army life. I'd like to wear a pair of civilian shoes and pants for a change. They don't tell us much so all we can do is guess and hope someone hits the nail on the head. I only have one thought in mind that is home. Everyone that's been over a little time has the same thing in mind home sweet home.

How you doing with the beer drinking much. Your Pal Joe

The day after Joe wrote this letter, history was being made on the other side of the now-peaceful world. In the harbor of Tokyo Bay, more than 200 Allied military vessels dropped anchor; the sight was one the Japanese never conceived when they designed their plans for war to control Asia just a few years earlier. Aboard the battleship Missouri, representatives of the Japanese government and military tearfully signed the document stating that Japan was officially surrendering. General MacArthur, representing the United States and the United Nations as directed by President Truman, signed the papers and stated, "It is my earnest hope and, indeed, the hope of all mankind, that from this solemn occasion a better world shall emerge out of the blood and carnage of the past." September 2 was declared VJ (Victory in Japan) Day in the United States. And again, as in the weeks before, nations celebrated in the streets.

The days of walking hilly miles to visit his parents' house at 12 School Street were over for Stanley. The house there, originally Sands Point School House when it was built in the late 19th century, had been a multi-family residence since 1930 and all of the days that the Palaseks lived there. It was where Stanley and Mary spent their wedding night, and where several guests were said to have spent their night sleeping in the bushes surrounding the house that same evening. It was home to all of the Palasek boys for much of their lives. With Willie being the only one still living at home after Alex joined the service, paying rent on the large portion of that house was not in the senior Palaseks' best interest any longer. They moved to the third house from the railroad station on Bayview Avenue, a mere third of a mile from the front door of the Nielsen Building where Stanley and Mary resided on Main Street. The small but pleasant Dutch colonial style house had only one bathroom, but it would be sufficient. Joe's bride, Margaret, and her son, Joey, moved into the house to save money with hopes that Joe would return soon and they would have a place of their own.

For several weeks, Stanley painted most of the rooms in his parents' new home on Bayview Avenue and was sorry the project was coming to an end. It gave him time away from his apartment, which meant fewer arguments there, although those were no longer as angry as they had been a few short years ago. Perhaps peace was possible, even in their little world. Stanley would also miss the simple meals he was enjoying from his mother's kitchen. One of his favorite dishes, though, would soon be available more often thanks to the end of rationing: a simple boiled chicken, served with boiled potatoes.

Stanley's brother Carl was doing everything possible to be sent home after his brief months in the service, claiming a need to care for his son and what he explained as a pre-existing problem with his hands. Though he did not use either reason as an excuse to avoid the draft, he now desired to return home. But for the time being, he was stationed and waiting in Naples, Italy. Alex, home on leave for two weeks shortly after the war ended, was more than eager to pitch in with the work at his parents' house before returning to his next assignment at Camp Gordon outside of Augusta, Georgia. The camp was entrenched in America's Deep South and therefore named after Confederate Major General, John Brown Gordon. It was not necessarily the best destination for a "yankee" like Alex.

In the Japanese city of Yokohama, Iva Toguri (who, as noted earlier, was nicknamed by Americans as "Tokyo Rose") was captured and classified as a traitor, due to her anti-American radio broadcasts and her status as an American by birth. She would, over a period of several years, be tried and sentenced to 10 years in prison for her words over the radio, with which she called American soldiers "boneheads" and told them they should give up fighting. After her release, she lived as a stateless person in Chicago and was eventually pardoned by President Gerald Ford in 1976.

***From John P., San Diego, CA, September 5, 1945** – Dear Stanley, I got your letter yesterday but I went to a ball game last night so I didn't have time to answer it. As it is now it looks like I'm leaving this base and soon, sometime this month. It may be overseas as the scuttlebutt has it. Anyway it looks like I'll end up with a royal screwing. No leave, no nothing. I can tell you this much if it is for overseas my heart certainly isn't in it. I'll let you know when it happens.*

I told you before a couple times that I wouldn't write home for money but I guess I'll have to make a hypocrite of myself because I could use some right now. I didn't shoot crap if that is what you're thinking. I just have to buy some gear I need and also have to develop a lot of film. S-o-o-o suppose you ask mom if she'd send me $15 and I'm not going to make a habit of it either. See what you can do?

It's news to me about Carl getting out. I haven't heard from him in some time now or Joe or Steve either for that matter. I hope they all get out soon. I hope Alex had a good time on leave though I guess it would be pretty hard for him since nobody's around and he doesn't drink. Well, I guess that covers the situation. John

Despite the peace settlements, war in one form or the other was far from over. Information was being brought forth that numerous Soviet spy rings were operating in the United States and Canada, supplying sensitive documents to the U.S.S.R. The Cold War was commencing. After more than 30 years of control and occupation by the Japanese, a new occupation began in Korea. The now "liberated" nation was divided at the 38th latitude between a Soviet Union-controlled north and the U.S.-occupied south.

***From Alex, Fort Gordon, GA, September 7, 1945** – Dear Stan, I arrived here in Gordon 2:30 A.M. (we missed the bus* cause we wanted to). I haven't slept since Tuesday night [the 4th] when I was home. I didn't get a seat on the train until I was almost in Spartanburg, S.C., I sat in the aisle, but people passing up and down, so I stood all the way.

They woke the company up at 3:45 A.M. so we just got our stuff at 2:45 A.M. got in our fatigues ate chow and went on a 8 mi hike to fire 8 shots apiece on a range. Coming back it got so hot guys were passing out left and right there was only a few of us left that they got trucks and rode us in. The temperature was somewhere around 95° or 105°. If it wasn't for the sand that's in this camp it wouldn't be too bad. The food here is swell it's prepared so you can eat it and enjoy it at least. The cadre here don't know why we came to Gordon, Georgia, they're going to close this camp in a few weeks. A lot of Bn's [battalions] shut down long ago. We are doing the same thing we did at Camp Croft, it's all review and they don't know what the hell to do with us.

How is the house coming along? Don't Willie do anything? I guess that's all for now solong and God Bless You All, Your Pal and Brother. Alex

From Steve, Compiegne, France, September 9, 1945
– Dear Stan, Once again I'm scribbling you a few lines to let you know that I am well and getting along disgusted or should I say discouraged. Why, well I am idling as usual turning in equipment every day. Rumors are thick as molasses, so far none are ever true. This kind of life is worse than dodging bullets.

Before I go on with my gripin, thanks ever so much for the letters. Stan I don't write as often as I have been. I keep repeating my lines and I am sure you folks must feel bored with such scrawny lines. I am tired getting lazier by the day. I do play cards also see lots of American shows. I went on a tour of Lourds. There is where the picture was made, "The song of Bernadette." It's a shrine built in the side of a mountain. In the church 81 masses are going on at one time, I tell you folks it's beautiful. The cripple leave their crutches to walk again. The multitudes sing Ave Maria, everyone knows in Polish. Some day I will describe to you.

You don't know what is the matter with Carls hands, its too bad. He should have stayed at home where he belonged, he had his choice. I do wish him good luck, regardless of how he feels about me or you. Solong for now folks, god bless you, I hope to see you soon. Your Pal & Brother Steve

Vidkun Quisling was one of the early post-war leaders to be brought to justice for war crimes. Quisling had at one point been a Commander of the British Empire, but after the invasion of Norway by the Nazis he led a puppet government in Norway under the control of the Germans. He was found guilty of embezzlement, treason, and murder, and put to death by a firing squad. In Japan, Prime Minister Hideki Tojo, who was being held accountable for the attack on Pearl Harbor, knew that he was to be arrested and tried for war crimes. In an attempt to avoid such a trial, he tried to kill himself with a gun. Tojo failed and was treated by American surgeons. He would alternatively be tried and hanged before a third year had passed.

The efforts, heat, and dust of moving into a new home in the late summer, combined with concerns for her sons, had taken a toll on Marjanna Palasek. Alone most days as her husband and son Willie worked, she fell ill from exhaustion and respiratory issues. Stanley would take time as needed to see that she got to the family doctor until her health improved. With the end of gasoline rationing, Stanley was more than happy to take his mother anywhere she needed to go in his car when possible.

From Alex, Fort Gordon, GA, September 13, 1945 –
Dear Stan, How is mom? Is she okay now? I may not be here for the full nine weeks. Stan could you please tell William to pick up my film it's in Bayles Pharmacy under the name Palasky. These good for nothings made em get a G.I. hair cut boy if mom saw me now she'd disown me. Also tell mom to send me my brown loafer shoes and a couple of white undershorts and T shirts, there's quite a few of them home.

How's the house coming along. I hope maybe someday I can repay you for all you have done for mom and all of us Stan. You may think I'm talking through my hat but someday when this is finished up and I'm out I hope I can repay you.

Boy its been raining all day and we been in it were sloppy wet all the way through. Hell I'm disgusted if they don't send us over soon I'll wind up in the guard house. The chicken shit we take in this place I could rip every damn Sergeant apart with my bare hands. Most of them are rebels and they love to ride our ass. I probably won't write for a while so if you don't hear from me, please no letter to the chaplain. Best write to the brig I'll most likely wind up there. Gets pretty tiresome sitting around the barracks. I guess that's all the troubles I've got solong Stan. Your Brother, Alex P.S. How is mom, is she better?

Chapter 27

When WW II began, many of America's activities changed. Baseball, the great American pastime, had been reduced to using players of lesser skill while professional athletes enlisted in various service branches. Now that the war was over, it appeared as if baseball would return to full strength in 1946. Players such as Bob Feller, Joe DiMaggio and Ted Williams, perennial all-stars, were among the thousands from all levels of professional baseball who left the game to serve their country. Not all of the ballplayers returned to their fans. Over 100 of these men did not come home alive.

Many of America's industries were changing as well. New companies had emerged with the intent to supply troops with the necessary tools and components to win the war. Companies that were already established changed their goals or production systems to meet the needs of the war effort, recognizing that their usual products might not be as in-demand (or necessary) during wartime. The need for war equipment outweighed the need for the production of tools to hit a horsehide ball. The Hillerich & Bradsby Company in Louisville, Kentucky, had for decades been a prime manufacturer of baseball bats. Their bat production slowed during WW II, and was replaced in part by the production of wooden gunstocks and tank pins. With the return of many of the sport's heroes, H&B was one example of a company that survived the production adjustment well. Others retooled for peacetime or closed their doors as they were not able to adapt to post-war production. Yet there was still work to be done by servicemen at home and abroad.

***From Alex, Fort Gordon, GA, September 22, 1945* –**
Dear Stan, How are you, how's mom pop and everybody? Well it's another one of those hot days here again but I'm glad I'm through training. They pulled our company in off the filed today and this time it's the thing we been waiting for. I'm going back on the high seas only a one-way ticket for a couple of years. They are issuing us all sorts of gear we are restricted to the company area. Where we go I don't know its anybody's guess.

Our Sergeant saw our shipping orders and we go to Fort Ord, California. I think we leave this Thursday or Friday. Well Stan I suppose that's all for now solong and God Bless You All. Tell Willie take care of my junk for me, I'll write to him later, solong sport. Your Pal and Brother, Alex

Six days later, Alex was aboard yet another military train for the long ride westward. As usual with such transportation, the ride was bumpy and engine fumes made the air hard to breathe as they rode across hot, humid southern states to California.

From Steve, Compiegne, France, September 23, 1945
– I am sorry for writing you folks such sob stories as to my predicament. But a fellow must tell some one of his troubles and I feel better. I have 60 points and I believe I will be moving in Nov. or maybe sooner depends on orders and how they come in. Three hundred low pointers have gone to Germany, Army of occupation. I know definitely I am going home it's this damn waiting that gets my blood boiling. I can only say my battle stars have helped me stave off the army of occupation. I believe I would go nuts if caught up in that lineup. I am feeling fine, playing cards, eat and sleep as long as I please. Signing off with best wishes and regards to all and I hope to see you all soon. Remain your pal & brother, Steve

Japan was now recovering not only from a losing effort in the war, but the sudden death of almost 4,000 people from a typhoon. In India, the English army had worn out its welcome rapidly once the war ended; leaders Mohandas Gandhi and Jawaharlal Nehru instructed the British soldiers to leave. In the United States, it was time for the World Series and the Chicago Cubs were indeed going to be in it once again. Local Chicago tavern owner Billy Sianis thought it would be nice to bring his goat to game four of the series, but the goat and Billy were ejected from the park —even though they both had tickets to the game. Before he left, Billy was said to have put a hex on the Cubs for their denial of his goat's entry. The Cubs proceeded to lose the series in seven games to the Detroit Tigers. As of the date of this writing, the Cubs have never won a league championship, their ticket to play in the World Series.

Stanley and Mary were doing their best to avoid conflict as their young boy was growing older. But tensions were beginning to rise at Stanley's work, which would often find their way to the apartment on Main Street. Prior to the war, CBS was primarily a radio network that experimented in local broadcasts in New York. As the priorities for technology and men increased during the war, less importance was placed upon television technology and a number of men left CBS to join the service. Now, with those same men returning home, CBS was reviewing how to reincorporate those men back into the CBS family. Rumors circulated about the company laying off recent hires to make room for previous employees. The uncertainty raised many questions and tempers in the halls of the network. Stanley, never feeling committed to any one employer at this point of his young life, was preparing himself for bad news while also keeping his eyes open for other possibilities at the rival NBC and Dumont television networks. He had rapidly risen to be a master technician and was involved in developing new technologies for CBS, such as the transmission of color broadcasts. His skills would take him far in the field of television.

From John P., San Diego, CA, October 3, 1945 – *Dear Stanley, I guess its about time I write. I owe Carl a letter, I guess also Steve and I haven't heard from Joe in a coon's age. I hope he really is on his way home this time.*

Everything with me is still fouled up like Hogan's goat. I still don't know what the score is. They are shipping guys out to sea every week and I'm eligible but that doesn't bother me much since I'd just as soon be putting time in in Japan or China as here. How many points have I got? Well, I don't have enough to buy a secondhand steak so I'm not giving civilian life much thought. I have a grand total of 31 points. They discharged a few men from here with three kids and I guess next they'll get rid of guys with two etc. Who cares anyway? I'm sure I don't.

Because this base is all fouled up they decided to pay us once a month. Which means I'll get paid in November some time and I guess I'm supposed to sit on my stern and twiddle my thumbs in the meantime. As it happens I'm flat broke.

Well, the nights here are pretty cool nowadays but the days are hot. The temp has been around 100° just like in Africa. There are quite a few forest fires around Dago, which have been going on for some time now. At night you can see the glare in the mountains and smoke billows up like the pictures of Nagasaki. Too bad the damned town doesn't catch fire since it's no damned good anyway.

Nowadays I have a crew of swabbies to boss around. I'm in charge of repairing a bunch of landing craft. It's pretty crazy work since we burn up the good ones for scrap and repair the damaged ones. As it is they have thousands of them around here rotting away which will never be used but they're all nuts around here anyway so I don't let anything like that worry me. It doesn't take any brains to fix up these barges so I get by even if I do have to listen to these lame brained leftenants. I still think I know more about shipfitting then they ever knew.

Well, I guess that does it so I'll knock off. Hope this finds you shipshape and taking your share of good spirits now and then. Let me know if Joe should come home suddenly. John

Stanley's longtime friend and fellow musician, Eddie Kaspar, returned safely from Europe. He told Stan in a letter how he barely missed grave injury or worse after the war ended. A fellow soldier on his boat crossing the Atlantic was playing with a pistol that he chose to bring back to the States on his bunk. Ammunition was prohibited for the men on the voyage, but many disregarded the rule. The soldier's pistol went off and tragically killed a fellow soldier as he lay in his bunk near Eddie, possibly dreaming of being safely at home after surviving numerous battles. Eddie had no desire for guns after being required to carry and use them against others, but he did bring back a German Luger he salvaged and sold it to Stanley. Eddie did have an interest in a shortwave radio receiver that Stanley was selling, but getting it to his new assigned base in California would be impossible.

From Eddie Kaspar, Camp San Luis Obispo, CA, October 4, 1945 – Dear Stan, Received your letter and was glad to hear from you. I have been pretty busy here and getting ready to be shipped out to some camp, I hope its near home. I sure would like to have that radio, but when I get out of this lousy Army, I would like to buy one, maybe I could get one pretty cheap. I've had about two weeks of training on television now, and its really the big thing in the future. I bet they really keep you busy in CBS. Well Stan I'll close now and be waiting for a few lines from you. Your pal Eddie

From Alex, San Francisco, CA, October 4, 1945 – Dear Stan, I arrived in California last night and so far I'm all right. They woke us up at 5:30 A.M. which isn't so bad. We had chow which by the way is the best I have eaten in the Army, no kidding the food is swell. They then sent us to the dispensary and gave us two shots, a check up, clothing issue and really put us through the mill. I may be here only from 7 to 10 days then it's the boat ride.

How's everybody at home, mom, pop, Stas, and Mary. Well Stan I guess that's all for now solong. God Bless All of You. Your Pal and Brother Alex

Chapter 28

The lives and destinations of many American servicemen in Europe were in flux. Joe, having acquired more than a sufficient number of points, spent a week in a staging area before he was able to board a westbound ship from Italy back to the United States. Steve watched as friends were shifted to temporary assignments where their presence was needed more, and expected such a change of venue for himself. Mary's brother, Adam, already received his reassignment and welcomed it for the change in scenery and climate further south in Europe, as the autumn days were changing from warm and sunny to damp and cold in Germany. John Palasek continued to wait for something to happen that would end his residence in San Diego. Alex, having moved north to Fort Lawton in the Seattle hills overlooking Puget Sound, was now one step closer to shipping out, but to where, he did not know.

From Alex, Fort Lawton, WA, October 21, 1945 –
Dear Stan, Well I moved again I'm a few miles from Seattle Wash. and this camp is really nice. It's an old C.C.C. camp it's spread out over the mountains. They tell us they have quite a bit of rain, we came in 2:00 this A.M. and it was raining like hell. The food is swell, the cook's are German P.W.'s let me tell you they can really cook.

One bunch came in this morning got a shot and they are going bye bye tomorrow. I may be here only a few days but if you write the address on this envelope will be the same from now until I get home. "1947" maybe. I'm still with the same bunch of guys we stick close together and when it comes to details one of us usually lands in charge of the group so you can bet your ass we don't do a hell of a lot. The rebels get the workout. We can keep the lights on as long as we want to last night, I should say this morning I darn near knocked the hell out of a bunch of rebels they decided to play poker when the guys want to sleep. By golly there are only a few of us New Yorkers here but we sure tamed down a bunch full of rebels. Women here are a dime a dozen there's dances every other night that's where most of the guys are, being I don't bother I decided to write home, I get pretty used to sitting around by myself, only when we go to town, we go as a bunch. I'll be out of here before the week is over. As yet we don't know where the hell we are going I hope I don't get stuck in Alaska or some frozen hole. Stan when I get to a decent place I'll write for my civilian shoes so tell mom if she could have them fixed up that is when I ask for them.

I heard from John once I was wishing I could see him but I'll have to wait now. So Carl won't answer your mail, nice guy, no shit I'm the youngest in the family but for someone who isn't out of his diapers he takes the cake, he holds grudges why? I know you never crossed his path, maybe someday he'll come down off his high horse and live with the "common people." Solong God Bless You All, Your Pal and Brother, Alex

Post-war technology and advances were briskly moving forward, many of which were inspired by technology developed for the war. Liquid-fueled rockets were being designed and demonstrated as possible ways to send geo-synchronous satellites into Earth's orbit. Simple innovative devices such as the clock radio became available and a ballpoint pen was now being marketed for the outrageous price of nearly $10 at Gimbels in New York City.

Justice was being swiftly served as trials were held for war crimes in Nuremburg, France, and Norway. In hopes of a more peaceful future, the United Nations was chartered and would soon meet in the Sperry Gyroscope complex in Lake Success, New York, where Stanley was working when the war began.

Alex Palasek was now assigned to the 4th Brigade of the 713th Engineers Combined Operations Forces, with its yellow on blue shoulder insignia and motto "Put 'Em Across." An amphibious force of the Army, they were trained in how to perform in combat when landing on foreign beaches and proceeding inland. It was their duty to be sure that personnel and equipment were delivered on shore safely. Similar to his duties in the Merchant Marine, he was also trained to maintain and assure the proper operation of the ship and the activities of the men on board. In a post-war world, monitored occupation of Japan and inventory of seized weapons were now to be a key part of his responsibilities.

From Alex, Port of Seattle, October 25, 1945 – *Dear Stan, I won't be able to mail this letter immediately. I'm a part of an advance party on this transport we're on ahead of the rest of the troops to direct and keep order. All we do is stand guard 4 on 16 off. This is a new ship, clean and it's a navy job, that means three meals a day. I guess we won't be going over for any great length of time. They navy treats us all right, there are thirty some odd marines here also, "sea going bell hops" do they think they are king stuff. Where I'm going I'll see the results of a bomb that was unpopular with the Japs, Nagasaki.*

How is everything at home, how is everybody, is Willie still sick, is he still at Plandome? I suppose the house is done. Well Stan I guess I'll cut this short Solong and God Bless You All, Your Brother, Alex

As October was ending, Stanley had one primary desire on his mind: that his brothers might all be home to share Christmas together this year. With Alex leaving the West Coast for Asia, his brother, John "hanging around" in San Diego, Steve stuck in Germany, and Joe out of contact for weeks, it seemed like a mere pipe dream to Stanley. He stayed close to his family and parents who were now around the corner with his brother Willie and Joe's wife, Margaret, and prayed for the best for all. Although he and Steve wrote often, Steve's wife, Stephanie, hadn't written to Steve in weeks. Being naturally closer to her own family, news traveled slowly from the Wrobel home up the hill to Main Street in Port Washington. Stanley had only found out recently that while painting her own apartment, Stephanie had an acute gallbladder pain and fell off a stepladder. Stephanie was taken to the hospital where surgery led to an infection, which nearly took her young life. Stan wrote to Steve to tell him about Stephanie, believing that Steve already knew; he did not. The hurt and frustrations were taking a toll on the man who had once written proudly of being a good soldier in "this man's army."

From Steve, Compiegne, France, October 31, 1945 –
Dear Stan, Thanks for the information pertaining to my wife. I haven't heard from her in one month now, I was worried and you have brought me the news as to what happened. I knew something was wrong, I feel bad and low as is due to this long drawn out waiting period. I am angry at my wife and her family, for not wiring me, I could have been home by her side. I know, because minor emergency cases come up and the men are flown home providing they have the points. I have points and eligible for discharge Nov 1st. I am not blaming my wife much because of her condition. But them at the house I feel so damn low it is not funny. I'll just take a slow walk and lose myself, I guess it doesn't matter. Who cares.

I immediately took your letter to my Commanding Officer, showing him facts. Trying to obtain an emergency furlough. He sympathized with me. The advice I got is they want proof. By that I mean a wire or cable sent through the Red Cross telling my C.O. that my presence is wanted, explaining the case. Then I would most likely be flown home with top priority. I know my wife can't move to follow through. One must get through to the Red Cross. Still my chance is good to go if she does this. I wish she would do this I would be discharged in no time.

Stan I don't know when I'll get home, that war ship gag is camouflage. Where are the 4000 ships we had during war time. In commercial use I know and so do all the rest. They got us here the job is over and now they say its ship shortage. What they are doing is discouraging the men in order to join the army again. They can blow it out their political hats.

What burns me up is, that I am eligible for discharge and the Captain keeps telling me I'll be home for Christmas. How can I be, the shipping is tied up in the states, longshoremen on strike, the limeys are taking their largest ships off the line, the dirty bastards after all we did for them, I am so disgusted its really not funny. Anyway I hope I can make home by 1947, seems like never. I am so close to the gangplank yet so far. But I keep going to the movies, have my ration of American beer, smoke like a chimney.

So long Stan, god bless you and thanks a million, I am sorry to write like this, But I can't help it. I remain your Pal & Brother, Steve

Chapter 29

An early winter was gradually approaching the Port Washington peninsula and the rest of the Northeast in November 1945. Mary's walks with her son to the park or the town dock to watch the boats were becoming less frequent. Stanley's hours at work, in order to accomplish more and hopefully retain his position, were getting longer as the days grew shorter.

Internationally, the United States Senate approved a measure to join the United Nations, thus becoming a force in the various assemblies and sub-organizations of this new governing body. The world was surprised by the news that General George S. Patton — who had fought, commanded, and survived dozens of battle campaigns throughout his life in the military — had died. His staff car and a military truck collided while he was traveling for a hunting trip in Germany. Within two weeks, he succumbed to grave injuries.

Patton was laid to rest, per his request, at the military cemetery in Luxembourg City, near the bodies of many men of the 3rd Army who fought under him.

Problems were beginning to heat up in what was to become the Cold War. The U.S. did not want Germany or the Soviet Union to advance in the use of rockets for weaponry or other "peaceful" purposes. The U.S. government set up a lab at Castle Gould, once a part of the many Gold Coast estates in the Port Washington village of Sands Point. Here, Operation Paperclip was begun to bring scientific minds together. More than 80 German scientists and engineers were given the opportunity to meet in the United States in order to further develop technology that the United States had seen in limited use during the war. The scientists included Werner Von Braun, a man whose concepts and designs in aerospace technology would, in time, be held in high regard amongst all Americans as the space race progressed. Alex Palasek found the post-war mood in Japan to be just as chilly as many Americans' feelings regarding the use of German engineers.

From Alex, Japan, November 2, 1945 – Hi Stan, How's everything out your way? Well, so far I haven't done a damn thing here. Everything here is starting to go G.I. inspection but that's only because there is nothing for us to do. The 2nd and 3rd Brigades of this regiment are going home, this the 4th Brigade is going to be the only one left overseas for occupation.

The Jap climate is much like N.Y. but now its cold as a b_____d. We went looking for a pool room last night and wound up in a billiards academy the Japs play 4 ball billiards so we quit there. One night another fellow and I walked into a Japanese schoolroom and had a hell of a time teaching them English. They catch on pretty darn fast the guy who is teaching them is a Jap he spent 34 yrs in California and speaks it fluently. He brings us beer and apples they'll do anything for a soldier. The rumors are getting better as to going to the Philippines. I hope so but if we set up there it means basic all over again.

Any snow yet, bet its cold there. Any news of John, Joe, Steve or Carl, or is he and his wife still on a high horse? It would be nice for mom if one could at least be home for Christmas I suppose that's all for now solong. God Bless All of you Your Pal and Brother, Alex MERRY CHRISTMAS in case I don't write later.

Young Alex was not to be in one Japanese location for any length of time, it seemed. Soon after his arrival, he was moving from one coastal port to another.

From Alex, At Sea Near Japan, November 3, 1945 –
Dear Stan, I guess it doesn't make sense writing out here in the middle of the ocean but maybe I can get some writing done out here. I'm still a week out of Nagasaki and it's the same old weather again storm's rain, altogether it's a pretty lousy trip. Nagasaki is only a staging area so I'll wind some place in Tokyo maybe. I sure wish they would put us some place to stay for awhile we have been on the hop since I came back from my furlough in August.
    Its cold as hell on this ocean, the ship is hot so I got a cold, sore throat and a headache, it's so damn monotonous. Tomorrow we cross the international dateline today is Friday, we ship Saturday so tomorrow is Sunday. Well Stan there isn't anything I can think of so I'll close for now, solong and God Bless All of You. Your Pal and Brother, Alex

Aware that there would be intense fighting and struggles while he was stationed in Europe, Steve knew it would be a difficult task to fight and lead as a good soldier; but he proudly served as he felt was his duty. Now, he was fighting a battle of politics and paper and could barely stand the ordeal.

From Steve, Compiegne, France, November 5, 1945 –
Dear Stan, According to what you say Joe is really on the way home and it sure is about time, it really drives a guy crazy sweating out this waiting line. As for Alex, maybe he won't have to leave for overseas I hope not even though the war is over I am quite sure no soldier could feel right in these god forsaken countries.
    As for myself Stan the situation is rather dark. I am not happy, I couldn't be any more. Seems like everything I ever planned, hoped for is shattered. One reason I am blue and now quite sure, I will spend another Christmas here. I hate to even think of it. Yes the

war ships are here, what good is it, they are bluffing themselves in Washington, not us, we are wise to this slow motion redeployment. Because the brass wants to hold men as long as possible, without men there would be no brass. I am disgusted. We wrote the different Senators to take up the fight for us. What happened to the 4,000 ships we had during the war. Out for world trade, the hell with the G.I.s no money in that. Speaking of money, I don't know the value of it anymore and don't care. My second misfortune, to my sorrow is the illness that struck my wife down so suddenly. A double operation to date costing $550 dollars which proves to me, money isn't everything. Why should all these things happen to us, we never hurt any one, I guess it was the hand of god. My wife I know feels the same, feels bitter towards the world, I understand. Still I could had been home in 24 hours, if proper steps were taken through the Red Cross. Maybe she didn't want me to know fearing I would worry. The world at times is so cruel, I really am baffled. Nothing matters any more I am just living from day to day. I shouldn't be writing like this Stan, But what can I say, or do, so many miles away, idling and wasting valuable time.

Well folks, those are wheels of fortune, ones that keep the world guessing, cheering some and breaking others, like a roulette wheel. With best wishes and regards to all, I remain your Pal & Brother, Steve Some day I will see you all (Be good.)

After months of being based close to the vessels he was working on for the Navy at the Port of San Diego, John Palasek was relocated. His new bunk was in a much less likely place for an able seaman to be located: the desert and mesas to the east of San Diego at Camp Elliott. Named for a Marine Corps leader, the camp was primarily a receiving station of the U. S. Naval Training and Distribution Center (TADCEN) where sailors going to or returning from the Pacific would find themselves prior to their next destination, be it home or another assignment.

From John P., Camp Elliott, San Diego, CA, November 6, 1945 – Dear Stanley, Well as you can see by my address I have a new home now. This place is about 15 miles outside of 'Dago' out in the hills away from civilization. I'm living in a crummy old hut, and I mean crummy. Even in Africa I lived cleaner than this. There are 21 guys in the hut besides me so it's really crammed. I sure hope I don't have to stay here very long. They gave us a physical this morning and we have to go through a lot of other crap like night vision tests, etc.

As things stand now I am subject to any kind of draft they put me on so I might get some sea duty in sooner than I thought. The way they look at it is if you haven't enough points to get out they do anything they please with you. There are two big drafts leaving for overseas I guess Monday and if I don't get on one of these then I guess I'll be stuck in this hole for a while. I still can't get a leave and I guess I'll go on getting a royal screwing like I've been getting ever since I came out here.

To me, the worst part about moving around is not getting any mail. When I've got a lot of time on my hands I'd just as soon write letters but after a while it gets like writing to myself. The only thing I'm interested in right now is finding out if Joe is home or not. It sure would be nice if he got home for Christmas. I hope you're in shape to drink a few kegs of beer with him like he always said he'd do when he came home.

Boy, I thought the Repair Base was big but this place has got it beat for size. You can stand at one end of the street and look down it and see barracks as far as the eye can distinguish. I don't know who you have to know to live in a barracks but I guess you have to really rate. Well Stanley, I'll knock this off and get outside and get in the chowline. I imagine I'll lose weight here because the chow stinks. Hope Joe is home when you get this and I don't think a telegram would get me a leave but send it and I'll try. John

Chapter 30

Life, for many Americans, was gradually returning to the way it was prior to the war. Every day, soldiers and sailors returned home, though not as swiftly as many would have hoped once the war concluded. Food staples such as coffee, sugar and meats were becoming increasingly available at prices that were not inflated due to demand, scarcity and "whatever the market could handle." The entire nation, as with much of the world, was beginning to feel like the enormous weight of wartime was becoming lighter day by day. However, those servicemen and women who had not yet returned continued to hope that they would hear from friends and family in letters, nearly as much as they desired to be back home with them.

From Steve, Compiegne, France, November 14, 1945 – *Dear Stan, Thanks ever so much for the letter I received this day. I now understand the situation as it is back home. Knowing that my wife is out of the hospital eases my mind. I have been worried and lost weight but I finally received a letter from her. Yes I can see the point that she didn't let me know that I wouldn't worry. I had no mail from Steph for a month until now. I at once had that certain feeling, telling me something was wrong. Well, all I can say is thank god.*

Well folks I am writing you for the last time from this town of Compeigne, as the seven twenty fourth is being deactivated here. All low point men are going to Germany. I am going to South France and the port of Marseilles. How long I will be there I don't know, I am not excited, still the change of scenery will do me good. Seems like a step closer to home, right on the water's edge. Keep writing. When your mail starts to return you can be sure I am on the way. Believe me I am fed up. I came in like all the rest to do my bit. The war is over and I am ready to go home. I have been ready for ages now. The peacetime army has its good points, providing one can keep his nose clean.

So Carl is home on furlough, well well that is also a bit of news, I wonder how he is doing. There really isn't much I can add to this scrawny letter of mine, so take care folks, God Bless you and here's hoping I may see you soon. Your Pal & Brother Steve

The Palasek family's prayers since the war began started to be answered in mid-November. Private First Class Joseph Palasek showed up at his parents' home on Bayview Avenue two days after calling his bride, Margaret, to tell her he was packing his gear at a base in the U.S. for the final time. Margaret had been nervously waiting, along with her husband's parents and Joe's brother, Willie, not knowing exactly what train would bring his arrival. The house, which sat across the street from the Long Island Railroad yard, was a wonderful sight for an exhausted soldier who had experienced war's hell for months on end. Joe's smile as he entered the house from November's chill radiated the warmth that only a family, safely reunited, could feel. Some 3,000 miles to the west, his brother John was about to set off to sea in the direction of his younger brother Alex.

From John, Camp Elliott, San Diego, CA, November 21, 1945 – *Dear Stanley, Well it turned out as I thought it would as far as my leaving here, I mean. I got a draft today and by the looks of things I'll get some sea duty in. The ship I got is the S.S. Talbot, DM #28 [Author's note: This is an error by John. The ship was actually the S.S. Tolman. The S.S. Talbot was decommissioned the previous month.] which is a Destroyer mine sweeper. Guess I'll be busy sweeping Tokyo Bay or some place for quite some time. I'm supposed to get the ship tomorrow which is Thanksgiving Day, of course. I imagine it's down here in San Diego someplace. My buddy from Long Island went aboard the C.V.E. Kalinin Bay yesterday so I was the last of the old gang to get a ship.*

I guess I won't get the mail situation squared away for some time. Also, I guess I can forget about trying to get home and I kind of figured I wouldn't get any leave as I wrote you before. I hope Joe is home by now. If he isn't, he sure has a slow ship. A friend wrote and said maybe Joe was swimming home. Well I guess that's all there is to this letter. I'll write you again soon as I get the score. John

Thanksgiving Day, November 22, 1945, brought more than the usual joy for many Americans. That week, The Saturday Evening Post featured one of its customary covers by the celebrated artist Norman Rockwell. It depicted a scene that many families were fortunate enough to associate with due to the war's end: a young American soldier in full uniform, sitting and peeling potatoes — something he may have done many times over the past years, particularly when assigned "K.P." or "Kitchen Patrol" in basic training. But the young man on the cover is grinning as he sits next to his mother, who smiles at her son with a peeler in her hand. Such a moment may have been similar to one that the Palasek family would cherish with Joe being home, even though four sons were still away. For the Rykowski parents, the photo may not have endeared itself to them as much. Though their boys Ollie and Adam were no longer in harm's way, they were nonetheless away from home and memories of their son, John, came to their minds and hearts yet again. Still, the day was to be one of gratitude for most Americans as the feast was to be larger than years past with the end of strict rationing. Even the Macy's Thanksgiving Day parade, with its enormous helium-filled balloons, had returned to the avenues of Manhattan after four years of strict helium shortages to reserve it for government use.

From Alex, Nagoya, Japan, November 27, 1945 –
Dear Stan, How are you, How's Mary + Stas? This city was the most heavily bombed city in Japan, it's leveled completely to the ground. The Mitsubishi airplane factory was in this city and it can't be recognized as a plane factory anymore. They are blowing up all Jap guns, ammo everything. They cut up the Jap's atom smasher. I've been assigned to an engine platoon, so I'll get a chance to learn Diesel Mechanics. This outfit is amphib's like Johnny is, and do the same job. There isn't as much chicken shit either as we had when I was with the infantry.

The is quite a slew of Polacks in this outfit, I don't hang out with any of them, also a bunch of WOPs. The fellows in the motor pool where I was told me how brave these guys talk now but in Lingayen Gulf, Philippines they were the worst chicken shit bunch that there was. Now we are taking inventory on the equipment here then they say we are going to the Hawaiian Islands or the Philippines. So far I haven't had any mail since Oct. 25. It's all tied up somewhere in one of these army post offices.

Well Stan I guess that's all for now I'll sign off so until I write again solong and God Bless You. Your Pal and Brother Alex

In Port Washington, Joe was happy to be home with Margaret and his son, but he realized that he was going to have to find a job to support his family — a task that would not be easy in a post-war economy. Every morning, Joe would go around the corner to the stationery store on the corner of Main Street and Haven Avenue for copies of the Long Island Press and Newsday in hopes that something worthwhile could be found in the classified ads. Day after day, he kept his disappointment to himself and his hopes high. On the weekends, he looked forward to the chance to spend time with his brother Stan and his wife. Their young boys, Joey and Stanley, would play together and the men would share a few beers and talk. Searching for work was not about to put much stress upon Joe – especially in comparison to what he had experienced overseas.

Chapter 31

From John P., Hawaii, November 30, 1945 – *Dear Stanley, Guess I better write some more letters while I have time to. Since we pulled in here yesterday I've been busy as hell fixing this, that and the other. We took on more fuel today and we're going out a few miles to make a speed run and gunnery practice also to drop some depth charges. Then we come back again and tie up for a while. I rate liberty tomorrow but I imagine there'll be a lot of repairs to do when they get through firing. I want to go see what Honolulu looks like and get a few beers. It's been about a month since I've been on any kind of a binge so any kind of beer will taste good. We're pulling out for Japan Monday. So all that scuttlebutt about us getting off is a lot of baloney. Guess I'd like to see that son of a bitch Hirohito anyway. Hope they don't drop any of those atom bombs anywhere near us because I'd hate to find myself at sea with no water beneath us.*

Most of the officers aboard seem to be pretty good Joes which helps to make things a little more endurable. Guess a lot of them are in the same fix I'm in and would just as soon be out. I'm enclosing a clipping from one of the local papers which proves what politics can do. Take note of who wrote it though. That takes the cake allright.

Wish I knew where Alex was and if he is in Japan maybe I'd run across him, who knows? But then I guess it's just not my luck as usual. This will have to be all for now I'll write again before we pull out. John

Martin Feinstein, a 23-year-old Technician Fourth Grade in the Army, wrote the article John referenced. Tech 4s, or T/4s, were skilled military personnel who were considered, as were Sergeants, to be non-commissioned officers and received increased salary. Feinstein was assigned as a writer for the Stars and Stripes newspaper, which was distributed to the military. His article, entitled "Senator's Son, With 18 Points, Ordered Stateside by Navy," caused a considerable stir both amongst servicemen and civilians when it was republished in the Honolulu Advertiser and elsewhere. The article describes the unusual reassignment of Navy Seaman 2nd class Paul T. Stewart who, according to a letter sent to The Stars and Stripes, "was bragging to all hands about his connections." At this time, Navy personnel were not being reassigned to stateside duty until they had 18 months overseas and accumulated 38 points. However, young Stewart, the fortunate son of Tennessee Senator Tom Stewart, was ordered to return in a letter that was said not to be typical of protocol. Stewart was to be reassigned to the Naval training site in Norfolk, Virginia. According to the article, someone of Stewart's time and points would typically be either reassigned elsewhere overseas or sent to a forward base in the country where he was stationed. The newly appointed commanding officer of the amphibious group in Waipo, Hawaii, Lieutenant V.A. Wade, stated with resentment in the article that, "Had I known this sooner, I would have sent him to a forward area." This was the beginning of a wave of such letters from Senators to return certain favored recruits stateside prior to their accumulation of the normal number of months overseas or points be they family, friends or sons of constituents. The somewhat bold exposé by T/C 4 Feinstein in Stars and Stripes fortunately did not harm his future, as he went on to become one of the founders of The John F. Kennedy Center for the Performing Arts. Mr. Feinstein sought the best for all, from servicemen to artists, for many successful years.

Though WW II was over, the world was not at peace. Indonesia had declared its independence from the Netherlands in 1945 and the beleaguered Dutch military struggled to maintain control of the area, considering it as a part of Dutch East India. The British, previously a controlling nation in the region, came in to attempt to regain a Western presence. Rebellions would last several years, pulling forces of many nations into this small region.

Nearly four years had passed since the devastating Japanese attack on Pearl Harbor. It was not long after that attack that the port was again an active base of operations for the American Pacific fleet, even though the ships Arizona, Oklahoma, and Utah still lay partially or completely beneath the tropical waters where they sank. The U.S. government was now investigating how such an attack could have occurred without warning, or if there were warning signs that were not properly investigated prior to the attack. For young John Palasek, having only seen the damp grey of Wales, the arid desert of Tunisia while overseas, and the Port of San Diego, the tropical annexed U.S. Territory of Hawaii was a very unfamiliar sight.

From John P., Pearl Harbor, HI, November 29, 1945 – *Dear Stanley, Well, here I am in Pearl Harbor. We tied up at 5 o'clock today which is exactly six days from the day we left San Diego. On the way over I heard that they're going to take on a whole new crew here and let all the guys off who'll have enough points to get out by February. I'll find out how true this is soon enough. I guess if I get off here I'll probably have a hell of a long wait to get a ship back home. All this is pretty screwy to me, I mean taking guys from the States and bringing then all the way out here and switching crews. Oh well, I shouldn't worry, it's a little late for that.*

Coming in to tie up we passed all those places where the damage was done and you'd never think a bomb had dropped here to look at it. The airfields are jammed with planes and there are more ships of all types in here than I ever saw before. The harbor lies between two mountain ranges and it's sort of like a bottle neck for ships since it's a narrow channel which leads out to sea. It's a wonder to me they didn't do more damage than they did.

From the sea the island sure looks beautiful and doesn't resemble any shoreline in the Atlantic that I've seen. I haven't been ashore yet to take a look around but I will as soon as I get paid which will be in two days. Of course I'll have to see Waikiki beach they all brag about back in the states. Bet there are as many whores here as anyplace even San Diego. Not that I want any part of them because I'd rather get drunk then pay good money for a dose of foreign clap.

    At one time I used to get a kick out of traveling but somehow I lost interest along the way some place. Distance doesn't mean much to me and a couple thousand miles more or less adds up to the number of days it takes the get there. One thing good about sailing these days is that you don't have to worry about showing any lights for fear of subs and stuff like that. We had general quarters every day which is a Navy custom since this is a man o' war. It's a destroyer minelayer not a sweeper as I probably wrote you. It has six five inch guns for the main battery. They're in pairs on two turrets, forward and one aft. If I were to write this before or rather a few months ago while the war was still on I'd be shot for treason or something. But here I am doing it right in Pearl Harbor too.

    I hear a guy croaking over the radio about the Limeys fighting in Java. What we ought to do is go over there and help the Javanese knock off some of those limey bastards that have been controlling them all the time. What the hell good is that United Nations bullshit which is supposed to prevent wars. Why in hell do they let the limeys keep fighting. I guess if you got a membership in the United Nations Clinic you can step all over anybody who isn't – Batshit!!

    While they're investigating what happened at Pearl Harbor maybe I could get a job to help them out as a committee of one. I'm right here and they're in Washington so what the hell do they know about it with their long-range calculations. When the Japs came everybody was probably busy shacking up with some local whore and they got caught with their pants down – some joke, eh?

    Well I still haven't gotten any mail so I guess it will be Christmas before I do. What with the warm weather here, I guess Christmas will be just another day on the calendar. I sure can pick some peculiar places to be on Christmas. What the heck, its nice and warm here and you don't have to freeze your ass off like you do back home about this time. Yeah. I know it sounds like sour grapes but I might as well look at it that way as any other.

    Well, I guess that's all I have to offer after six whole days away from the states. My, my, and I'm not even homesick. Amazing isn't it. So I guess I'll put this letter in a bottle and hope it drifts *through the Panama Canal alright so it'll get to the east coast. You do the same when you answer it and I'll get it by the time I get home some time. What? Another leave? John*

Chapter 32

No one on Long Island was surprised when winter arrived as an unwelcome force in 1945, as it was every year. Yet somehow, the winter sky did not appear to be as steely grey as it had in the past. The north wind seemed to be more of a crisp tingle on your cheeks and nose than a heavy, cold, wet rag pressed against your face. Knowing your loved ones were at home (or, hopefully, soon to be home), safe from the weapons of enemies, made the season feel more bearable than previous winters. The change in character was slow and somewhat restrained in its acceptance by many — much like the first, tenuous time on ice skates, knowing something good would come despite the potential first tumble onto the pond's rigid ice. Radios played the fitting song, "It's Been a Long, Long Time" by Harry James, almost hourly. Families were lining up in front of the Beacon Theater to get tickets for the film "The Bells of St. Mary's," starring Bing Crosby and Ingrid Bergman, and admiring the Christmas tree that sparkled in the theater's front lobby rather than piles of goods to be recycled for war production. Even though not every soldier would be home in time, things were surely going to be better this Christmas.

From John P., Pearl Harbor, HI, December 4, 1945 – *Dear Stanley, Well, to date I still haven't received any mail. Right now I have some time so I'll do some more scratching. I made two liberties so far to Honolulu and bought some junk and tanked up on some schnapps. One night I even had Schlitz beer, which is something I couldn't get in Dago for 25 cents a bottle. All I can say about this island is that it's just like being in the States and anybody who's been stationed here for a few years certainly has nothing to bitch about. I see quite a few women Marines and waves around brave souls.*

Boy, we're loading up on stores to the gills. When we shove out of here about Monday we're supposed to make a few stops at some of the islands like Saipan, Okinawa. Looks like this "can" intends to be out for some time. This afternoon I watched a transport, which was tied up astern of us, load up with sailors going back home. They had a band to see them off playing "California Here I Come" and wound up with that "Aloha" tune. It probably would have made me homesick if the damned ship wasn't heading to California. (Oh, yeah?) Very touching, indeed.

In our shipfitter shop on this ship we have one of those double silex pots [Author's note: Proctor Silex coffee pots] and it's always going. We also have two irons to press our whites at night and when we're not making coffee on the presses we're making eggs. Sometimes our chow is better than they have in the galley too. Boy they sure work the ass off the seamen. Especially under way and as fouled up as shipfitting is in the navy I'm kind of glad I am one. The skipper of this ship is a commander and he likes the rough weather they tell me. They say he doesn't come out on the bridge unless it is rough and when it is he's so happy he grins all over and clicks his heels in the air for joy. That's what the seamen tell me that stand the lookout watches. He looks like an ex pug [Author's note: pugilist, boxer] to me and he's Regular Navy so he and I have nothing in common. I made him a star out of brass for the flagstaff on his gig, which they use when he goes ashore. He hasn't used it yet because we're moored to a dock. Hope it makes him happy and also hope he stays out of my way.

Well that is all since I'm down to the bottom of the page. I'll write again when I cook up a good sea story. John

The city of Nagoya, Japan, prior to its WW II focus on production for the war, was already an industrial city. It was also the location of several old shrines and the historic Nagoya Castle. Before the war, it was not unusual for Americans to be hosted at the homes of influential businessmen interested in bringing their products to the U.S. The vast number of aircraft that were being built there for the Japanese war effort far surpassed the production of tea sets and had made repeated and heavy Allied air attacks necessary. After the war, factories that produced products more appropriate to peacetime were rapidly reestablished; their owners once again wanted to attract American dollars.

From Alex, Nagoya, Japan, December 9, 1945 – *Dear Stan; I finally received part of my mail and I sure was glad to hear everyone is allright. I guess Joe should be home by now, Steve said he was waiting and is disgusted and can't blame him, he tired of all the chicken that a peace time army has.*

So far I haven't been doing much. Monday I'm supposed to start work, learn how to run the crane. I got a few souvenirs and as soon as I get some more I'll send them. The weather here is turning pretty cold now, but we aren't going to stay here we are supposed to go to Hawaii and I hope its time. This afternoon at 1:00 o'clock we go to a Jap's house, some sort of party, then at 7:00 tonight we go to a nip's house. She works in the Dai Nippon Brewery. I still don't drink or smoke so I'll be okay.

I'll write a letter later on its near 11:00 and I want to go to confession. Solong God Bless All of You, your Pal and Brother, Alex

Chapter 33

Christmas Eve of 1945 in Port Washington, New York, was exactly the type of night many would imagine a Christmas Eve to look and feel like in this region. It was cold, around 30 degrees, and a graceful snow was occasionally settling upon the ground — just enough to reflect the lights and transform the dark ground with a dusting of white. For many who celebrated the holiday, it was a night to finish gift shopping or decorating the tree for the children to see the next morning. It was also a night for some grateful families to immerse themselves in the joy that loved ones were finally home to share the holiday together. Yet for others, emptiness lingered, as their brave men were not yet home. For the Palasek family, each of these dispositions were in their midst. Joe was with his family at his mother and father's home, just around the corner from his brother Stanley. Steve was still trying to return from Europe; his wife, Stephanie, and her daughter, Regina, were at her parents' home near Sandy Hollow Road, deeply missing his presence. Stanley's most recent letter to Steve was returned as "Not Deliverable." Even without a war in progress, past history made this a cause of unease. Alex, too, was still in Nagoya as a part of the Allied occupation in

Japan. Some 400 miles to the southwest of Alex, John Palasek had landed in Sasebo, Japan, a strategic city to the Japanese Navy months ago, which was now severely damaged by the war. Stanley's wife, Mary, asked if they could go to her family's home in Roslyn on Christmas day, as they were all concerned about Adam in Europe and Ollie in the Pacific.

From John P., Sasebo, Japan, December 24, 1945 –
Dear Stanley, I guess I'll have to start writing some letters now that the trip is over and the rolling has stopped. The last two days and nights were really rough and I mean rough. We hit a storm about 600 miles off Okinawa and we were kept busy pumping out the chain locker all the time. [Author's note: The chain locker is the location below deck where the anchor chain is stored and open to the environment at the point where the chain passes through the ship to the anchor.] To add to this we were traveling through an area where a lot of mines were floating around loose and thank God we didn't hit any or none hit us those two dark nights. It's not a very nice feeling to know there are loose mines floating around especially in rough weather like we had.

We're anchored in Sasebo harbor, which is pretty big as harbors go and you wouldn't think that Jap ships were all over this place a few months ago. Coming up we passed Nagasaki, which is among a bunch of hills and we couldn't see much of it and there probably isn't much of it to see anyway after that A-bomb flattened it out.

A week ago the sun was scorching and now it's pretty nippy out which reminds me, tomorrow is Christmas. I haven't had any mail in quite some time now and I'm wondering if I'll get any tomorrow. But if I don't, what's the difference. I'm used to it by now. Just found out there is no mail for this ship at all so – it'll be Christmas tomorrow anyway, such as it is.

All told, it took us 18 days actual sailing to get here and now that we are here I don't know what's next. Tomorrow is a holiday so there won't be anything doing and I won't find out what's on the menu till Wednesday.

I suppose I could go on with this letter and describe topography etc. but I'm not exactly in the mood for that so I won't.

It's a hell of a place to be Christmas is all I can say. On the way here from Enewetak I had a slight accident. The fire main busted one night and flooded a compartment and while I was working at it trying to bust a lock to get at a valve, a piece of steel flew off and hit me in the arm. The way the blood gushed out I thought I'd cut an artery but after I got a tourniquet around it, it stopped and it turned out that it was only a vein that was cut. My arm is o.k. now but it's still sore at the elbow. Anyway I was lucky I didn't get it in the eye.

After this letter I guess I won't write for a while till I get some mail. Not that I don't want to but for the past month I've been writing more or less to myself and soon as theses dodoes around here catch up with our mail everything will be straightened out. I know we'll be here a while because we need quite a few repairs so I'll wait till I get some mail before I write again which will be this week, I hope. Alex

And so, Christmas of 1945 came and went: in a joyous way for some, and for others, with hope for a better tomorrow and a deep sensation of loneliness.

Chapter 34

January 1, 1946, was the first New Year's Day in several years on which Americans woke without being at war. There were still matters to be addressed by governments and militaries in an attempt to assure lasting peace, but one could finally go to bed without the likelihood that an air raid drill might suddenly shatter the silence of the night. In Japan, Emperor Hirohito stood witness to American General Douglas MacArthur's forced purge of undesirables from the Japanese government. Hirohito also came forward to his people, of his own volition, to renounce the earlier Japanese ideal that the Emperors (including himself) were of divine origin, thus making the Japanese people superior to all others on Earth. He stated that it was time to become a part of the rest of the world, not to be sovereign rulers of it.

Stanley was more content and secure in his job at WCBS-TV since the first of the year, as he was moved from operation of the transmitter to the more exclusive development lab. Here, he would work on a different transmitter that would be capable of sending out color television signals. When the year's first weekend arrived, it was time to enjoy another Saturday drinking beer with his brothers Joe and Willie. Sunday, the family was together at the boy's parents' home, where Margaret whispered to Mary the news that she and Joe were expecting their second child. More smiles came to all when word came from Stephanie that Steve's company was, indeed, back in the states. The news brought Stephanie release, as her worries over her husband's return were becoming more than she could bear. The family hoped that it would only be a matter of weeks before they saw Steve again. It was also rumored that Carl was on his way home from Naples, Italy, but no one had heard anything for certain from him or his wife. Even though the war was over, Willie surprisingly continued to deal with fatigue and twitches, which were diagnosed as a symptom of nervousness. Within 10 years, the little-known disease of Muscular Dystrophy and its symptoms — unrecognized by his doctors at the time, and virtually untreatable — would take Willie's life.

  The next morning, Mary received a phone call that brought delight to her heart. "Hey sis," were the first words she heard. She instantly knew that it was her brother Ollie, home after being in the South Pacific. By noon he was at her apartment door, with his huge grin that evoked tears of joy. Her brother Adam was still somewhere in Germany, and Mary and Ollie talked over a long lunch of sandwiches and coffee of how they hoped he would also be home before long.

  Beginning in 1910 and continuing until WW II began, Angel Island in California was considered the Ellis Island of the West. Thousands of immigrants from Asia had legally entered the U.S. there, just off the coast of Marin County. It was now to be the final departure point for the last Japanese prisoners of war who were held in the U.S. In January 1946, the last of these prisoners prepared to board a ship there for the long voyage back to the Far East. Most would find their homeland to be different from when they left. The ravages of war, the sadness and bitterness of their people, and the obvious presence of American servicemen would be unhappy reminders of a failed war against the West.

From Alex, Nagoya, Japan, January 5, 1946 – *Dear Stan, Well how's everything back home? Hope this letter finds you in the best of spirits, both kinds or are you on the water wagon? I'm down this diesel school out of Nagoya, we are in a Jap airport and it's a seaplane base. We are now living in tents and its cold as hell we are about 30 ft. from the water our tent is on the seawall. I had quite a few pictures taken in a studio as soon as I get them I'll send them, also souvenirs I have.*

I got another letter from Steve he seems plenty worried about Stephanie he should be on the way home he's disgusted and I don't blame him. I meant to write him but by the time he receives my letter he'll be home I think so I'll wait. Guess I'll be here for a year or so, I shouldn't gripe I'm damn glad the war is over, so in a way I'm lucky.

I received a letter from Willie he said for me to list the things I want, if the post office won't let a package through, tell the post master go take a flying ____ jump at the moon. Hey, is William working? Please answer me with the truth because that makes me worry. Even if he wasn't, you'd say he was but please tell me the truth.

So you had quite a bit of snow, well we got some here but it's all gone now we got some snow flurries but that's all. I suppose I'll can the chatter for now solong, and God Bless You. You Pal and Brother, Alex

Before that week was over, more good news came: this time for Joe Palasek. Having little luck finding a job in the want ads, he had returned to the pipe factory where he had worked before the war. It was located just a few miles from his parents' home, in the Manhasset Isle section of town. The manager was more than happy to see Joe and offered him a position as a foreman. Joe gladly accepted the chance to support his now growing family and quickly made plans to move to a house he would rent on Charles Street, only a mile from his parents' house. His parents would let him take the furniture he was using, plus a few other pieces, to his new home. This gave Marjanna the opportunity to shop for a few new pieces of her own, and to set up a newly furnished room for her son John when he eventually returned.

The Long Island Rail Road (or as its daily users called it, the LIRR) had been a part of life in Port Washington in ways that could both lift one's spirits and tear at one's heart, particularly over the last five years. It was a convenient way to travel to Manhattan, or to Flushing or Jamaica, Queens for the rare treat of seeing a show or shopping. The station platforms were also the last place to say farewell to loved ones, where many servicemen shared hugs and hopes that they would soon return safely, though not all of them would do so. Since getting a job at CBS, the LIRR was Stanley's daily transport to and from Manhattan, along with thousands of others clustered on the dull grey electric coaches. More than once, Stan had to remind himself of what an infinite improvement it was over the soot-filled train that took him upstate to the Navy two years earlier.

Monday, January 7, seemed like just another one of those routine days as Stanley boarded an eastbound train for home at Penn Station's track 20. With the winter sun having set earlier, the glass roof of the station merely rendered a reflection of all the commuters below it. As the train departed and rumbled through the dark tunnel deep beneath the mud of the East River toward Long Island, and as the train lights flickered as they usually did, Stan glanced up from his technical books and noticed yet another fortunate soldier about five rows away returning home. The insignia on his left shoulder was the same as Steve's company. Perhaps Steve would be home sooner than they had hoped. Suddenly Stanley realized, that among all the trains that would leave Penn Station for Port Washington that day, and all the dozens of cars on those trains, and with all of the commuters on board, his brother Steve was no longer across the ocean but a mere five rows away. Stanley closed his book and yelled across the seats, "Steve!" Steve recognized not only his name, but also the familiar voice that had called it out for years. He turned his head with a look of disbelief. Steve jumped from his seat and went to hug his brother as Stanley slowly rose from his bench seat. There were smiles and a few tears shed, but only of happiness as they couldn't seem to exchange words quickly enough. Stanley took out a few pieces of writing paper as he talked with his brother and wrote brief letters to his brothers Alex and John, telling them the news that Steve had returned on the same train he was riding.

After crossing the grey slate concourse in front of the Port Washington station, where cars and taxis were picking up riders, the two brothers went up to Stanley's apartment and surprised Mary as she prepared dinner. They poured two beers to share. Steve had little to say about what he had experienced overseas; he would keep most of the specifics to himself forever. He merely wanted to know what was new with Stanley, the family and Port Washington. For now, one beer would be enough. Steve took his two duffel bags of gear in hand and nearly ran across Main Street and down Irma Avenue's hill, passing the spot where he would one day have his own home. Making a left at the end of the avenue, he regained his composure and took a deep breath. Slowly he walked up to the front door of his in-laws, and returned to his wife and daughter, safe, sound and happy as any man could be.

Chapter 35

The world was changing rapidly with the arrival of peace. Just in the month of January 1946, technology that was originally developed for the war effort was modified for uses other than combat. A radar beam once designed to invisibly detect aircraft was fired from New Jersey to the moon, and received back on Earth after a few moments — proving that communication with objects in space would be possible. A rocket-boosted jet flew from California to the East Coast in just over four hours. This event inspired Stanley remark in his diary, "One could have lunch in New York and four hours later in California. What will science do next?"

Peaceful projects were not the only concepts being developed for America. Bikini Atoll in the Pacific was designated as the site to further test lethal atomic weapons. Russia was also sprinting to develop its own nuclear device. Change in Europe came as the welcome mat to refugees was rolled up. An agreement to return German refugees was signed by 18 European nations that had offered wartime shelter to scores of displaced citizens, and Sweden was to return thousands of refugees from the Western Soviet Union states, as well. Stateside, changes were occurring beyond those of scientific advancement, pitting citizen against citizen; striking workers shut down the meatpacking and steel manufacturing trades, two American industries that strongly supported the war effort. It seemed nations and individuals alike were shifting from collaboration to achieve peace, to a competitive landscape fueled by what was in one's own best interest.

The USS Henry A. Wiley was a minelayer built on Staten Island, New York in 1944, just an hour from the Palasek home on Long Island. The ship departed Japan in mid-January to make its final voyage home to the states after faithful service in the war. Shipfitter 2nd Class, John Palasek, was on board.

From John P., West of Hawaii, January 28, 1946 –
Dear Stanley, I guess it's about time I broke out my writing gear and turned to a letter just to let you know what the score is to date. I hope everything's o.k. at home and I don't know whether it is or not since I have had few letters since November and I don't expect any more, naturally since I'm homeward bound or at least headed in an eastward direction. We are at present about 14 hrs out of Pearl Harbor and we're supposed to drop the hook there sometime tomorrow morning.

We came back exactly the same way I travelled to Japan on the Tolman that is; via Eniwetok and Pearl from where we are supposed to head for San Francisco and the Mare Island Navy Yard soon as we change skippers at Pearl which will probably take several days. Boy we had rough weather all the way except today. This is the rollingest pig iron bastard I ever hope to be on. We popped quite a few rivets from the strain and I hope it stays together for just six days after we leave Pearl and then I can start thinking about whether I'll sell apples on some corner or good humors, depending on the weather of course. Speaking of weather I hope it will be warm around Long Island when I get there I'm used to warm weather and it was pretty cold in Japan and I froze my ass off.

I guess Steve'll be home by the time you get this letter and Carl is probably shipped out. I hope you'll write Alex and tell him I'm on my way home because I imagine he'll be wondering why I don't answer his mail and thinking I'm still in Japan and I don't want to write him till I get squared away.

Coming back we passed the date line on midnight Saturday so it became Saturday again and it was quite a long day if you ask me. Seems funny to be sailing along, or should I say rolling along, and keep pushing your clock ahead 1 hour every few days and then suddenly push it back twelve hours. Oh well, I don't intend to cross any more date lines for a while now so I don't worry about it. I won't worry about the next war either because I know it will only last about 1 hour. John

Stanley was again becoming anxious about his job at CBS. He had discovered that even though he was working alongside Peter Goldmark (the inventor of the 33 1/3 speed, long-playing record) on color television using a mechanical three-colored wheel, he was still subject to a layoff similar to other CBS employees. Rumors indicated nothing would change until May, but the pressure was on to spend more time at work and show he was essential to the project. Stanley wrote in his diary that February, "I am still on color television. There is not enough time to sleep, work and do all that a person wants to do. The days pass into nights, the nights into weeks, weeks into months and so the years pass. How time flies. Yes time flies! It seems a short time ago when I was peddling my bicycle for Horowitz delivering papers. Then came the labor work then roofing, slating, cat and dog hospitals, finally wiring testing, then was Sperry, Press Wireless and now CBS. The war is over but it still takes its toll." Fortunately, many of his brothers were (or would soon be) home, thus making letter writing less of a concern.

One war was undeniably over, yet others still simmered. France, which had a controlling interest in Vietnam, was battling against rebels there, known as the Viet Nimh. Unlike recently seen battles in WW II, this war was not being fought against France by a uniformed force with a battlefield show of strength or typical strategies. Instead, the rebels were difficult to detect among other citizens, and were often hidden from view until they fired upon the French nationals using guerilla warfare. Soviet influence was establishing a Communist-led government in North Korea, further raising tensions as the country became increasingly separate from its neighbor to the south. Stalin stated that his nation — which now predominantly used its proper name since 1922, the USSR — must concentrate on defending itself against capitalist development in the world, thus making another war inevitable.

***From Alex, Maizuru, Japan, February 11, 1946** –*
Dear Stan, How are you, how's everything back at the house, well so far I'm all right I got here in good shape. I drove a ¾ ton from Kyoto to Maizuru, it was snowing and raining so I took part of a roof of a jap house with me. The streets are so darn narrow like the driveway back home, honest, we crossed the mountains okay though I had a few scare's when I started to slide, if you remember I never drove anything bigger than a wheel barrow back home. Here all they said was get in Polack and start driving. I'd hate like hell to pay for one of these army trucks.

I'm stationed in a jap naval barracks college, steam heat, its real pretty mountains all around best of all there is a ski run right behind us. It snowed the past few days so there's about 2 ½ foot of snow outside. I was down in a jap torpedo factory, and picked up a depth micrometer made in R.I., U.S.A. sub base, nice huh using our own tools against us.

I'll send most of the stuff home soon as I can. I'm trying to get a jap pistol if possible. Well I hope everything home is hokey dokey solong God Bless You Your Pal and Brother Alex

February brought with it more wonderful creations that would change the world over time. The U.S. Army gave its first public demonstration of the ENIAC computer. Weighing in at 30 tons, the massive machine could calculate rocket trajectories in only 10 days — a vast improvement, since it would take months for a mathematician to calculate that information. The ENIAC would lay the groundwork for computers for decades to follow. On a more passive note, the first frozen French fries were marketed and sold at Macy's in New York. They were met with little public praise.

On February 15, John Palasek found himself at the Long Beach, New York Naval facility where he once departed to San Diego. This time, he was there not for reassignment, but for discharge. The next day, Saturday, he was reunited with brothers Joe, William,

Steve, and Stanley, as well as Margaret, Stephanie, and Mary at his mother's house. He had lost a few pounds since he last went through New York, but looked well and drank much of his own weight in whiskey and beer that evening. Around 11:30 p.m., Stanley put him safely into the new bed in what was to be his room. It was the first of many nights that the brothers would again enjoy each other's company over drinks, picking up where they left off as if no time had passed since their last reunion.

Chapter 36

Returning servicemen found it difficult to find good jobs. Steve was considering finding a partner and scraping together $3,000 so he could start his own beer distribution business. John was trying to sell his brother Joe (with some success) on the idea that the two of them should pack up and go work in Europe; just what they would do for a living had not yet been determined. Stanley was fortunate enough to still have a steady job that paid a respectable wage, but he would need a loan if he were to fulfill his hopes of moving out of his apartment to a home of his own. On a March Saturday, all were surprised when a package arrived at their parents' house from Alex in Japan. Carefully folded and packed within the travel worn box were kimonos, handkerchiefs, and other silk items, including two flags bearing the "Rising Sun" of Japan.

From Alex, Nagoya, Japan, March 9, 1946 – Hi Stan, How are you, how's everyone back home. So far I'm all right but we are pretty busy here so I don't have much time to write letters. Our outfit is breaking up so we are working Sat + Sun. I got a letter from John, he was in Pearl Harbor, but his letter was a month old so maybe he is home by now, I sure hope he is, as far as Carl goes like I said before if he wants to live in his little world well he can go fly a kite him + violet together.

So you are still with CBS that's good from what I hear the job situation is really tough, when I get back it will be lousy, you see we hear quite a bit about the stripe happy civilians, figuring if you never had stripes in the army you weren't any good, I'll worry about that when I get back which is still quite a long way off. I hope you don't mind me scribbling I'm a little pissed off, but otherwise okay, hope this finds everyone at home the same solong and god Bless You All, Your Brother, Alex [Note: The postscript to this letter had both "Alexander Palasek" and "Port Washington" translated into Japanese writing, or "kana."]

Servicemen were coming home at a steady pace and though work was hard to find for many of them, such was not the case for Major League Baseball players. With many of America's sports heroes (who were now also war heroes) returning home, spring training in Florida for the 1946 season was in full swing from the Atlantic to the Gulf shores. With gasoline becoming readily available to all again, travel plans were being made, often to the sound of singer Nat King Cole's swinging hit extolling the concept that one should "Get Your Kicks on Route 66."

On March 24, 1946, Mary got the phone call that she most anticipated: Ollie had just returned home from the Roslyn train station after picking up his older brother, Adam. Stanley and Mary immediately drove to her mom's house on Powerhouse Road in Roslyn. One by one, Mary's other brothers and sisters came to the house to celebrate another family reunion. Mary was grateful to have her whole family, less one precious brother, together again. She also looked forward to many other nights to spend together, making up for lost time. As with many families, the Rykowskis felt that this was the correct time to take down the pennant in the front window of their family homestead. They folded up the red banner, which had a blue star for each son who had served bravely and one gold star for their son and brother, John.

With all the good spirits among the Palasek and Rykowski families, there were still matters in the world that could cause worry, or heartbreak. An underwater earthquake near Alaska resulted in a tsunami which killed more than 150 people on the northern, shores of Hawaii. War trials continued in Europe for those who were behind the Nazi extermination of approximately 10 million innocent people. Most of these trials were rapidly followed by executions of the guilty parties. The U.S. military command in the South Pacific believed an excessive number of U.S. military men were consorting with the Japanese. Without saying it openly, one of the major concerns of the

U.S. commanders was that personnel were frequently spending time with prostitutes, which tarnished the noble and honorable reputation the government expected of its servicemen abroad. In response, General MacArthur signed orders that would halt "fraternization" between American servicemen and Japanese citizens. This order unfortunately (and quickly) led to segregation in many public places, thus suppressing the Japanese in their own homeland.

One soldier in Japan who was not concerned over this separation was young Alex Palasek. Although he might never back down from a confrontation (family back home heard he had beat up a local who challenged him at judo one evening), he believed that hard work was plenty to keep him occupied and out of trouble. He was rarely in one place for long, constantly moving around the island of Honshu. A brief stay to work in Nagoya was followed by a week or so in Kobe before Alex returned to the Tokyo area. Although Stanley would write several more letters to Alex over the next few weeks and months, Alex sent few replies. Had the war continued longer, the family would have been seriously concerned — but given the arrival of peace, the family felt confident that Alex was doing well. Besides, rumor also had it that he was sending most of his correspondence to a young lady back in Port Washington rather than to his family.

From Alex, Yokota, Japan, April 8, 1946 – *Dear Stan, Well I moved again. I came back from Kobe for the third day and finally they told me to pack for good. I'm attached to the Eastern Airforce. I'm with the engr's [Author's note: The Army Corps of Engineers] again anyway we are building an airstrip 2 mi long for B-29s. We are about 30 mi from Tokyo but we are up on top of the mountains and way back in the hills, no town or nothing near us. We are living in Quonset huts, the chow is worse than all hell but never mind that. I'm split up from the rest of my pals some are here but in different companies. This strip will be finished in June and then this outfit will deactivate.*

I'm supposed to start driving a 4 ton diamond T in a day or so I'll let you know the laydown then so for now solong and God Bless You Your Pal and Brother, Alex

The loud arguments and verbal battles were continuing at the Nielsen Building at 62 Main Street, but seldom at the apartment of Stanley and Mary. Instead, the racket came from new neighbors who were fighting in the apartment below. This noise joined the rumble of the trains below and the new fire whistle erected on nearby Haven Avenue that was tested daily at noon and six o'clock. By that summer, Mary became aware that she was pregnant with her second child. Instead of "going to the show" at the Beacon Theater to get away from the bickering between each other, Mary and Stan were now going to the movies with four-year-old Stanley. With the joy of a second child on the horizon, they were discovering, for now, what it meant to be a family and they were enjoying it.

Chapter 37

Despite the war's end, some matters were less than harmonious as 1946 progressed. Without the need to do what was necessary in order to support a war effort, workers were now directing their concerns to their own desires rather than that of the nation. Much like dominoes in a row, one union after another went on strike to demand the wages and benefits they dared not request during wartime. Continuing strikes by meat cutters, coupled with new ones by railroad workers, coal miners, longshoremen, and several other unions, made everyday items difficult to acquire once again. With almost all power plants in the 1940s dependent upon coal for fuel, power cutbacks became common. The ongoing steelworker strikes meant new cars could not be produced, as hopes to replace an old clunker or buy a new appliance were put on hold.

August brought Carl Palasek home from Europe to his wife, Violet. Rather than return to their rental, they took over Carl's brother Willie's room at their parents' home. Fortunately for Willie, who suffered from double vision and other bothersome symptoms periodically, this living situation didn't last long as the first in a long series of breakups and reunions commenced for Carl and Violet. Better news arrived as fall began and Margaret and Joe welcomed their second child, a daughter they named Patricia. The entire Palasek family, minus Alex, celebrated the christening at Stanley's small apartment as he was chosen to be Patricia's godfather.

On October 30, 1946, a telegram arrived at the Palasek home on Bayview Avenue. During wartime, telegrams were too expensive for casual communication and typically brought the worst of news to loved ones. This message was not from Japan or any department of the military; it was from the distant state of Washington, from Alex, to let his family know that he was back in the United States. Eight days later, on November 7, Alex was a civilian knocking on the front door of his parents' home. The final piece of the family puzzle arrived home in the same condition in which he departed (save for the addition of a few pounds, much of it in the form of muscle that a hard-working young man might acquire). The Palasek and Rykowski boys, who had survived the trials of being abroad and the dangers of war, were home together at last on Long Island.

The morning after the presidential election that November, America woke to unexpected news. Thomas Dewey was greatly favored to win the election over incumbent Harry S. Truman — partially due to the stress the nation faced as a result of workers' strikes, but also due to the fact that Truman had risen to the presidency as a result of Roosevelt's death rather than on his own merit. Many people doubted his ability to lead a rebuilding nation. Upon accepting his election to the office of President, Truman held aloft the *Chicago Tribune*, which ran the headline "Dewey Defeats Truman." At year's end, President Truman officially declared that the hostilities of the war were over.

As time passed through the end of 1946 into 1947, the married Palasek sons — Joe, Steve, Carl and eventually Stanley — were buying homes of their own. With a growing family, Stanley knew his Main Street apartment could no longer serve their needs. He also left CBS for a new, better paying job at WABD, a New York station of the DuMont Television Network, though that job would only last for one year.

In Port Washington, a new street of dirt and gravel had been laid in what was once the sand pit between the Baxter and Mill Ponds. It was the same sand pit where Stan and his brothers would hunt rabbits and play golf on their imaginary golf course of their childhood years. Stanley was able to secure a loan to build a two-bedroom, Cape Cod-style house (with space upstairs for more bedrooms) at 23 Bayside Avenue. Mary was ecstatic that she would finally have a home of her own with a yard where her sons could play.

When it was time to move from the apartment, Stanley took all the letters he had saved from his brothers and brothers-in-law, and searched for a box in which they would all fit. The cardboard box from Flagstaff Foods of Perth Amboy, New Jersey was the perfect size. The letters were placed inside, and the lid was folded shut. Stan loaded the box in his friend Eddie Kaspar's truck, alongside the furniture, clothing and other household items that were headed down the hill to their new home.

After 35 years as a television technical director at WPIX-TV in New York, during which, on July 17, 1959, he became the first in his field to operate instant replay in a baseball game, Stanley retired to play golf as often as the weather would allow. The pleasure would only last a few years. Months after diabetes took his life, Stanley's wife Mary was cleaning out the second-floor den to create a sewing room. She had been living on her own in the Bayside Avenue house for years, since her three sons had all grown and moved on to start lives of their own. As she was sorting through the den's contents, she came across many items she felt were worthy of nothing more than the trash. She decided to set aside the dusty box of old letters, moving them to a spot in the basement where they would be out of the way.

Sixteen years later, Mary passed away. Her three sons (Stanley, Sherwood and Mark) joined together to clean out the house before its sale. Anything they didn't want to keep would be sold in a tag sale. As that tag sale neared its end, her youngest son, Mark, realized they had forgotten to look beneath the basement staircase, behind its makeshift plywood door. Where he hoped to find overlooked treasures, he found a gaudy ceramic lamp, three empty suitcases from 40 years earlier, and, far beneath the bottom step, a dusty cardboard box. Mark immediately knew what the box contained, having seen it once several years ago.

There was indeed a treasure under the basement staircase. A treasure to be shared.

Stanley Palasek (age 14) with his father, Stanislaus

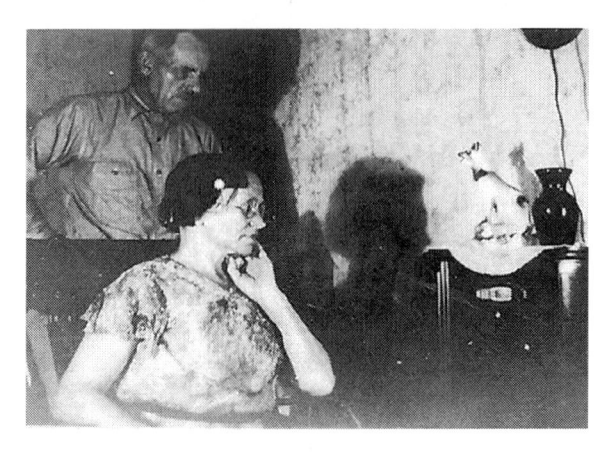

Stanislaus & Marjanna Palasek

Stephen Palasek and bride, Stephanie Wrobel

Stanley Palasek and bride, Mary Rykowski

PFC Joseph Palasek

PFC Joseph Palasek in Italy

Adam Rykowski on right, escorting First Lady Eleanor Roosevelt

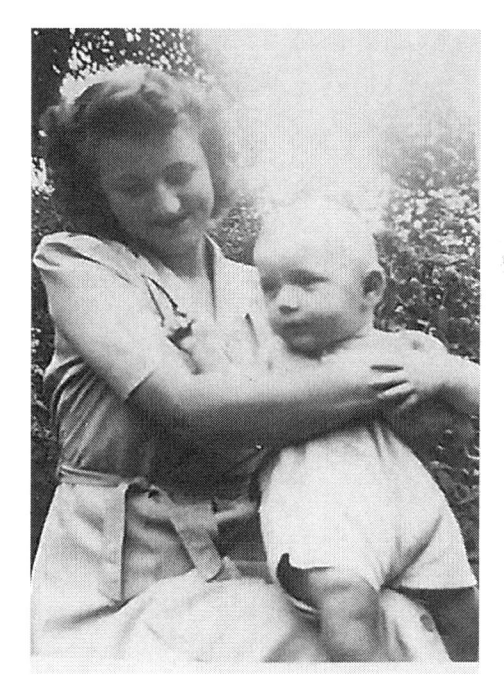

Mary Palasek and Stanley Jr.

PFC John W. Rykowski

Ship Fitter First Class John Palasek

Sgt. Stephen Palasek

Private Alex Palasek

V-Mail Christmas Card

John Palasek (Right) with fellow sailor, Maurice

Postwar Party Christmas 1946

Front row, seated on floor left to right, both photos: Stanley Palasek Jr., Alex Palasek, Willie Palasek, Steve Palasek, John Palasek.

Back row on sofas, left to right, top photo: Evie Tyma (daughter of Al & Evelyn), Stephanie Palasek, Al Tyma, Mary Palasek.

Back row on sofas, left to right, bottom photo: Al Tyma, Mary Palasek, Evelyn Tyma, Theadora Rykowski (mother of Mary & Evelyn)

Acknowledgements

My sincere thanks go to my friend and editor, Natalie DeYoung, who was always patient with my terrible punctuation and grammar, and encouraged me for well over two years with kind words and delicious caramels. My thanks also go out to my brother, Stanley Jr., for help with our family photos and memories, as well as to my cousins (first, second, and removed), who helped me fill in blanks to complete this story. Thanks also to my dear Aunt Stephanie for her memories, as conveyed through her family to me; sadly, she passed to be with her beloved husband, Stephen, before I was finished writing this book. My gratitude obviously goes to my parents, Stanley and Mary, for not tossing out these precious documents, and for all the stories they shared once upon a time. Gracious love must also go, as it does daily, to my dear wife, Irene, who allowed me the space and time needed to write and the warm hugs when I needed them.

Finally, thanks must go to all of my uncles, who rose to the call of duty and served the urgent needs of America and other nations without hesitation. Most of all, this book is dedicated to the memory of my uncle, Private First Class John W. Rykowski of the 602nd Battalion of the Third Army. Though I never knew him, my mother's love for her brother somehow filtered down to me. His burial flag, insignia, and certificate from the President for meriting the Purple Heart have been on the wall of my office with his photo through every step of this book, and will continue to be there. His body, originally laid to rest in Champigneul, France, was later moved to the American military cemetery in Epinal, France, where I had the privilege of placing a flag and roses in 1999 as the first family member to visit his grave. His name is among the WWII dead on the Roslyn, NY clock tower. You have all made me very proud.

Made in the USA
Middletown, DE
02 September 2016